In the Case of Our Fate

The Diviner's Legacy: Book Two

E.K. BARNES

Printed in the United States of America

www.ekbarnesauthor.com

First Printing, 2021

ISBN: 978-0-578-91493-0

The title font was set in
Luminari by Canada Type
The text type was set in Iskoola Pota
Cover art and design by KT Barnes
Copyedited by Jessie Campbell
and Rita Ray

OTHER WORKS BY E.K. BARNES

WHEN THE DIVINE ARE DEAD

MISSED WHEN THE DIVINE ARE DEAD AND DON'T MIND MAJOR SPOILERS? CATCH UP BY SCANNING THE QR CODE BELOW OR VISIT WWW.EKBARNESAUTHOR.COM/RECAP

TO
GRANDMA
*WHO PASSED THE YEAR
I WROTE MY FIRST BOOK*

OTHER WORKS BY E.K. BARNES

WHEN THE DIVINE ARE DEAD

MISSED WHEN THE DIVINE ARE DEAD AND DON'T MIND MAJOR SPOILERS? CATCH UP BY SCANNING THE QR CODE BELOW OR VISIT WWW.EKBARNESAUTHOR.COM/RECAP

TO
GRANDMA
*WHO PASSED THE YEAR
I WROTE MY FIRST BOOK*

TABLE OF CONTENTS

Acknowledgments // i

Prologue // 2

1. Can We Agree That Battle Scars Suck? // 3

2. My Brother Is a Butthead // 15

3. Frank Almost Puts Me on Death Watch // 27

4. If There Was a Cure… // 42

5. My Sister Has an Idea // 57

6. The Adventures of Our Liquid Gold Hearts // 71

7. My Best Friend Is a Douchebag // 82

8. Jay-Jay Has Too Many Secrets // 98

9. The Invasion of the Sad Girl // 108

10. Dad Tries to Give Us the Talk // 120

11. So I Might Have Gotten into a Fight // 134

12. Serena Protects the Enemy // 147

13. My Parents Are Conspiracy Theorists // 158

14. Big Pharma Has to Be Stopped // 170

15. The Curse of Star-Crossed Lovers // 180

16. Rebecca Feels a Little Stabby // 198

17. Priori Labs is Lying to You // 209

18. Aaron Is a Slimeball and Serena Knows It // 221

19. A Dragon Takes on Mile Square // 234

20. Olga Picks a Fight with the Chosen One // 248

21. Serena Finally Cracks // 258

22. Why Hadn't I Considered the Possibility? // 269

23. I Meet the Spirits of the Past // 283

24. Savanna Stops Being Selfish // 297

25. That Did Not Just Happen // 308

26. Jay-Jay Knows Which Words Will Hurt // 317

27. The Second Law of Thermodynamics // 326

28. I Almost Kill Jay-Jay… Again // 339

Epilogue // 350

Alphabetical Index of Diviners // 356

About the Story // 357

Glossary // 360

Own Voices Recommendations // 361

About the Author // 362

ACKNOWLEDGMENTS

There are many people I didn't have room to thank in the acknowledgments for *When the Divine Are Dead*—people who played an integral role in my English language arts education or who supported me in other small ways.

First, I want to thank my fifth-grade teacher, **Mrs. King**, who spent a lot of energy attempting to get me out of Title I reading—a program for children in my school district who struggled with reading comprehension. She worked with me to make sure my test scores accurately reflected my ability. Mrs. King was also privy to many short stories I wrote during our writing time. One story in particular—told from the perspective of a stiletto shoe—still stands out in my memory. It was during this time when I began to imagine Bradley's world, creating characters that would stay with me forever.

Second, I'd like to thank the first English language arts teacher of my secondary school education, **Mr. Daniels**.

I remember sitting in his class while we were studying *The Outsiders* by S.E. Hinton. I was stoked to learn that Hinton was a teenage author. I sat at my desk, thinking,

"If S.E. Hinton could write something so poignant and raw from a point of view that wasn't her own at fifteen, surely, I can too." Learning about S.E. Hinton inspired me to pursue my writing dream. It was during my junior high years when I obsessed over world-building and character arcs. I added new characters like Jay-Jay and Serena, who would later play a significant role in this series.

It was also in this language arts class when I was taught the conflicts of persons. It was the first time I considered that a person's conflict could be with themself. This idea became a constant in my writing, allowing my characters depth and relatability.

I will never forget the day Mr. Daniels grew intense about scene description. He wanted us to be detailed with our writing, down to the sweat slicking a character's skin. As a thirteen-year-old girl, I found this gross and unnecessary but grew to understand its significance. Mr. Daniels went on to read us a paragraph describing a beach using the five senses. Scene description was always something I struggled with. I tended to write my stories too quickly, preventing my characters from stopping to smell the roses. When I was writing *When the Divine Are Dead* and this sequel, I forced myself to slow down to describe Bradley's environment. What he saw, tasted, seen, and heard, as well as how he felt, brought the story to life. I would think of this lesson mid-sentence, laughing at my younger self whenever I had to mention something unsavory.

Most importantly, Mr. Daniels taught my class the value of the human experience.

It wasn't a year later when I decided to integrate my love for fiction into my essays for school. I used snippets of Bradley's life experiences to draw my readers' interests into the reality of non-fiction. Although my teacher that year did not seem to appreciate it, my classmates—including my friends **Madie** and **Alicia**—oohed and awed over my painstaking description of Bradley's mental state.

I would also like to thank a girl I met at summer camp between my seventh and eighth-grade years, whose name I can't remember. At the time, I was working on a screenplay for an animation unrelated to this series. She held an interest in my writing and hoped one day I would become famous.

I'd also like to thank the last English language arts teacher of my high school education. **Ms. Fox** was one of only a few teachers in my high school who attempted to accommodate my undiagnosed social communication issues in the classroom. I will never forget the day she went out of her way to congratulate me on a poem I wrote regarding the assassination of John F. Kennedy, or the day she told me I had a great voice following a poetry presentation.

Another person I would like to thank is **Jason**—a friend from high school. He insisted on meeting with me a couple of years after our high school graduation. We sat in a coffee shop as he drained me of every bit of writing advice I could offer. At the time, he wanted to write a fantasy series. I discussed with him my longing to dig back into a series I had abandoned years before. Since then, I counted down the days until I finally began my last attempt at writing what would later become *When the Divine Are Dead*. This is the sequel to that book.

I will always and forever thank my friend **Nery**, who has continued to support my writing. She insisted that I not delete a certain sentence in this book that is politically risky. She went out of her way to gather a group of online friends to rig the poll I had posted on Twitter asking whether I should keep it.

I can't forget to thank my copyeditors, **Jessie** and **Rita**, for continuing to work with me on this series despite busy schedules and major life events. I will forever be grateful for their enthusiasm and attention to detail. A similar thank you can be given to my sister, **Kaitlin**, who designed the cover and was one of the first to read an early draft.

I would also like to thank **my parents** and my cousin **Brandon**—who were all too eager to read a copy of *When the Divine Are Dead* in the first few weeks it was released. My dad, who rarely reads and had never read any of my books before the first book in this series, devoured *When the Divine Are Dead* in a matter of days. His coworker **Jamie** was also among the first few readers.

I would also like to thank my cousins **Justin** and **Gabrielle**, who have minor characters named after them in this book. **Ankhita**, a girl I grew up with, and **Britney**, my former college resident advisor and fellow author, also have minor characters named after them.

I also don't want to forget to thank **Brandi**, **Katherine**, and my cousins **Jordan** and **Kylie** for either ordering a copy of *When the Divine Are Dead* and/or supporting and sharing social media posts. I want to also give a quick shout-out to **Jennifer** for leaving a generous and detailed review of that book on multiple platforms.

Lastly, this book is dedicated to my grandmother, **Barbara**, who passed from ovarian cancer on November 9th, 2011. The year I wrote my first book, which was an early version of *When the Divine Are Dead*, was the year she passed. I made sure this book was released on the anniversary of her passing in honor of her wonderful influence on my life.

I hope you enjoy this sequel.

CONTENT WARNING can be found at
www.ekbarnesauthor.com/contentwarning4

"There are such things as
false truths and honest lies."

— *Romani proverb*

PROLOGUE

Stepping away from Marcie, I gasped in a lungful of air, trying to breathe against dense fog. I'd felt this before, the memory of it stinging my eyes with fresh tears. My heart sank, darkness clouding the bright relief I had been feeling moments before. My vision blurred, Marcie's red hair the only color I could see before I bent over, sobs erupting from my lungs. I blindly felt in the dark for a solid object to keep me upright, but Marcie's hands gripped my arms instead. I could hear her voice, but I couldn't make out the words. My legs shook from my weight. I wanted to fall, to hit the ground with so much force I would crash through the floor and sink into the dark abyss of the underground. Something tugged at my gut, like an invisible string was attached to it, and someone was pulling, the material expanding, stretching like a rubber band. *Snap!* I felt the pull of the rubber suddenly bounce back, slamming into me with full force.

Something was wrong. Something was very wrong.

1
CAN WE AGREE THAT BATTLE SCARS SUCK?
BRADLEY

"We stole the fortune-teller's kid. Right in front of her eyes too!" The blonde woman with the twigs in her hair seemed to barely contain her excitement. She paced the traveling RV, rehashing what had occurred on the street. It was the ultimate sleight of hand, a dozen witnesses missing every important detail. The plan had been for Garrett to nab me while everyone was paying attention to her. She was wild and bruised—the kind of person people couldn't ignore as she searched for her non-existent missing child. She'd tricked my mother, my father, and all the people who loved me into averting their eyes for a fraction of a second.

"Wasn't I a good actress, Garrett?" The woman kneeled behind the driver's seat of the RV, pleading for reassurance with her honey eyes. Garrett had a fat cigar crushed between his teeth, the smoke and its accompanying aroma swirling inside the cabin. He smiled into the rearview mirror, his yellowed, decaying teeth sending a brand-new chill down my spine.

I hadn't had time to scream. The man had snatched me so quick. It wasn't until after the fact when I realized what had happened. By then, I had no way to alert my mom and dad and little sisters that I was being taken. A whimper escaped my lips, saltwater spilling from my eyes, as my hands dug at the foam of the small booth seat. The woman turned toward me, extending her hands forward to trap my face in between their span. Her long, brittle nails tapped against my temples.

"Don't cry, child," she cooed, her thumbs wiping away a few of my tears. "We saved you from the bad witch lady." The woman smiled proudly at her triumph. She was missing a tooth—an incisor. Half her face was layered with bruises, new and old. The clothes she had on didn't match the season—a tank and cutoffs in late October. Her breath smelled like a mixture of candy and cigarettes.

I pressed myself against the wall, the chains around my ankles clinking with the movement.

"I want my mommy," I whimpered. I was only five. My mom was my whole world. My monthly voyage to kindergarten was the only thing to separate us.

The woman frowned, my plea igniting a sudden darkness in her eyes I hadn't noticed before. Her grip around my head tightened—my bones felt as though they were being crushed under the pressure. Gritting her teeth, she addressed the man. "This child is evil, Garrett! I thought he was supposed to be different from the others."

Evil? I tried to pull away from her grip, but she was holding on too tightly. I couldn't be evil. I'd heard the stories of the devil, *o Beng*, who struggled against God, *o Del*, to reign over our lives. Mom had taught me about our religion. Dad had brought me to church. Our house had rules to maintain the balance of our dueling deities. If we strayed from those rules, we would experience the consequences of bad karma, or *prikaza*, and our ancestors would dish out punishment. Had I done something to allow the devil into my life? Was I now unclean? Were my ancestors punishing me?

Garrett took a long drag from his cigar, unsurprised by the woman's assumption. He breathed the smoke out without coughing, answering the woman calmly. "They're all evil. That's why we take them. They're the spawn of the devil. We can't let them mature, or they will end us all. The world as we know it will cease to exist."

Hot tears flew down my cheeks. Had my mom not burned all my hospital clothes to please our ancestors after their last punishment landed me in that unclean place? Surely she had missed something. Maybe my punishment hadn't been big enough. Maybe I was truly *marime* this time—cursed and unclean, evil, as Garrett had said. How easy it was to fall to *o Beng*.

The woman let go of my face, pouting. "I wanted him to be different." She glanced at me scornfully. "He's so cute. I want to keep him."

Garrett roared with anger at her admittance. "He is evil! He must die!" The RV swerved a little on the road. A car honked. The woman cringed before stalking to the back and folding into herself on the floor. She didn't say another word as she tugged at the loose strings of the carpet. I wanted her to keep pleading with him, to convince him I'd already paid my price. I didn't have to die. I'd be good this time—stay clean by living *Rromanija*. It was no use, though. I knew I'd fail.

Garrett didn't stop driving until we reached the woods. The brakes squealed as he slowed the vehicle to a stop, yanking the transmission into park. He tugged at a curtain behind the driver's seat until it covered the width of the RV, removing all the front windows from my sight. I heard him leap into the colder air of the autumn night, losing track of him until the side door flew open to reveal his full frame. He half smiled, half grimaced, studying me with hungry eyes. My heart leaped into my throat at the sight, unsure of exactly how he planned to kill me. The woman in the corner shut her eyes as he yanked the door closed behind him. He loosened his belt as he lunged at me, my scream lost in the forest to anyone who might've cared.

★

Someone was shaking me, my name echoing from a distance. My screams soon changed from the shrill, high-pitched tone of my childhood into the deeper sound of my teenage cries. In less than a second, I was upright, sweat slicking my skin. My eyes burned from the sudden influx of light, my lungs heaving wildly as I gasped in lungfuls of air, trying to rid my senses of Garrett's haunting acidity. My mom was standing at my bedside, her caramel eyes wide with worry.

"It's a nightmare, Bradley," she whispered, shaking my arm. I flinched from her touch, dropping my face into my hands. It was the ninth anniversary of my kidnapping, and although I had only spent two days with Garrett and the woman, my brain forgot sometimes that I wasn't still there, being punished for whatever evil I had done to deserve such a fate. It had been so long, yet still as I grew older, I knew more. I understood more. I think the memories might've hurt more too.

"I don't want to go to school today," I mumbled. I didn't ask, just stated my desire, knowing my mom would go along with whatever I wanted. Halloween was when I was given the most control of my day, even when I felt I had lost it all. Mom and I held horrible memories of that fateful holiday. Her guilt was often palpable. On many occasions, she had tried to take the blame for what happened—tried to blame it on her own marime—the uncleanliness she'd taken upon herself when she married my dad. He wasn't Romani. He didn't take on much of her culture when they officially united. After I was kidnapped, Dad tried to stamp the idea of marime out of our household. I always thought it was because he was selfish and unwilling to change, but after all these years and after all we had been through, maybe he had a point. Marime was as hurtful to our family as my dad's belief in sin and a punishing God. Our constant bad luck either meant we'd challenged our ancestors into a constant state of retaliation or we'd become so sinful that God had to punish us with more darkness. Either way, I'd given up on pleasing any of them years ago.

Mom tugged absentmindedly at the end of my navy fitted sheet. "Does an omelet sound good to you?"

I shrugged, rubbing my eyes. "I'm not hungry."

"You need to eat," she protested.

There was a long pause before I dropped my hands from my face. "Fine."

Lately, she'd been cracking down on managing my diabetes—the disease my doctor diagnosed me with shortly before Garrett had taken me. I had a bad habit of ignoring my symptoms to the point of needing medical attention. Not that I didn't care. It was more like I didn't want to have to care.

She left before I glanced at the clock—almost six in the morning. The house would be quiet for a few more minutes. I could already hear my twelve-year-old sister, Paige, shuffling around next door.

I forced a shiver, shaking my limbs in an attempt to rid the nightmare from my thoughts. Can it be called a nightmare if it actually happened? My life was more of a living nightmare.

What I hadn't realized then was that Garrett wasn't referring to evil little boys who broke from Rromanija. He believed all children of the divine were devil's spawn. He knew we would develop powers as we matured, believing we would bring an end to the universe. He wasn't the only one to genuinely believe this, but I had remained naive to the sheer amount of hate that existed toward the diviners until recently. I've had several near-death experiences, but the ones starring neo-Nazis were the worst by far. It turned out that a group called the New Order had been targeting me for a while. When Garrett failed to kill me as a powerless child, the target on my head seemed to grow bigger. My family was relatively safe from them while we lived in the Chicago area, but the second we moved to Indianapolis at the beginning of August, we became targets again. It took the New Order a month to execute their plan, somehow using me and my marime to bring our defenses down. Several of us barely made it out alive.

I made my way downstairs as the unmistakable scent of eggs wafted through the downstairs entryway. Sliding onto a bar stool in the kitchen, I watched as the eggs quickly changed from their liquid form to a mountain of yellow fluff. Mom loves to cook. I could have sworn it was pretty much the only thing she'd done since we moved to Indianapolis. She'd had so much free time with us kids in school that I think she was bored. When we lived in New Mexico and, later, the Chicago suburbs, Mom ran a fortune-telling business out of our home.

She'd gained an entire community of loyal but curious clients. She hadn't been able to do that in Indianapolis, though. It wasn't a safe enough space. We had to keep a low profile to avoid drawing unwanted attention to ourselves.

I ate my omelet in silence as the rest of the family got ready for work and school. My eight-year-old brother, Blake, was upset that the schools in Indy didn't do anything to celebrate Halloween. Since Mom and Dad never allowed him to go trick-or-treating, the school's Halloween party was usually his only chance to dress up and collect candy.

"Rebecca is an *artiste*," Paige said, smiling as she pronounced the i like a long e. She gestured to her own face, the entire left side coated in swirls of paint. Our ten-year-old sister, Rebecca, had re-created an elaborate work of art. It was very Van Gogh-esque. If I hadn't known my sister to be unusually talented with a paintbrush, I would have thought it was professionally done. It was impressive. Too bad the paint would be a direct dress code violation.

Mom frowned, although I could sense a hint of pride in her eyes. "I really don't feel like answering any phone calls from your principal today."

Paige crossed her arms in defiance. "I'm not taking it off."

Mom brushed a few strands of Paige's dark hair behind my sister's shoulder. Pursing her lips, she nodded wearily. "I know." Out of all of us, I think Paige is the most stubborn. Once she makes up her mind, it's tough to talk her out of it. Mom could probably already see she wouldn't, the call from her principal ringing in a vision. Mom could really see the future—her business wasn't all a sham. It would be a shame for Paige to have to wipe the paint off.

Mom's refusal to argue with Paige struck a chord of envy inside Blake. "Not fair!" He stomped his foot. "If she gets to wear face paint, I get to wear a costume!" It was a fair assessment, but he was fighting a losing battle.

Dad cleared his throat from behind me, and I flinched at the unexpected noise. "Sorry, Brad," he apologized, his hand resting on my left shoulder. I shrugged it off. Dad never seemed to grasp the concept that I hated my nickname. Coupling it with physical contact was worse.

Before Dad could talk some sense into my brother, Blake turned to me, furious. "This is all your fault!"

I dropped my fork onto my plate, the metal clinking against the ceramic. Blake knew he was in trouble before Mom could sputter his full name out. "Blake Alec Chambers!" He was already rushing up the stairs.

Gripping the edge of the counter, I tried to keep myself from doing the same as my brother. Frank, my mentor who also happened to be the school resource officer, had been working with me on fighting my impulse to run from my problems. I'd been doing it for too long, and it was hindering my progress. I'd also made a promise to my girlfriend, Savanna, that I would at least try to break my habit of running off when conversations got tough.

Mom tried to meet my gaze, but I couldn't reciprocate, not when I was focusing all my energy on staying put. "This is not your fault," she tried to reassure me.

I couldn't do it. I couldn't keep sitting there. It was too hard. Not with Dad and Mom and Paige staring at me. I tried to make a run for it, but Dad was ready, throwing his arms around me to lock me in place. "Your mother and I would appreciate it if you stayed where one of us could see you." So much for getting what I wanted out of the day. I gritted my teeth. Blake was right. This was my fault. Because of me, he couldn't be a kid—a normal kid, anyway. Our youngest brother, Jesse, who died from an inoperable heart tumor earlier in the year, never got to go trick-or-treating either. Paige and Rebecca didn't remember going, although they had before I ruined the tradition. It wasn't fair to them to miss out. There'd been complaints before, but nobody had truly challenged the rule. They understood our parent's reasoning.

"You should take him," I whispered. Mom and Dad looked at each other. I could tell they were debating the pros and cons. I tried to relax, feeling my heart rate slow, beat by beat. Dad was still holding me against him. He didn't need to do that anymore. I wasn't going to run. Attempting to outweigh the cons, I continued. "Savanna can take him. I'm sure she'll be up for it. Or any other diviner, really. If you can get Rebecca to go, I'm sure they'll stay safe. They can stay close by in the neighborhood." We didn't live in such a bad neighborhood.

"No," Mom answered with finality.

Dad pulled away. "Think about this, Clarinda."

She shook her head vehemently. "No. I can't watch both boys at the same time. I can't worry where Blake is every second of the night and still keep an eye on Bradley."

"Mom." I groaned. "I'm fine." She didn't need to watch me. What did she think I would do? I had learned my lesson from the year before—no alcohol.

"Don't lie to me." Mom jabbed her finger at me, her voice crackling with the fresh onslaught of tears. I can't stand it when people cry. Their tears throw me into a sense of helplessness. I want to make them stop, but I don't know how. My throat burned from trying to hold my tears back.

"Rin." Dad rounded the island counter to comfort Mom. He has a thing for nicknames, but I think my mom's the only one who likes hers.

I really wasn't going to drink or, for that matter, do anything stupid. I wasn't sure where I could get a hold of anything, anyway. It wasn't like Mom or Dad had a liquor cabinet. Besides, drinking hadn't ended well for me last time. The memory of that night was probably what was fueling Mom's anxiety.

Paige cleared her throat, tapping at an invisible watch on her wrist as Rebecca popped into view.

"I gotta take the kids to school," Dad mumbled, kissing the top of Mom's head. She sniffled but let him go. As he reached for his briefcase, he shouted at the ceiling. "Blake! Let's go!"

Mom wiped the tears from her cheeks. "Let him stay." She sighed. "Maybe we'll go to the candy store or something."

"Ooh, get some Milk Duds!" Paige shouted as they hustled out the door.

"Don't we already have candy?" I asked, glad for the subject change. I craned my neck to see into the dining room where two large bowls and six bags of assorted candy were taking up space.

Ignoring my question, Mom drummed her fingers on the countertop, her lips pressed tightly together. She stayed like that for a while, her eyes focused elsewhere. My stomach dropped. She wasn't going to let anything go. I'd be trapped with her and her anxious fumes all day.

2
MY BROTHER IS A BUTTHEAD
BRADLEY

As if I hadn't already suspected where her mind had gone, Mom stated as the three of us headed to the van, "I don't want a repeat of last year."

Yep. Who could forget last year? Except me, that is. I didn't remember much of last year's Halloween antics, but I'd gathered a good chunk of the story from Olga, an old friend from Illinois.

Three years ago, the school counselors made us all sign a piece of paper promising that we would never drink alcohol or do drugs or smoke or whatever. Nobody took it seriously. Well, I shouldn't say that. A good quarter of the school didn't take it seriously. I already had a reputation for being one of the "troubled" kids, so people assumed me and my friends, Chad and Olga, were getting drunk or stoned every weekend or something. I mean, Chad and Olga smoked cigarettes every once in a while, but as far as I knew, that was the worst of it. Until last Halloween.

Chad spent all night at his youngest sister's freshly planted grave, shooting up whatever drug he could get his hands on. I was only with Chad for a few minutes earlier in the night, so I wasn't there when the cops took him away. I had left the graveyard with Olga after his erratic behavior sent her over the edge. See, Olga was pissed at Chad because they had apparently slept together earlier in the week and he was pretending like he didn't remember it, which pissed *me* off because Olga didn't deserve to be treated the way he always seemed to treat her—like she was expendable. Her admission made me want to punch his lights out. If I had been lucky enough for her to like me back, I would have treated her better than he ever could. She always clung to Chad, though, never interested in me as more than a friend.

Olga and I found ourselves at some party where—surprise, surprise—I drank way too much. This wouldn't have been too big of a deal—I mean, normal teenagers do this all the time, right?—if I wasn't also type one diabetic. But because I am an idiot, and because nobody thought to warn me at thirteen about the added dangers of me consuming alcohol, the night took a turn for the worse.

I apparently passed out at the party, and nobody thought to do anything. They were having too much fun drawing on my face when I started seizing. It was the first time I'd ever had a seizure, a symptom of hypoglycemia I never experienced. I didn't believe anyone when they told me. According to Olga, everyone started freaking out about calling an ambulance because they didn't want the cops to bust the party. Olga got into a knock-down, drag-out fight with the kid whose house it was. I wish I had been conscious to witness that. She called the ambulance herself, the cops came to break up what was left of the party, and I landed in the hospital.

"I'm not saying you can't drink," my doctor had said to me the next day. "You have to be smart about it. Excess alcohol consumption can lead to low blood sugar. Alcohol tells the liver not to release sugar into the bloodstream. What happened last night happened because you were on insulin. The balance between the amount of insulin and glucose in your system didn't level out. Those symptoms that you usually experience when that happens would have stood out to you if you had been sober. The problem last night was that you weren't sober." He'd raised his gray eyebrows at me, drumming his fingers against the back of my chart. "Some of my other patients with diabetes have said they've experienced similar symptoms when drunk as they do when their hypoglycemic. Is that how you felt last night?"

The problem was I couldn't remember.

That was why my mom was not letting me out of her sight this year. That was the only Halloween I wasn't plagued by memories of what occurred in New Mexico, but that was because Chad and Olga's drama overshadowed virtually everything.

Life in Indianapolis was different, though. I didn't know if it was because Frank had been trying to put his bachelor's degree in psychology to use in our recent sessions or if it was because of the whole New Order fiasco in August, but I couldn't seem to rid my head of the chaos. The nightmares had gotten worse. They hadn't been like that in years. I knew Mom had noticed the regression too.

"Don't worry, Mom," I grumbled, climbing into the passenger's seat.

Blake was still acting sore toward me as he buckled his seatbelt in the backseat. "Why do you have to go with us? You don't deserve any candy."

"I don't want candy," I shot back.

"Maybe you should eat a bunch, see if it kills you," Blake retorted.

Mom's hand hit the power lock on the doors. For a second, I considered unlocking my door and leaving since the front doors didn't have child locks. She swiveled to face him, her brown eyes boring into Blake's. "I am so sick of your attitude." Her voice was low, holding a threatening edge to it. Mom was usually the calm parent, but Blake was testing her last nerve. "I felt bad for you this morning, so I was going to take you to the mall, buy a costume, and go to the candy store, but now I'm thinking your father was right. We should have forced you to go to school today. So, give me one reason why I shouldn't march you right back inside and ground you."

Blake crossed his arms, staring straight back at Mom like her threat didn't matter. "You always give Bradley special treatment."

My heart skipped a beat in the resulting silence. "You think I get special treatment?" I asked, my teeth bared. The hairs on my skin prickled. My mind reeled, sending me back nine years, reliving a short snapshot of a memory. I shuddered and brought the back of my hand to my mouth. Blake had no idea what it was like to be me. Nobody did. I sucked in a deep breath. The hand at my mouth trembled. With my other hand, I fidgeted with the lock.

"Everyone always treats you differently," Blake explained. "We have to go along with what *you* want. You're afraid to go trick-or-treating, so now we don't ever get to go. You can't eat what you want without getting sick, so we never get to eat what we want. You couldn't be around your friends anymore, so we had to move away from all *our* friends. I wish it was you who died instead of Jesse."

I finally shoved the door open. "Me too!" I shouted, my voice shaky, leaving him with our distraught mother.

I didn't want to go inside the house, so I looped around to the backyard. I could barely see where I was going as I stumbled past the gate, my eyes stinging with tears. I tried to blink them away, but my brain couldn't stop replaying Blake's frustrations. "Me too," I whispered again, a lump gathering in my throat.

Jesse may have died from an inoperable heart tumor, but he wouldn't have been in the hospital in the first place if it weren't for me. I got him shot a month before his death when Chad had gone on some kind of revenge rampage to make us even. Chad's sister Lenora would still be alive if I hadn't ducked from the path of his bullet six months before that. Turns out, Chad believed in an eye for an eye instead of turning the other cheek. There was my karma again. Upsetting *kintala*, the spiritual balance of the universe, led to my brother's death. I wish Chad had shot me instead. He had several opportunities to do so. He had a gun trained on me more times than I cared for. And yet, here I was, still standing, still breathing. I lowered myself on the grass in the far corner of the yard, thinking about it too long, remembering the moment I could have stopped him. If only I hadn't been so afraid.

I don't want to die. I just want the pain to end.

It was a while before I lifted my head, catching sight of my mother through the back sliding glass door. She was pacing in the kitchen, a cell phone plastered to her ear. She kept wringing her hands, blinking away tears.

Mom and Dad were the only people in the house who owned cell phones, and even then, Mom rarely used hers. My parents didn't like the idea of us having them. I don't know if it was because they thought we were too young, that phones were distracting, or if they were afraid our enemies could track our locations. It was probably a mixture of all the above. It didn't yet bother me not to have one, but Paige was always begging. Mom would smile and point at the landline. "You already have a phone." Dad would grumble about how he wasn't paying for her to talk to boys.

Mom hung up and leaned over the counter, burying her face in her hands. She was usually able to put up a calm front on Halloween, especially after I stopped being a kid. This year was worse for her, though, but not because of my nightmares, last year's fiasco, or our new place. It was worse for her because this was also the first Halloween without Jesse. That realization made me feel even worse.

Dad arrived home around noon. I caught him pulling Mom into a hug before disappearing from my line of sight. It was tough to pull Dad from his work at the broadcasting company. He only left for emergencies. I guess somehow this counted as an emergency.

Mom pulled a tray of chocolate cupcakes from the oven. I don't know why Blake thought I controlled what we ate. Between the mountains of Halloween candy and Mom's newfound obsession with baking, there was enough sugar in the house to last months. I knew Mom was going to force me to eat again. I had a bad habit of starving myself and letting my glucose levels get too low. When I did eat, I had to check my glucose levels all the time to make sure I didn't need to inject myself to break down the extra sugars. I was constantly having to balance between the two scenarios.

After the events of the past year, my mom thought it best at the end of August to have the doctors install an insulin pump that automatically injects the clear liquid when my glucose levels get too high. It sounds cool at first, but there was a good reason I never had one. If nobody knew I was diabetic before, they'd know when they saw it. Sure, if my clothes were baggy enough, I could tuck it out of sight, but to me, it felt like wearing a big neon sign that alerted everyone I met that, yep, I had diabetes. Mom liked it because it gave her peace of mind. I thought it was annoying because I couldn't go over an hour without wearing it. This meant I had to sleep with it plugged into the circular canula on my stomach. Also, I see the bills. I know how expensive it is to keep me alive. It was a bigger deal when I was a kid, and my parents were still scraping by financially. They weren't anymore after years of my dad's career climbing. I think I was part of the reason he started working so hard. The price of insulin had skyrocketed over the years.

I huffed, pulling my right shoestring loose. I stared at it for a second before retying it. I didn't remember wearing shoes the night Garrett took me. Squinting at the laces, I tilted my head, trying to remember that detail. I thought I remembered everything about those days in the mountains, but somehow, this detail was evading me. Had I worn shoes? I had to have been. My mom wouldn't have let me leave the house without them. Why couldn't I remember? Was I finally losing pieces of those horrific nightmares? I wasn't sure how I felt about that theory.

While I wished to forget, the memories had somehow become a part of me. How would I live without them?

My mom's voice startled me out of my concentration. "Sandwich?" She held what looked more like a wrap than a sandwich, cellophane keeping it safe in case I didn't eat it right away.

I didn't answer and returned my attention to my right shoe. I pulled at the string, holding it tight. Maybe the amount of force would jog my memory. Something sparked through my veins, causing me to drop it, but the memory didn't come. "Was I wearing shoes that night?" I asked.

Mom blinked, taken aback by my question. I never asked her anything about those days. I never talked about it. She sighed and sat next to me on the grass. "They fell off." She bit her trembling lip, trying not to let the memories bring more tears. Her voice cracked as she said, "Bradley, I failed you." There came the waterworks.

I swallowed the lump in my throat. I shouldn't have brought it up. I should have let it go. I wanted to move past this already. I struggled to think of something else to focus my attention on, but her wails were too distracting. "Mom, you know you did everything you could, right?"

"No." She shook her head between sobs. "I could've been paying more attention." She paused, drawing her shaking fingers to her lips. Her eyes darted, gazing at nothing. "That lady was screaming, and the girls were crying." Her voice trailed off, her brows knitting. "Gretta.

The police told me her name was Gretta Thoring. She was taken from Colorado Springs when she was a little one. She'd been missing for twenty years. Her parents had an empty grave for her and everything. They thought she was dead." Mom shook her head as a new wave of sobs came. "I can't imagine not having you here today—for you to be gone twenty years, for you to not recognize us or remember us, for you to not know your name."

This was news to me. I never knew the blonde woman's name or her background. Garrett always called her a profanity. She did everything he told her to do. I thought it was because she was afraid, but now I think it might've been more than that. I'd seen it in one of our old neighbors, and I'd seen it in Olga—women who fell in love with the men who hurt them, women who sympathized, made up excuses. How convenient for Garrett to create someone so complacent they'd do his bidding without supervision. When they had the chance to run, to escape, they would choose to stay instead. Gretta—a woman who didn't even know her own name— screamed and fought when the cops came to her aid.

"Garrett!" she had shouted herself hoarse, her eyes never leaving his body. What allegiance. What sick, twisted loyalty.

He'd let her live.

"Mom, he was gonna kill me," I clarified. I wouldn't have been like Gretta if the police hadn't found me. I would've been fed to a mountain lion. She knew that, right? Well, maybe not the mountain lion part.

Mom nodded, curling her lips over her teeth, a strange high-pitched sound emitting from her vocal cords. The noise shot my heart rate up, sweat sticking to my skin. It didn't last long. She clamped her mouth shut, her lips still wobbly. She tried to wipe the tears from her cheeks, but fresh ones sprouted to replace them. "Frank told me about the other kids," she finally admitted. Great. I was going to have to have a talk with Frank the next time I saw him. He couldn't go blabbing my secrets to my mother.

There were other kids that Garrett had stolen before me—kids whose decaying bodies I sometimes saw when he threatened me.

"Why didn't you tell anybody?" she asked, flabbergasted.

I could feel my blood beginning to boil. I could smell it rushing through my nose, through my face. My hands shook. I didn't know why I was suddenly angry, but I couldn't stop it from erupting. "There's nothing that could have been done for them!" I shouted, flying to my feet. I left her wallowing in the grass as I slammed the sliding glass door shut behind me. I wanted the day to end.

Dad bounded down the stairs. I tried to pass him, but he caught my arm. "I want you and Blake to stay out of each other's business for the rest of the day."

"Don't worry," I growled, yanking my arm from his grasp. "I don't feel like seeing his face right now."

Blake was nothing compared to my own torturous memories.

3
FRANK ALMOST PUTS ME ON DEATH WATCH
BRADLEY

"I didn't see you at school yesterday."

Savanna's words jarred me from my stupor. I blinked, lifting my head from the desk. I couldn't believe we were already in our sixth class of the day. I'd been in a daze the entire day. Savanna bit her lip, her thin dark eyebrows pulling together above her blue eyes. "Ursula and I came by your house last night, but your mom said you weren't feeling well."

"I'm fine," I lied. Savanna and her sister lived across the street from us. I shouldn't have been surprised that one of the many rings from the doorbell had been them. "I just don't like Halloween."

"That's an understatement," my godsister, Serena, said with a harrumph as she passed us on her way to her desk. I shot her a glare that she missed. Serena had only been back to school for a month after her supposed quarantine for mono. We all knew the real story, though. She'd been recovering from whatever massive internal damage the neo-Nazis had caused. Nobody really knew what happened to Serena in the bunker. The only information I'd been able to dig up was that she'd lost a kidney. There were no broken bones, no visible bruises, nothing to indicate what they'd done to her.

"What does she mean by that?" Savanna demanded, placing her hand on her hip. Savanna was probably the only diviner in the school who hadn't heard the long, dark summary of my past. She'd heard bits and pieces, and I preferred it to stay that way. The less she knew about me, the better. Our mutual friend Jay-Jay was pretty good at keeping my secrets. Serena, on the other hand… well, I just hoped Savanna never asked her directly.

Serena's and my parents had been best friends since they were our age, which meant pretty much every piece of my family's gossip reached her ears. She'd been the one to blab my past to Jay-Jay. I was sure she'd inevitably blab to Savanna too if I wasn't careful.

"Bradley Chambers, if you are keeping secrets from me—" Savanna was cut off by Jay-Jay's sudden entrance.

"You've been going out for two months, Savanna. Give him some time." Jay-Jay slung the laptop bag he used as a backpack over the back of the chair next to mine. Savanna silently deliberated for a second before slinking away to her seat in the front row. She always listened to Jay-Jay. They'd been friends since kindergarten.

"That was new," I said, referring to her impatience. Savanna had waited weeks for me to get the courage to talk to her. After two months, though, she'd grown apprehensive, desperate to know me better.

Jay-Jay smiled, taking a seat. "She knows I've seen more of the future, and she hates waiting for something she trusts is most definitely going to happen." Jay-Jay'd been the one to initially see us together. He had visions like my mom.

"What'd you see?" I asked, curiosity getting the better of me. Since the day Savanna and I first met, Jay-Jay'd been dropping hints that Savanna and I were destined to be together, but he'd never once been specific about his visions. At least, not to me.

Jay-Jay wrinkled his nose, shaking his head. "I already feel like I'm intruding. I'm not about to make this awkward."

Oh God. What had he seen?

Something in my facial expression must have been amusing to him because he busted into laughter. "Relax." I didn't think he realized how impossible that was for me to do with everything going on. I tried to breathe slower. His smile dissipated. "You should tell her, though. Sooner rather than later."

I choked on my breath, my heart beating faster at the thought. There went all my effort. Wasted. I caught sight of my godsister from the corner of my eye.

Jay-Jay had been avoiding eye contact with Serena since the bunker. It drove her nuts. Not because she wanted him to talk to her but because she couldn't have a normal argument with him. She seemed to think he knew all along what the New Order would do to her—and I thought she might've been right. Jay-Jay was the one to alert us to the enemy. He also knew they would capture Serena. He'd been skimpy on the details, but it was highly plausible Jay-Jay had known more than he had let on. I wasn't sure how I felt about it, especially since I knew psychics only see absolutes—they can't change what they see in their visions. Serena should've known better. Both our moms have the same ability.

"Not until you face Serena," I said. He winced at the reminder. "Seriously, dude, you gotta admit something."

Jay-Jay traced his front teeth with his tongue. For a second, I didn't think he was gonna respond. Finally, he sighed. "It's the burden of the psychics to know too much. While some think knowledge is power, we often find that knowledge is sacrificial, for we know what we'll lose."

I blinked. Was he quoting the Bible? Socrates? Some other famous thinker guy?

He glanced at me from the corner of his eye. "Your mom taught me that."

Oh. Well, I was close. Jay-Jay had been speaking to my mom—psychic to psychic. Should've known.

"I was talking to Mr. Lindt just now." Mr. Lindt was Serena's telepathic father. Serena, Jay-Jay, and I had just left his classroom where he taught algebra. I wasn't wondering what had held Jay-Jay up, but I was given the answer anyway. Jay-Jay continued. "I was asking him about unknowns. You remember that speech he gave on the first day of class?"

I shook my head. I was lucky to remember anything from algebra class.

"I didn't know he was a telepath at the time, but it got me thinking. He said he loved the mystery of the unknown. That's weird, right? Coming from a telepath? Those people have all this useless, trivial knowledge of everyone. So I decided to ask him about it. Turns out he also finds his powers are a burden. Sometimes he hears things he doesn't want to hear. He's lucky he can turn it off, tune it out. Psychics don't have that luxury."

Serena had once told me about the day she grew into her powers. Mr. Lindt hadn't seemed at peace at all not knowing what would happen to his daughter. It's one of the few events psychics like his wife can't see. Even they don't know how a new diviner's power will turn out. In that case, how could he love the unknown? Wouldn't his life continue to be a hundred times better with his gift? Wasn't it better to know? He couldn't possibly be at peace blocking everyone's thoughts.

It all sounded like a bunch of bull to me—diviners pretending they're at peace. It was the one belief I had adopted from my grandfather since moving to Indianapolis. Diviners are never at peace. In a short time, I'd seen how correct Grandpa Anderson had been. The hypothetical enemies he rambled on about were real the entire time. Little had I known that they'd been after me since New Mexico. Those other boys—the ones whose decayed bodies are buried throughout Sangre de Cristo— they had probably all been diviners too. If they weren't, they were targeted for being Romani. Funny how there's a stereotype regarding Romanies stealing children… when Romanies, as well as the diviners, are the ones being kidnapped.

Diviners come from multiple lines of Romani ancestries, forming their own branch of identity following the holocaust, or the *porajmos,* as Romanies call it. A long time ago, Romanies were banned from England, Portugal, Spain, and other European countries. An entire race or ethnicity became *illegal.* Our ancestors couldn't walk outside or be seen without persecution.

Since I look white like my dad, it's hard for me to imagine that level of racism. Garrett targeted me because my mom was a fortune-teller. But even in England, it was illegal to *pretend* to be a "gypsy." People used to paint their faces brown and dye their hair black and dress in overly sexualized costumes, demeaning an entire group. The only reason it was illegal was because it confused the police. People still do this here in the States—especially at Renaissance fairs. Some countries would even ship the Romani people here to be slaves. Slaves!

I was already getting myself worked up by the time Mrs. Scar cleared her throat halfway through her lecture on the European Renaissance. I'd learned a lot in the last month or so regarding that part of my heritage, and it pissed me off.

A PowerPoint slide of old sixteenth-century artwork accompanied Mrs. Scar's lecture. The works of Rafael, Michelangelo, and the rest of the Ninja Turtles gang overlapped on the screen. That's when I saw it in the bottom left corner—a painting from Caravaggio. I'd seen this painting before—a Romani woman stealing a ring from a man's finger as she read his fortune. A copy of this artwork hung proudly on Olga's bedroom wall back in Itasca. She drew a different meaning from it than I did. I saw it as another stereotype portraying Romanies as thieves. Olga found it funny, almost metaphorical—the ring a symbol of the man's heart. The woman isn't simply stealing a valuable object but the man's love and becomes the object of the man's desire.

I know better though. I know what people thought (and still think) of the Romani people. I know antiziganism when I see it. Oh God, that was another word I hated. The word itself was antiziganist. It stemmed from the German word *zigeuner*, or "traveler"—another stereotype.

I'd been surprised by how many people cared about my mom's lineage. "I don't scam people," Mom had to explain on multiple occasions when we lived in Illinois. "I genuinely try to help others overcome their fears, their addictions, their grief. I truly believe that it's my calling in life to make the world a better place one person, one fortune, one session at a time." My mom had helped so many over the years—whether they were believers or not—that most of her clients never accused her of stealing or scamming or making things up. They knew in their hearts that what she said to them was always either true or well-intentioned. Her gift had even saved lives.

Our old fundamentalist church wasn't so keen on the idea and, on multiple occasions, had tried to push us out, but Mom would stand her ground. "We can't make positive change if we run," she'd said. We moved anyway.

It's an old Romani tradition that women provided for their families by telling fortunes, whether they were psychic or not. They would learn the craft from their mothers or grandmothers—and yes, *some* would steal— but it was one of the only ways the women knew to make money. Others—both men and women—would perform on streets, singing or dancing or some other form of entertainment. They were seen as beggars, poor, filthy— referred to as untouchables. Several Romanies traveled— many still do—because they feared that staying in one place for too long would bring trouble. While they learned to speak many languages, Romanies were known by outsiders to be traditionally illiterate, believing that the Romani language lacked sophistication or written words. This isn't true, though. It was just difficult for Romanies to access formal schooling in their countries. My great-grandmother, whose family had settled in Poland, learned to read Polish from a neighboring Jewish girl, but even after decades of living in the States, she struggled to read English. Mom has been worried about Great-Grandma Anderson's eyesight when she'd briefly reappeared in our lives. She could hardly read at all in August.

Romanies were always lower class because they were never allowed to succeed. My great-grandmother's grandparents were driven to alcoholism. They were the last nomads in my family line. Their children, who held very few good memories of their parents, stayed in Szczurowa. Their entire family, except for my great-grandmother, was murdered during a Nazi raid. My blood boils for them.

I slammed my textbook closed. The sound startled half my classmates. Mrs. Scar paused her speech to assess my body language. I made her nervous. I'd run out of her classroom before—not because of anything she said or did, but still. She knew me as a troubled kid because Frank had strict rules for my teachers to contact him immediately if I jumped off the rails. I felt kinda bad for her. It wasn't her fault I had no patience.

I tried to walk calmly out of the classroom but dropped a few things on my way. I left them. Someone— probably Jay-Jay or Savanna—would get them back to me sooner or later.

Frank met me two-thirds of the way to the front offices. "What's wrong?" he huffed, holding out his arms questioningly. I kept walking toward the offices, my hands shaking. I wanted to break something. The second I was through his office door, I chucked my textbook and a journal to the ground. They slid across the carpet, the journal slipping away before the book hit the wall.

Frank quickly shut the door behind him. "You're going to have to tell me what's going on."

I kicked at the leg of a chair, lightly at first and then with full force. My toes stung as the chair tipped, nicking the wall in the process. It had been a while since I'd let myself get angry like that. I usually tried to run it off. I punched the wall—furious, hot, wet tears sprouting from my tear ducts. I was so tired of everything that continued to happen to me. I was so tired of living my life. Why did I constantly feel like I was fighting? Whether it was against a visible enemy or not? Why couldn't I mentally escape from the memories, from the pain, from the hurt? I didn't want to be like that anymore.

The last time I blew up in Frank's office, it was pretty much about the same thing. I couldn't seem to move forward, to remove my curse. I drew my fist back, ready to shoot it forward again, but an invisible force held my hand.

"Stop," Frank ordered.

"Let me go." He wasn't physically touching me, but I knew it was him holding me back. Like my sister Paige, Frank was telekinetic. He could stop an object in motion simply by focusing on it. He was more controlled than my sister—her powers were tied to her rapidly changing emotions. She could destroy our house if she weren't careful.

Frank shook his head firmly. "Not until you tell me what's going on." I gritted my teeth but didn't explain. I didn't know where to begin. I wanted to hit something— to feel physical pain to match my emotional turmoil. He huffed. "Seriously, Bradley. I can't have a broken wall or a broken fist on my conscious."

I tilted my head. That was an idea. I'd broken my wrist when I was six. It was another bad memory— another example of my misfortune. My mom had a different opinion. I had walked away from a car accident that killed five people. To her, it was a miracle, but I had lost my best friend. "What's a little extra force?" I asked through gritted teeth, fighting Frank's telekinesis.

Frank stepped in between me and the wall, angling his shoulder in the path of my extended fist. "If I let go and you hit me, that's battery against a police officer, which the State of Indiana does not take lightly."

I closed my eyes, sucking in a lungful of air. He was right. I didn't need yet another thing to feel guilty about. I tried to yank my arm back, but Frank still had a telekinetic hold on it. "Let me go," I grumbled, opening my eyes again.

He pointed to the toppled chair as the resistance melted. "Sit." His nostrils flared, and his brown eyes lit with fury. I obeyed, righting the chair before plopping in it. Frank leaned against his desk, his arms crossed. "Is this still about New Mexico?" My hands shook thinking about it. Frank sighed. "Bradley, do you know what PTSD is?"

I let out a strange laugh. I'd heard of it before, but he couldn't possibly be implying that I had it. "I'm not a soldier."

Frank leaned forward, attempting to meet my gaze. "In many ways, you've been through a lot more than some of the soldiers I've met who've come back from the Middle East."

I laughed, which came out as strangled and high-pitched. It took a minute to stop myself. Finally, I smirked. "Tell that to the guys who come back dead." They'd been through so much they hadn't made it home. Maybe that was the preferred way to go. At least they didn't have to live with the anguish.

"This isn't funny, Bradley." Frank shook his head. "I have no doubt in my mind that this is something you struggle with. Your parents are worried about you, and frankly, you're starting to scare me." I laughed at his transparency, and he continued. "Post-traumatic stress disorder can be dangerous to try to fight alone—"

"I'm not gonna off myself," I interrupted, realizing where he was headed with his public service announcement. I paused, annoyed, exhaling. "I'll be fine—give me a week." I'd be better once Halloween week was behind me. I'd have to be.

Frank narrowed his eyes, suspicious. "That's not code for 'give me a week to put my affairs in order,' is it?"

"If it was, would I tell you?" I asked. It was probably not the right thing to say, in hindsight.

Frank reached for his desk phone, dialing an extension. My heart pounded in my chest, blood rushing through my ears. He wasn't calling for backup, was he? Surely, he wasn't going to force me to go see a legitimate psychiatrist. I was fine. Besides, what was the likelihood of finding a psychologist who would understand the culture I was raised in—who wouldn't be concerned when I started rambling about the powers of the diviners? What were the odds of a diviner in the mental health field living in or around Indy?

Frank spoke into the phone, pressing it close to his face. "Hey, Hope. It's Frank. Can you send Jay-Jay Jones to my office for a few minutes?" Hope. That had to be Mrs. Scar's first name. There was a pause as he listened to whatever my history teacher was saying to him. He glanced at the clock. Class would nearly be over. "Tell him to bring his stuff then, that's fine." He hung up the phone and glared at me. "How 'bout you try lying to me with a psychic in the room?"

I rolled my eyes. "Why didn't you call the telepath from down the hall?" Mr. Lindt would have been a better choice if he wanted to test my sincerity. Serena's dad was probably in the middle of teaching a class, though.

Frank frowned. "He left for the day." Mr. Lindt *left?* But hadn't Jay-Jay just spoken with him? He seemed fine when I saw him less than an hour before, not that I was paying attention. Frank didn't elaborate. Maybe one of his other kids had a doctor's appointment or something. The Lindts had four children, after all.

★

It didn't take long for Jay-Jay to knock on the door. He seemed nervous when Frank let him in, shooting me questioning glances.

"What'd you do?" he whispered, taking the other seat.

I let out a short laugh. It almost sounded normal this time. "Frank's being paranoid."

"About what?"

Frank jabbed his finger at me. "I just need to know that he has plans to stay alive."

Jay-Jay glared at me. "What the hell, man?"

I shrugged. "You know I'm not going to die soon. You were literally just telling me about your visions." He hadn't been specific, but it had seemed I starred in several.

Jay-Jay huffed, studying his hands. "That doesn't mean anything," he mumbled.

"What d'you mean?"

My best friend flexed his jaw. His eyes looked watery. My heart beat a little harder in my chest. He was starting to make me nervous. I tried to remind myself that the future can't change. He'd seen me in the future, so obviously I wasn't going to die. What was his problem?

After several long seconds, he held out his hand. "Give me your hand." He didn't look at me, his eyes on his knees. I gave him my hand, trying to feign confidence. I wasn't going to die. Especially not by choice. That wasn't my style.

His dark eyes were unfocused as he searched through the glimpses of my future for something significantly wrong. After a minute or so, he abruptly yanked his hand back, gasping in a lungful of air.

My heart stopped.

4
IF THERE WAS A CURE...
BRADLEY

"Why would you do this to me?" Jay-Jay moaned, covering his face with his hands. I shrank in my chair. Was I going to die? I wondered how it would happen. *Would I let the diabetes end me?* That sounded painful and drawn out. *Maybe I would swallow a bunch of pills. Could I stab myself with a kitchen knife?*

Jay-Jay slid his hands far enough down his face to reveal his eyes. Frank caught his gaze, his eyes pleading for an answer. Jay-Jay's voice was a whisper. "I don't want to know things. I always see too much."

Frank's apprehensive shoulders fell, his hand lifting to rub his eyes with his thumb and middle finger. "I shouldn't have involved you."

"No, you shouldn't have," Jay-Jay spat, his face twisting in anguish. If only he'd gotten over what had happened to Serena before Frank dragged him into my mess.

I swallowed a hard lump in my throat, forcing the question out with my breath. "Am I going to die?"

Jay-Jay looked at me like I'd suggested we storm the Capitol. "Of course not." He stood and left the room, the bell ringing in perfect synchronization with his exit.

I tried to talk to Jay-Jay during our last class of the day, but he was icing me out. Actually, he was icing everybody out, just like he'd been doing to Serena since the whole Nazi fiasco.

Serena most definitely noticed, her upper lip curling into a smile of satisfaction. "What'd you do to Jay-Jay?" She crossed her arms expectantly. She was enjoying this. She had to be. Now we knew how she felt.

Savanna nudged Jay-Jay with her elbow to no avail, shooting me a questioning glance.

Serena's ex-boyfriend smirked from the row in front of us. "Cat got your tongue?" Ever since Kase and Serena split, he'd been sitting farther away from her but still within earshot in case something diviner-related came up. He didn't want to let go of his connection to other diviners when his family had been actively ignoring their gifts. The Schwartzes wanted to be normal so bad—craved it with their entire beings. Kase was to do everything in his power to appear ordinary. He played the role of high school football jock too well.

I glanced at Jay-Jay. Was this what his recent attitude change had been about? Did he no longer want to be a diviner? I knew he was starting to hate his visions, but I didn't think it had reached the extent that he wanted to be normal. I didn't know much about Jay-Jay—having known him for only a few months—but he always seemed to be in tune with his ability. Everything he knew about the diviners he learned from Savanna's family. He was a "half-breed" like me. Growing up in a single-parent home—a single parent who is an undivine—neither he nor his mother had known anything of what Jay-Jay would become. Receiving his powers was a surprise.

I can't imagine not ever knowing about the diviners. I'd always been told that when I turned ten, I'd inherit a random diviner ability. It had given me something to look forward to. It was exciting. I grew up with tales and children's fables like the story of Ankhita the Deceiver, who, like Olga, could transform into various creatures. Jay-Jay had none of that knowledge. Four Decembers ago, he woke from a vivid dream involving a snow day that wasn't in the forecast. Turned out, he'd already lived the day in his sleep. Everything happened exactly as it had in his dream.

The last bell rang for the day, snapping me out of my thoughts. I blinked, trying to refocus on the present. What was I worried about again? Oh, right. Jay-Jay and his ominous vision. As if Jay-Jay was answering my unspoken question, he slipped me a piece of paper before quickly disappearing into the throng of students. Unfolding it, I studied the nine words he had scrawled in his chicken-scratch handwriting. "If there was a cure, would you take it?" My heart skipped a beat. What did he mean by that? A cure for the diviners? No way. My abilities were crap, but I wouldn't get rid of them if I had the chance. They were a part of me. Besides, I was finally learning how to put them to use. I could make objects disappear—a handy trick to have if I were ever kidnapped again.

Savanna leaned over my shoulder, trying to see the message Jay-Jay had handed me. "What does it say?"

I crumpled the note, stuffing it in my jeans pocket. "Nothing," I muttered irritably. How could Jay-Jay want to bail on us? How could he want to deny the part of him that connected him to an entire community of diviners?

Savanna draped her arm over my shoulder. We were the same height. Her voice was low, sad. "Why don't you tell me things?"

It took all my focus not to shake her off. "Because I don't know everything." I didn't. I had no idea what Jay-Jay had seen. The past I knew well—lived in it sometimes—but the future was always something that evaded me. I knew she wasn't asking about Jay-Jay, though.

She pulled away. "I'm not stupid, Bradley. Don't treat me like I am." She could never be stupid. Savanna was smart—smarter than me anyway. She had a focus that I would never have. It bugged her more than anything when people assumed the opposite. She was gorgeous. Her eyes were a startling blue, contrasting her brown complexion. Her thin hair was long and straight, although often it was pulled into a ponytail for cheer. She'd tugged it loose hours ago, letting it fall to her waist. I wished I had the patience to give her more of my attention, but I'd already ruined the afternoon.

I rolled my eyes, stuffing my textbooks into my backpack. "I know you're not stupid, Savanna. I just don't want to talk about it."

She followed me out of the classroom, trying to match my pace. "Don't give me that crap." Her voice started to shake, tears sprouting from the corners of her blue eyes. Grabbing my arm, she pulled me to a stop. "Something is going on. First, you ignore me. Now, Jay-Jay. He saw something bad, didn't he? Why don't you all want to tell me? Is the New Order back? Is my life in danger? My sister's? My parents'?" Her voice kept climbing octaves as she continued to guess. Then it returned to a low, broken sound. "You?" She searched my eyes, one hand on my upper arm, the other holding my hand, pleading for an answer. Pleading specifically that it was not me the New Order was after.

I thought about that for a second—the possibility that the New Order had returned. Its members spanned across the country and, although several of them had died the night we were in the bunker, I doubted we'd seen the last of them.

Savanna's eyes searched mine for answers, my breath catching in my throat at her nearness. She stared at me with her ocean blue eyes as if she were peering into my soul, considering the possibility that maybe one day we'd be pulled apart and begging the universe that it would not be so. Experts say it's unlikely that anyone would meet their soulmate in their teenage years. It was moments like these, though—with her eyes peering into mine—that I believed we perhaps surpass all the odds.

I knew I'd have to tell her everything. Maybe not at that second, but soon. I also knew there was no way I could sugarcoat my past for her. She'd have to hear all of it—well, maybe not some of the more gruesome details. Still, it wouldn't be pretty.

I lifted my free hand to sweep away her thin brown hair and rested my hand on the back of her head, my fingers intertwining with her roots. Leaning in, our noses touching, I stared into her eyes, whispering a promise I hoped would stay true. "I'm not going to die." She deserved that much reassurance in the present. She had to know I wouldn't die—not according to Jay-Jay, so she didn't need to worry so much. That's when I kissed her. The thought of breaking my promise scared the hell out of me, but I didn't want to think about the possibility. I was a survivor—I always had been—and I hoped to God everyone around me would be too.

A horrible thought occurred to me. What if Jay-Jay had seen *her* death? If he was *that* upset? No. He couldn't have, could he? My heart leaped into my throat, pounding violently. Savanna was Jay-Jay's oldest friend. He'd nearly wrung Serena's neck when he'd realized how much she had put Savanna's life in danger last August. It would explain why he had shut down—why he wanted to be cured.

I suddenly didn't want to let go of her, let her out of my sight, let her out of my thoughts. If it was Savanna who would die… or almost die… or whatever it was that made Jay-Jay so upset that he had to ignore everyone as he did Serena, how long did I have with her?

Savanna pulled away first, gasping for air, her cheeks flushed. "You gotta let go of me." She laughed breathlessly. I hadn't realized I was holding her so tightly. I relaxed my grip on her reluctantly. The hallways had mostly cleared. Savanna blinked, losing her dazed expression. She glanced at the hallway clock. "Shoot." Trying to pull her hand out of mine, she tried to skip away. "Coach is going to kill me if I'm late for practice."

I pulled her back. "Don't leave." What if this was the last time I'd see her alive?

She smiled, placing her index finger on my lips as if to silence me. "I have to. We have state finals coming up."

I continued to keep my hold on her hand, gazing into her eyes, worried that any of these moments could be the last I saw of her. She hadn't picked up my newfound apprehension. *Good.* Slowly, I let go, let her return to her oblivious, seminormal life—a life that hopefully wouldn't involve anything more traumatic than she'd already experienced. I forced a smile, working to hide my fears. "Have fun."

She pecked me on the cheek. "I'll call."

Then I was alone.

★

I climbed into my mom's van a few minutes later, my mind preoccupied with the unknown of Jay-Jay's visions. Could my fears be right? Was something going to happen to Savanna—to the girl he'd been telling me all along was the key to my destiny?

"You got a little bit of lipstick," Paige pointed out, trying to embarrass me as she rubbed the stain from my cheek. I didn't fight her. Normally, I'd care, but under the current circumstances, it didn't matter if Savanna had left the proof of her kiss on my cheek or my lips. I only cared about how I'd been pushing her away, keeping my secrets to myself, holding in my pain as to not alter her emotions. I cared that I'd taken her for granted, taken the strange promise of our destinies intertwining as proof that we'd make it. What if our destinies, all this time, involved losing the other? Like the story of Orpheus and Eurydice I had learned in the Latin class Serena had signed me up for. Or the story of Romeo and Juliet we were reading in English. I'd lost people close to me before. I lost my best friend back in Niles and my brother in Itasca. I seemed to have also lost pieces of myself. I didn't want to be lost anymore. I didn't want to *lose* anymore.

Mom glanced at me in the rearview mirror as she drove through the neighborhood, worry lines creasing her forehead. When she parked the van in the driveway, she turned to me, her hand on my knee. Mom tried to never touch me unless she was desperate for a vision. I flinched too much, reminding her of the moments she felt she had failed me. The others started to leave, making their way inside the house. She frowned, her eyes glassy. "That can't be right," she muttered.

"What did you see?" I asked, grabbing for her hand as she pulled away.

She moved too fast, slipping from my grasp. "I'm sure it's nothing," she reassured me, attempting to smile. Mom wasn't so great at hiding her emotions. Like Paige, she was practically an open book.

"No." I shook my head, swallowing the lump in my throat. She climbed out, and I hurried to follow her. "No, no, you can't say something like that and not tell me what's going on. Not with Jay-Jay acting all pissed at me."

"Jay-Jay's mad at you?" she said innocently as if she hadn't seen whatever Jay-Jay had. She headed toward the front door.

"Mom!" I chased her down the walkway, reaching the door before she did. My hand curled around the handle, wanting desperately to control our conversation. "Is Savanna in danger?"

Mom tilted her head, scratching her scalp. Running a finger along her hair, she pulled a strand or two back in place. "Bradley, let me ask you something. Be honest." She pursed her lips, staring at a second-story window. I waited for her to ask her question. Finally, she looked at me, her eyes narrowing. "If there was a cure, would you take it?"

I took a step back, the heels of my feet hitting the door. *What?* My hand quickly dug into my jeans pocket, procuring the note Jay-Jay had written not too long ago. I unfolded it, rereading the words. It was the same question. My heart thudded against my chest, my breathing growing unsteady. With shaky hands, I held out the piece of paper. Why was everybody asking me this? Was this still about our powers, our gifts, our divinity? If it was, my answer was still the same. No way would I want to be "cured." Were my mom and Jay-Jay seeing a future where I was?

She raised an eyebrow at the note but didn't say anything, waiting for my reply. How was I supposed to answer a question like that without any explanation or context? When I didn't respond, she glanced at her feet. "Frank called me this afternoon. He's worried you're going to try something stupid."

There was the anger I was feeling over an hour ago, coming back to haunt me. I stiffened. "I thought Jay-Jay convinced him I was fine." Seriously. What was everybody's sudden obsession with my well-being?

Her lip twitched. "Psychics only see absolutes." Wow. Was she seriously doubting Jay-Jay's ability to see my future? If I died, he would have seen it, and I was pretty sure my mom would have been freaking out if she'd seen it too.

"Death is a pretty final absolute!" I shouted. "You can't get more absolute than dying!"

Mom held out her hands, taking a deep breath, her tone still calm. "Don't get defensive with me. We're only trying to cover our bases. Your dad and I don't want to lose another kid, especially now that we're going to have more of them."

"Mom?" My anger dissipated as quickly as it came. "Wha…?" Surely, she wasn't trying to tell me she was pregnant. I shook my head at the idea. That was impossible. She had a vision. If she were pregnant, her powers wouldn't be working.

She sighed, her shoulders slumping. Her lips curved into a frown, lines creasing her forehead. "I'm keeping Paige home from school tomorrow. We're about to get a distraught phone call from the Burnetts." She turned her head to look at the tree in our front yard, watching as the orange and brown leaves started to fall.

The Burnetts? Our old neighbors from Itasca? What could possibly be so important that Paige would have to miss school.

When she turned back to me, her eyes were wet. "Bailey Burnett's not going to make it through the night." Oh. Right. Mr. Burnett was given six months to live. That was at the end of July, right before we moved. He was the father of Paige's best friends back in Itasca. He'd beaten cancer before, but he wasn't expected to beat it a second time. They'd received the news on Rebecca's birthday, three days before we left town for good.

My heart stopped. "Does Paige know?"

Mom shook her head.

The events of that July day burned in my memory. Mrs. Burnett had rushed in to see my mother, to beg her for good news when she had none to give. My mother had a vision, proving the doctor's prognosis correct. Had she seen more than that? How did Mr. Burnett dying have anything to do with the number of kids in our house?

Mom saw my question forming before the words left my mouth. "Karston's having a tough time with the loss, so we'll be taking in the kids."

Karston was Mrs. Burnett's first name. The last time I saw her, she was a wrecking ball of panic. That wasn't a fair assessment, though. She'd just learned her husband wasn't going to make it. The Burnetts had three daughters—twelve-year-old twins, Sage and Seth, and a one-year-old, Tuesday. If they were coming to live with us, the house was about to get chaotic. Great. I had a hard time imagining having three Paiges around. I could barely stand the one. I wondered if that was why Mom kept the extra bedroom upstairs empty. Had she known all this time that the Burnetts would come to live with us? Had she had a vision that far—a little over three months—into the future?

"Hey, Mom?" I asked, scratching the back of my neck. "I'm curious. How far in the future can you actually see?"

She smiled, cupping my face in her hands. "Enough to know that if you try anything funny in the next few months, you won't succeed." Geez. If I wasn't going to die, then why was everyone concerned with my life? Why were they still pestering me? So what if I tried to end it all? What was the big deal if my attempts weren't going to kill me?

I grimaced. Maybe this was more about "the cure." In a way, that would be like killing a piece of myself. But why would I do it? "And Savanna?" I asked, figuring I didn't need to explain my reasons for asking.

Her smile disappeared, her expression neutral. "I don't want you to worry. There's probably a perfect explanation."

My heart pounded violently against my ribcage. She was being vague. I hated when psychics were vague. "What's nothing, Mom?" I asked, my teeth gritted in anticipation.

Mom didn't say anything for a moment, her eyes flicking over my expression as if to check my stability. Could I handle whatever information she had to throw at me? Probably not. I still wanted to know. "I can't see her," she finally said, her tone cautious.

Holy. I gripped the doorknob tighter, trying my best to keep myself grounded in the moment. She may have said she didn't *want* me to worry, not that I shouldn't, because this was big. Mom seems to have a bit of a blind spot for people who have premature death written into their destiny. Maybe not with Mr. Burnett, but she had with Jesse. She couldn't see my brother at all in her visions. Was it the same with Savanna? Could she not see her because otherwise she'd witness a death she didn't want to see? Maybe Jay-Jay could learn whatever trick Mom possessed to avoid those types of visions. Maybe, just maybe, Mom was too scared to look. I'd be.

"Mom." I grabbed hold of her wrist, squeezing it so that I might trigger a vision. She gaped at me, shocked that I'd gone as far as to grab her, but she didn't pull away. "See anything?" I asked, begging her to dismiss my fears.

She stood still for a few seconds, searching through pieces of my future for clues. After what seemed like too long a pause, she let her shoulders slump, her eyes refocusing. "I can't see her," she admitted again. I let go, my heart plummeting into my stomach. She continued, "I don't think it's anything to worry about, though. This happens sometimes when a certain vision could upset the universal balance. If more than one psychic is watching a particular event it could interrupt the signal. That's why I didn't see the trouble with the New Order ahead of time. Jay-Jay was already hyperfocusing on that event. If I were you, I'd ask your friend what he saw."

Yeah. Been there, tried that. All that got me was a vague question about a cure and an intense level of anger that could mean one thing—something bad was going to happen to Savanna.

5
MY SISTER HAS AN IDEA
BRADLEY

The whole no cell phone rule had never bothered me before. It wasn't like I had a lot of friends to call or text. Emergencies came and went, sure, but I survived without one. This was different, though. I wanted nothing less than to call and text Savanna, begging her for a quick reply so I would know she was safe. I paced the front room, watching the driveway across the street, waiting for her to come home from cheer practice. The house phone stayed in my hand, and I set her cell number to number six on speed dial. I'd never programmed anything on speed dial, but this seemed like as good a time as any.

"Bradley, come eat dinner," Mom called from the dining room. I ignored her, stopping to peer through the window for the thousandth time. I knew Savanna wouldn't be home, but logic didn't matter to me.

I hated that I couldn't drive yet. Serena and Jay-Jay were already signed up for driver's ed in the spring, but Savanna and I would have to wait almost another year before we became eligible.

I hated that Mom seemed so chill about this. It wasn't too long ago she was freaking out about not seeing Rebecca in her visions. She and Dad completely flipped when they noticed. (So maybe that was because Mom had temporarily lost her ability, but still.) How could she sit there so calmly? Was it because Savanna wasn't one of her own? Did she not care what losing her would do to me?

Jay-Jay had pointed out earlier that day how we'd only been with each other for two months. It felt longer and yet not enough. It was like time stopped when I was with her—nothing else mattered. Well, mostly nothing else.

I hit the six button again, putting the phone to my ear. It rang for too long before I got her voicemail. I listened to her recorded voice, thinking of that cliché in movies where a loved one keeps paying their dead spouse's phone bill so they could hear the sound of their voice. I scowled at the thought, hanging up. I didn't want to be one of those people. I paused, glancing at the screen. Why was I acting like she was already dead? She couldn't be, could she?

Rebecca set her fork on her plate, climbing out of her seat as I redialed. She was scowling as well, her brown eyes rolling with annoyance. It wasn't common for her to be annoyed so easily. She was soft like our mom—calm and sweet. I backed away slightly as she marched to me, grabbing my arm. She tried pulling me to the table, but my ten-year-old sister wasn't exactly the strongest person in the family, at least not physically. It was easy to resist her attempt. She groaned, balancing on her tiptoes as she reached to touch my face. I yanked myself back. "What are you doing?"

Rebecca hopped, still attempting to touch my forehead. "Testing a theory."

"With your powers?" I asked, angling myself beyond her reach. She nodded. She definitely had my attention. Rebecca didn't use her powers willy-nilly. Great-Grandma Anderson had called her the Chosen One. We weren't sure what all that meant, but we did know one thing—she could accomplish more than the average diviner. I'd seen her destroy half of Fort Ben with a small movement of her arms. If she could do something like that, could she tell me if something was going to happen to Savanna? I leaned toward her with my hands on my knees, and I braced myself for her verdict.

My sister stopped jumping, pausing to roll her shoulders like she was preparing to pitch a baseball. "Hold still," she ordered, gently placing her fingers on my temples. I obeyed, stiffening my muscles. Wouldn't want to mess up whatever she was doing by flinching. Mom watched us, her eyes wide, her knuckles gripping the back of her dining chair. Rebecca pushed her fingers upward like she was massaging my temples before letting go, pulling her hands shakily away. From what I could see from the corner of my eye, she appeared to be holding an invisible string. Her whole body trembled, her upper lip curling into a concentrated snarl. When she closed her hands into fists, a drop of blood dripped from one of her nostrils.

I dropped to the floor, gasping in chunks of air that stung my lungs. After a few seconds, my lungs felt like they were expanding, adapting to the change in my environment I didn't understand. It was like I was breathing for the first time, my mind clear of the fog that was usually there. My shoulders relaxed from their tightly wound position, the weight gone for once in my life. I studied my hands as I propped myself against the wall. They were calm, unshaking. The difference was astounding. I'd never breathed like this before. The strangeness of it all was refreshing.

Mom jumped from her chair, reaching my side in a matter of seconds. She placed her hand on my shoulder, and for once, I didn't flinch at the touch. I smiled, feeling useless memories fade away and not caring one bit about never being able to see them again. I was free from their burden. This was a game changer.

"What did you do to him?" Mom asked Rebecca, frantic for no reason.

I laughed. It was like Rebecca had pushed the emotional reset button on my brain. All the trauma was wiped from my memory. Tears of joy escaped my eyes as I reached for the phone in the middle of the floor. "I have to call Savanna."

"Apparently nothing because he still wants to call Savanna," Paige pointed out, joining us in the front room.

Mom glared at Rebecca. I couldn't understand what her anger was about. She was the one who wanted me to be cured of my "PTSD," as Frank called it. I thought this was it. This was the cure! It wasn't about my powers at all. It was about my trauma. The cure for my… my… I wasn't sure what to call it. Whatever. The point was, I was free. I'd been living with the cure practically my whole life!

I bounced to my feet, pulling Rebecca into a bear hug. "I don't think I've told you lately how awesome a sister you are."

"What about me?" Paige asked, offended.

I pulled away from Rebecca, whose smile mirrored my own, nodding to Paige. "You're okay." I laughed. Paige stuck her tongue at me as I pushed the phone's six button again. As I held it to my ear to listen to the dial tones, Mom practically growled at Rebecca.

"Undo it, now." Her voice was dangerous, completely out of character.

I shrugged it off, but Rebecca's eyes widened, her childish voice jumping an octave. "No!"

Savanna's voice came through the phone—her usual voicemail message. I hung up, getting ready to defend my sister. She never challenged Mom. Ever.

Dad's eyes flickered nervously between Mom and Rebecca, probably as confused as I was. Blake continued to shovel food in his mouth like nothing was happening. He'd been pretending I didn't exist all afternoon.

"Rebecca Valerie—" Mom started in on my sister's full name. If she wasn't serious before, she was now.

Rebecca wailed, stomping her foot, tears falling down her face. "Mom, no!"

I didn't understand either of their reactions. Shouldn't Mom be glad? Why was Rebecca suddenly crying at the thought of undoing whatever she'd done to me? I was already forgetting what it felt like to be me only a moment ago, but I knew it was something I didn't want back. Why was Mom fighting this?

"He was in pain, Mom!" Rebecca shrieked, defending her position.

Pain? What would that feel like? I wondered. I wasn't afraid of a little pain. *Bring it on!* I felt like Kase Schwartz, who was always geared up to win—whether it be in football or against a pack of neo… neo… darn, what were they called again?

"You took away his pain?" Paige asked, studying me. She tested the theory, pinching my arm.

An "ow" was all I could muster, but I didn't flinch away. She frowned, disappointed. Maybe I didn't like pain, but it wasn't so horrible that I would avoid it if necessary.

Rebecca stepped back before quickly turning, fleeing for the stairs. She stopped where the steps turned at a ninety-degree angle for one last defensive move. "I just didn't want him to suffer anymore!" Rebecca disappeared, running out of our sights to avoid Mom's illogical wrath.

Mom chased after her. As she grabbed the railing, she pointed at Paige. "Don't let him leave your sight."

I bounced on my heels. That sounded like a challenge. Paige crossed her arms, eyeing me suspiciously. "What'd she really do to you?" Silverware clinked against glass in the dining room, followed by Dad's feet thudding on the carpet.

I widened my smile, feeling like Genie from Aladdin. "I'm free." This was my time to escape—to be even freer. Dad was almost within reaching distance. I'd have to act quick. Making a mad dash out the front door, I made my escape.

Dad seldom attempted to catch me. He'd failed at it too many times. It was easy to outrun Paige. She used to be a gymnast—more of a stretcher than a runner. It was how Paige befriended the Burnett twins—the ones whose father wasn't going to make it through the night. It was also where all three of them made enemies with Olga's sister, Imogene.

I ran as fast as my feet could take me. It felt good, the cool air rushing through my hair and my clothes as I passed house after house. The high school wasn't too far from our neighborhood—maybe four miles—so I pushed to make it there before sunset. I'd run the distance before.

It took about an hour for me to reach the gym doors, but they were locked when I arrived, the parking lot deserted. Savanna wasn't there. I knew I had to see her, but I couldn't remember why. Barely pausing to catch my breath, I ran the four miles back to our subdivision. I considered joining a marathon as I dashed back. I missed running. Maybe I'd join the cross-country team. My doctors were always begging me to exercise more.

I was running south on German Church Road, the first houses of our neighborhood in sight, when I tripped and blackness overtook me.

I woke on the cold sidewalk, a strange light blurring my vision. A paramedic leaned over me, and the light disappeared. I thought maybe he was a police officer at first. He was dressed all in black with badges sewn onto the outfit. Red, white, and blue lights flashed from the boxy vehicle on the curb, illuminating the darkness.

"Can you tell me your name?" they asked, their fingers prodding at sore spots on my head.

"Bradley," I answered, my throat parched. I coughed. Probably should have brought water on my voyage.

I heard a familiar bleep from a police cruiser, but when I tried to tilt my head to see it, the paramedic fought my movement. A car door slammed.

"Who you got here?" a familiar voice asked.

"Frank!" I shot up, fighting the paramedic as he tried to hold me still. I swiveled my head to see him, battling the dizziness the movement caused.

"Dizzy?" the paramedic asked.

"No," I lied, blinking Frank into sight.

Frank crouched to get a better look at my face. "What are you doing here at night besides losing a battle with the sidewalk?" Angry disappointment clouded his voice. "I thought you weren't going to try to kill yourself."

I laughed, shaking my head at his inferred accusation. It was a ridiculous assumption. Why would I want to do that? I mimicked putting a gun to my head and shooting it, teasing Frank. I laughed at his visibly growing anger, his brows pulling together.

He narrowed his eyes. "Are you high?"

Another ridiculous question. Did he ever know me to do drugs? Okay, so maybe one drug. I threw my hands in the air. "On life!"

He growled. I guess that wasn't an adequate answer for him. Oh well. That was *his* problem.

Enough of his stupid questions. I started questioning *him*. "What are *you* doing out?" I asked, waving my free hand in the direction of his cruiser. Frank rarely ever worked the beat.

Frank stood, placing his hands on his belt. I took note of his hand's proximity to his taser. "I'm covering a shift for a friend." I swear he was a different person on the streets. His sense of humor was shot. He enjoyed his job at the school more. He claimed it was more fulfilling.

I stood, much to the paramedics' dismay, and felt the urge to disclose my real reason for being outside in the darkness. Of course, I couldn't be normal about it either. Smiling, I opened my mouth, letting lyrics tumble out of me off-key. I had to hum half the melody because I didn't know the lyrics too well. It was one of those love songs that was always playing on the radio stations.

Frank pointed at a medic. "Make sure you test him for narcotics." Geez. What was it gonna take for him to realize this was me without… what was it Rebecca took away from me?

"That won't be necessary!" My mom's breathless voice came from nowhere as she and Paige bounded up the sidewalk. I stopped singing. When Mom reached Frank, she whispered something under her breath. Frank's eyes widened in disbelief.

Paige grabbed my hand, tugging me in the direction of Dad's parked car. I hadn't heard the additional vehicle over my carefree singing. "Come on, birdbrain. Let's go home."

I twisted my arm free. "Not until I see Savanna first."
Paige groaned.

"This is going to be a lot of paperwork," Frank muttered to my mom, crossing his arms over his vest. Mom mimicked his action, initiating a staring contest between the two. I watched them, unblinking, interested in who would win. Cop versus psychic. Olga would've loved to see that. She'd call it a riot. I thought about calling her. We hadn't spoken since Jesse's funeral.

My eyes slid to Mom's shoulder. Something was missing. She didn't have her purse on her. She must've left it in the car. Tearing my eyes from the staring contest, I ran to the car and threw open the driver's side door. Paige ran after me, whining my name the entire time. Lunging for Mom's purse—which was lodged between the two front seats—I dug for her cell phone. It had to be in there somewhere. I could use it to call Olga—to catch up on life.

I noticed the keys in the ignition before I found the phone. I'd never driven before, but how hard could it be? People do it all the time.

Paige realized where my train of thought was headed as I pivoted my legs to reach the pedals. Her eyes practically bugged out of their sockets. "Bradley, don't!" She fought with me for a second as I tried to close the door, but I eventually won. She was no match for me. "Mom!" she screeched.

I turned the keys, listening to the engine roar to life. Mom and Frank reached the door seconds after I had hit the power lock. I laughed as they pounded their fists on the window, squinting through the tint. My foot hit the gas, the engine revving, the car staying put. Right. I guess it would have helped to put it in gear first. I grabbed the gear shift and tried to yank it back, but it didn't budge.

What? My eyes flickered over all the buttons and knobs, trying to figure out if there was a trick to making the gear shift move.

The doors unlocked by themselves, and Frank pulled the door open. Right. I was trying to escape from two telekinetics. Why did I think that would work well again? Grabbing my upper arm, he yanked me forcefully out of the vehicle. Something popped in my shoulder before he slammed me against the car.

Despite my arm and shoulder being in pain, adding to the headache I'd been ignoring, Mom was the one who yelped, her hands flying to her face. "Don't hurt him!" The paramedics stood frozen in place behind my mom and Paige, watching the scene in stunned silence, their foreheads puckered in confusion. Cold metal cuffs looped around my wrists, the color draining from my mother's face at the sight. Frank must've won the staring contest. It wasn't the first time I'd been arrested, sat in the back of a police car, or spent a couple of hours in a holding cell. Officer Joey's favorite pastime back in Itasca was finding a reason to do any of the above to me. This was a first with Frank, though. He usually wasn't this aggressive.

"Did the streets change you?" I asked fearlessly as he shoved me into the back of the squad car. This was the first time I'd been arrested since I discovered I could successfully make objects disappear. Frank's watchful gaze in the rearview as he drove must've meant he knew this too. I could Houdini my way out of the car if I wanted to. Still, it was more fun to watch him squirm.

I was surprised when he pulled the cruiser in front of my house. Mom pulled around us and into the driveway. Dad was standing in the doorway, the lights from inside illuminating his silhouette. As Frank led me across the grass, Dad addressed Mom. "Is it a full moon or something? Because our kids have been weirder than normal this week." I glanced at the sky, but I couldn't see the moon from that angle.

"Sunday, hun," Mom replied, sighing with exhaustion. Huh. So it was soon. For a brief second, I pictured us all as werewolves, ripping out of our clothes and changing into animal form. As a lowly shapeshifter, Olga could do it.

Footsteps pounded on the concrete driveway. We all turned to see who they belonged to. My heart thudded dangerously in my chest. Not from fear but from excitement. Savanna. It was Savanna! She rammed into me, my face in her hands, her lips fusing to mine. I willed the handcuffs away, having found a reason to free myself from their bondage. My fingers lost themselves in her hair. Hands wrenched at my sides, Frank and Dad pulling us apart. Paige pretended to gag.

Savanna's blue eyes seemed to glitter in the dark. "I figured out how to do a triple side flip today, you wanna see it?" She bounced as she said this, gearing up for the tumble trick. I didn't think she was going to take no for an answer, too pumped from her newfound talent.

I nodded. "Hell yes!"

She cheered, sprinting to the van, trying to make her way on top of the vehicle to gain some distance. Mom's voice grew nervous. "Um, Savanna, honey, I don't feel comfortable with you—"

"Don't worry, Mrs. Chambers." Savanna stood stick-straight on the roof of the van. "I've done it before. I can do it again." She smiled, bending her knees.

"Frank," Mom warned, refusing to take her eyes off my girlfriend.

"I got her," Frank answered as Savanna flung herself off the roof, flipping sideways in the air once, twice… I smiled as she flipped a third, her face inches from the ground. Frank pulled me back, thrusting himself forward, his face stuck in total concentration mode. Savanna's body froze, centimeters from certain injury. He let her down gently, Savanna squealing in delight the whole time.

"Did you see that?" She sprung to her feet, her hands flying up in a V shape. "I flew!"

Frank rubbed his forehead like he was fighting a headache. "Did Rebecca take the whole damn neighborhood's fear away?" Fear? Was that what this was all about?

6
THE ADVENTURES OF OUR LIQUID GOLD HEARTS
BRADLEY

Savanna ran to me again, and this time, I caught and spun her. *So this is what it's like to live without fear,* I thought. *I could get used to this.* Maybe that's what I needed to learn—to not be afraid of Savanna or her theoretical opinions.

Frank pointed at the second-story window, his expression sharpened with severity. He then pointed to the ground in front of him—a silent demand. I caught a glimpse of the upstairs hallway curtains moving, but it was only for a second, Savanna's lips recapturing my attention.

"I'm about to put the fear of God into that girl," Frank muttered before he grabbed my arm again, partially yanking me from my girlfriend.

Dad had left the front door wide open, the lit entryway making it easy to spot Rebecca's tentative figure through the storm door. The hinges creaked as she opened the door, peering at the scene. I'd never seen Frank so angry. His face was bright red—almost purple—

even under the dim outdoor lights. Rebecca bit her lip, stepping onto the porch. Her brown eyes were glued to the ground, her body trembling as she awaited Frank's shouts. Frank continued to pull me toward my sister as I pulled Savanna behind us.

"Are you trying to get people killed?" Frank's voice was low but harsh, air whooshing through his teeth with his words. Rebecca's face reddened to match Frank's, tears streaming down her cheeks. She shook her head. Her tears didn't quench Frank's anger. "You realize that's what could have happened tonight? These two could have killed themselves—"

"Like Romeo and Juliet." Savanna smiled at the thought, leaning her head on my shoulder. I tilted mine over hers, our heads resting against each other's.

Frank ignored her, continuing. "They could have killed other people—"

"Oh!" Savanna jerked her head excitedly, bashing her head into mine. *Ow.* "Like Bonnie and Clyde!"

I rubbed the side of my head until the brief pain was gone.

Frank grumbled something unintelligible under his breath. Rebecca lifted her head, eyeing Savanna with suspicion. She started to wipe the tears from her eyes as Frank persevered, listing the many things that *could* have happened but didn't. "They could have crashed cars, broken bones, landed in jail, gotten into fistfights—" That all sounded fun.

Rebecca broke him off this time, stomping her foot. "He doesn't want me to give it back to him!" I wasn't sure what she was talking about. I wasn't afraid of a little fear. "If I could give it back to him in doses, I would," Rebecca explained, the tears returning. "But I don't know how to do that. If I give it back, it'll hit him like a truck."

"Then hit me," I said, taunting her. "I can take it!" Fighting a truck? I could be like Superman, even if he wasn't my favorite superhero.

Savanna shrugged, uninterested. "Well, she didn't do anything to me."

"That's the other problem," Rebecca whispered, running her hand over her face to wipe away more tears. "She's right."

We probably all could have guessed that, but still, everyone stared at Savanna in silence, the confirmation soaking in. Savanna let go of me to perform a couple of cartwheels in the grass. Dad mumbled something about getting her parents, but Mom held his arm, looking like she was calculating something in her head, her eyes rolling to the night sky. A large hoop materialized in Savanna's hands, and she placed herself inside it, her hands gripping one part of it, her feet another. Circus tricks seemed to be of interest to her tonight. If she wanted, she could have a bright future in acrobatics. Savanna rolled with the hoop as if she were stuck inside a tire, her body upside down, then right side up, over and over again as she headed into the street.

"Rebecca, do it now!" Mom screamed.

Rebecca's cold hands touched my arm and then a rush of heat overtook me. It burned like a fire, running from my arm to my shoulders, quickly consuming my body.

A black sports car squealed as it turned onto our street, speeding toward us. My heart stopped, my lungs catching. Frank looked like he was pulling on an invisible rope. He yanked his arms back, Savanna spinning backward, knocking her grip loose from the hoop. The car sped past, barely missing her.

The fire continued to burn inside me. I couldn't breathe. Savanna scrambled to the edge of the driveway, her expression falling from hungry excitement to unparalleled horror, her brown skin the lightest I'd seen it. Her blue eyes unfocused, she let out a high-pitched bloodcurdling scream. The bass from the passing car drowned the noise for a second, but as it disappeared around the corner, the scream rattled Mom and Dad—they scrambled to her aid in search of the culprit to her fear. The lights across the street flickered on from her house.

I closed my eyes, my heart shattering into a million different pieces of glass. The shards poked and prodded my chest, painful enough to keep me from moving.

Rebecca let go of my wrist, stumbling, her quiet tears returning. Endless apologies tumbled out of her, but they were barely audible over Savanna's loud crushing sobs. I couldn't move to comfort either one of them. I was frozen in place, watching the memories return before my eyes.

Savanna's parents were shouting their daughter's name, asking questions to assess any injuries. At one point she cried, "Don't touch me!" After that, Mr. Huckleberry started cussing out my parents, adding to the chaos.

"The car didn't hit her!" Paige shouted across the lawn, floating between the crowd of parents and me.

"Car? What car?" Mrs. Huckleberry asked, her head swiveling to search for the vehicle that had nearly injured her daughter.

The temperature outside seemed to drop considerably, icing the fading burning sensation on my skin. I breathed in a shallow lungful of air, wary of the shards in my heart, and subsequently breathed the air back out. The memories started to fade from my vision. The glass shards dulled inside me, Savanna's wails diminishing with them. I caught Paige's eye before she swiveled her head back toward the end of the driveway. Savanna was hidden behind the sea of parents, Mr. Huckleberry's back blocking most of my view. I winced as a shard nicked me, returning my gaze to my sister. Paige was staring at me again, her mouth hanging open, her brown eyes wide.

"They're connected," she said at a normal volume. When nobody reacted, she said it louder. "They're connected!" A couple of heads turned. Mom nodded. The psychics all knew there was some kind of bond between

Savanna and me, but this—the connection between our fears—I wasn't expecting.

"Is there any way to break it?" Dad asked Mom. She glanced nervously at Rebecca.

Even though my youngest sister had her head buried in her lap, she managed to sense Mom's attention. "You can't," she mumbled the answer into her legs. "It's cosmic." I didn't think they could hear her from the end of the driveway, but Mom nodded. I wanted to ask more, but I was still fighting against the pain. What did she mean our connection was cosmic and that it couldn't be broken? That sounded like some next-level folklore. I could handle the idea that we were predestined to meet. Soulmates wasn't exactly a new concept. Being connected emotionally? Nope. Not cool. That was too much.

"You okay?" Frank asked me. I sucked in a deeper breath, several of the dull shards pricking me. I nodded anyway. I was expecting much worse. Rebecca made it sound like a near-death experience. Maybe it was. I had kind of built a tolerance to them. Frank glanced at the crowd of parents surrounding Savanna, who had seemed to calm herself into sniffles. He looked back at me, unconvinced as always. "Why aren't *you* on the ground?"

I breathed in again, testing myself. "It's *my* pain." Wincing, I breathed back out. "I know it best." It was a theory, but as far as theories went, it made no more sense than what Rebecca had said.

Focusing my attention on my seemingly all-knowing sister, I asked, "How'd you know you could do that? Take away a person's fear, I mean." Even though she had to give it back, the feat was still impressive.

Rebecca shrugged without lifting her head. "I just knew."

Okay. Seriously. How did she "just" know? Maybe she could do anything she put her mind to?

Rebecca stretched her arms, slowly lifting her head. Her blotchy eyes gazed past me to the group of people. "Tell Savanna I'm sorry. I didn't know what I did was going to trigger the connection."

"Trigger?" I coughed, the point of the shards scraping around inside me. "What do you mean? We were already connected." Everybody knew that. Jay-Jay had explained the whole connection thing months ago.

Rebecca shook her head, but instead of disagreeing, she said the thing we already knew. "You were connected by a string of fate." She tilted her head like she was listening to something none of us could hear. Her eyes focused on something far away, and she said, "It's rare, maybe rarer than me." Her lip twitched at the mention of her uniqueness. "Most people don't have a soulmate. They fall in love with each other *thinking* they've met their soulmate. It's not true. There isn't one person in the world that we each are destined to meet and fall in love with. Our fates constantly change as we go through life. A psychic can't touch us and know who it is we'll meet at the altar unless we've already met and started dating or courting. You and Savanna are different. Psychics could see the other person through you before you had met. That's not normal. It's usually the first sign that a couple is fated." She blinked a few times, refocusing. The skin between her eyes scrunched with guilt. "I forgot to take that into account when I took your fear away. The emotional connection between fated couples is supposed to develop slowly over time, but I triggered it when I messed with fate." She started to cry again. "I just wanted you to be happy for once. You've been having such a tough time lately." Rebecca buried her head behind her knees. "Mom's going to kill me."

Mom. Right. She had to know something about this. That's why she wasn't surprised.

I turned to the crowd. Savanna and her mom were missing. Mr. Huckleberry was shouting at my parents. "I want that boy to stay away from my daughter!" He had one fat finger jabbing in my direction. The heat drained from my face. I could breathe painlessly now—the shards gone—but Mr. Huckleberry's anger shot a new pain through me. He was right. Savanna wouldn't be in pain if it weren't for me. Maybe we should stay apart. But how?

Mom was trying to stay calm. She glanced at the sky, studying the smog for a moment as she counted breaths. Her voice was back to her usual soothing tone when she responded. "Do you want to try telling two teenagers they can't be together?"

"They're fourteen!" Mr. Huckleberry sputtered. "They're hardly teenagers!"

"Then what would you call them?" Dad crossed his arms. "Enlighten me."

I didn't wait to hear his answer. Of course, my parents would defend our relationship. They had dated all through high school.

I walked inside. Grabbing the phone from the socket, I pressed the number six for the thousandth time that day, holding it to my ear. Part of me didn't want her to answer, but the other part wanted so desperately to make sure she was okay.

"Hello?" Savanna answered, her voice hoarse.

My breath caught in my throat. It took a moment to shove the words out. "Are you alright?"

She breathed in deeply, snot and mucus accompanying the sound. I waited for what seemed like forever before she responded. Her words were choppy. "How do you hold that much inside all the time?"

I didn't answer because I didn't know, but somehow it felt easier now. As if accidentally letting another person into my world had somehow diminished the pain. I'd been dreading this moment, dreading telling her any part of my past, dreading her reaction. What happened instead was way worse than I'd imagined. If I had told her, she wouldn't have had to feel everything. "I'm sorry you had to feel that all at once."

"Feel?" Savanna sniffled. "Bradley, I *saw* everything."

She *saw*? *Oh no.* I began pacing the floor, my breathing growing less steady by the second. She saw. She saw everything. Even the parts I never wanted her to know. *No.* I pulled the phone away, resting my forehead against the wall. *This can't be happening.*

"Bradley?" I could hear Savanna's voice shouting through the phone. Tentatively, I brought it back to my ear. "Are you panicking? Don't panic."

That was sage advice. Sure, let me automatically continue to breathe like a normal person. Easy.

She lowered her voice. "If I can feel you then you can feel me, right? So, *feel* me. Feel my breathing." I listened to her forcefully steady breaths. I wasn't sure how I was supposed to feel her emotions when mine were this overpowering. I also wasn't sure I wanted to know what she was feeling. Disgust? Disappointment? Doubt? She knew now that I wasn't good enough for her. She knew everything. I closed my eyes, trying to focus on the sound of her breaths.

"You're wrong." Savanna interrupted me. My eyes flew open. Had I said something?

"What?" I groaned, frustrated.

"You're wrong about me," she clarified.

"No, I'm not," I snarled. Her breathing disappeared from the speaker. "Savanna?" She didn't respond.

I glanced at the phone. She hadn't hung up, but I couldn't hear her either. *Fine. If this is what she wants, I'll do it.* I groaned and closed my eyes again, focusing solely on the idea of her, sitting in her bedroom across the street, her cell phone at her feet. A strange warmth touched my heart like a drop of rain. The drops kept coming, pounding into my chest, aching, transforming my heart into a puddle of warmth. My lungs breathed in sunshine, thriving in the clarity of the false day. I could breathe clearly and calmly, and yet, there was still a dull ache in the thrum of my liquid gold heart.

"What is that?" I whispered, more to myself than to her. Water pooled above my fingers as they wrapped around the phone. I readjusted my hand, the saltwater tears sliding down my cheeks like miniature waterfalls. It was a glorious place to be—Savanna's heart—and yet, I couldn't quite comprehend it.

She sighed, her breathing returning on the other end of the line. "That is my love for you, Bradley Chambers. That is my love." Her voice cracked on the last word, faltering into a shimmer of quiet sobs.

I slid to the floor, mimicking her cries while basking in the warmth of her beautiful, unconditional love. I hadn't recognized this feeling, but I swore I would never forget it for as long as my heart continued to beat.

7
MY BEST FRIEND IS A DOUCHEBAG
BRADLEY

The events of last night had caused me to forget about Mom's plans. I'd fallen asleep to the gentle thrumming of Savanna's heart and, for the first time in a long time, slept soundly. Mom and Paige left for Itasca shortly before sunrise, their beds empty by the time my alarm jolted me awake. They planned to be gone all weekend for Mr. Burnett's funeral before returning with his three kids. This meant Dad had to drop us off at school. Since he had to be at the office early, we were forced to be early ourselves. I wasn't sure when the last time was that I'd been dropped off early enough to catch the breakfast crowd.

The cafeteria wasn't nearly as crowded as it was for lunch. A group of students played *Magic: The Gathering* at a table in the corner as I pretended to catch up on homework. I was behind in several of my classes but still finding it nearly impossible to focus on the pages in front of me. Schoolwork was always the farthest thing from my mind. Besides, Frank would make me work on some of it during success time. That was what this school called their study hall—success time—but I was always forced to spend it in Frank's office, either doing homework or being psychoanalyzed.

Jay-Jay appeared behind some of the students and their collectible cards, peering over their shoulders to examine what they had. At the sight of him, another memory from the day before resurfaced—his ominous vision. Jay-Jay smirked to himself, passing the table, and froze when he spotted me. He definitely hadn't forgotten. Pretending like he hadn't seen me, he slid into the breakfast line, chatting with a girl who clearly wasn't interested. His nervous desperation struck a chord of guilt within me. Maybe I didn't need to question him right away. After all, maybe his vision had already happened. Frank had managed to save Savanna's life twice last night.

When Jay-Jay paid for his food, he stepped out of the line awkwardly. His shoulders slumped as he reluctantly took the seat across from me.

There was a new topic I wanted to grill him on. Had he known about the emotional connection between Savanna and me? He had been the first to point out that we were destined. I cleared my throat. "What do you know about the fated?"

Jay-Jay took a bite of his dried biscuit, his expression blank. As he chewed, his eyes narrowed. Finally, he swallowed his bite of food. "The what?"

Had he been listening? For a moment I wondered if he was playing games with me. He had to know already. "Rebecca said Savanna and I are fated," I explained.

Jay-Jay shook his head, shooting a quick glance at the ceiling. "I don't know, dude." He waved his arm dramatically, his eyes wide. "I'm not some magic all-knowing source of diviner knowledge." He stabbed at his scrambled eggs with his fork. I wished I'd known what he'd seen in his vision that had him so on edge. I missed the carefree Jay-Jay I had met on the first day of school. This one was turning into a real douchebag. I couldn't get a straight answer from him on anything. Did he truly not know about the fated? Was his whole "you're destined to be together" speech purely a hunch? After a few minutes of chewing, something behind me caught Jay-Jay's attention. He leaned in. "Do I smell like marigolds to you?"

I blinked, confused by his rapidly changing tone. First, I was a nuisance, then I was a friend? Not in a million years was I expecting him to ask if he smelled like flowers. "Dude, I'm not gonna smell you." I leaned away.

He didn't push it. Leaping from his seat, he made a beeline toward... I turned to see who it was. Oh. Serena. She was standing a few feet behind me, twirling the ends of her shoulder-length hair as she flirted with a guy twice her height. I was pretty sure the guy was a junior on the basketball team. I'd seen a photo of the team when they were handing out schedules. Being one of the only white guys on the team, he'd stood out. Was Jay-Jay finally talking to Serena again?

Serena spotted Jay-Jay coming her way and scowled. "Oh, look—it's boy wonder."

"And hello to you too, Cruella," Jay-Jay quipped.

She crossed her arms. "As if I had the time to kidnap one hundred and one dalmatians."

"That's why she hired two goons to do it for her," Jay-Jay replied, leaning in. "All talk, no play." My eyes flickered between them as they bantered, feeling like I had missed something important. I thought they weren't speaking to each other.

The basketball player side-stepped out of the conversation before disappearing into a passing crowd. I didn't blame him.

Serena's eyes narrowed—her head tilted to match Jay-Jay's stare. She curled her lips into a crooked grin. "What do you know?"

He ignored her question. "You're right. Maybe there's a better name for you." He pretended to think, but I suspected he already had one planned. "Tristesssa." He exaggerated the *s* sound. Like a snake ready to strike. It wasn't like him to act that way, but Jay-Jay's shifting attitudes were starting to become the norm. This was a taunt—deliberately chosen to upset the one person he was supposed to make amends with. He nodded to himself, seemingly satisfied with his choice. "Yep. The sad girl."

I didn't get the reference, but a slight tinge of red stained Serena's cheeks. She gazed around, uncomfortable with his word choice. No one but me was paying attention to their conversation. Everyone else was off in their own worlds. If she'd seen me, she hadn't acknowledged it. "Locker room talk?" she finally asked, setting her jaw.

Jay-Jay shrugged, beginning to walk backward on his way to our table. "Guess you'll never know."

Serena followed him, angry, stretching as she matched his pace, her mouth as close as she could get to his ear. She was at least five inches shorter than him. "Listen, you little psychic weasel. I don't need any crap from your almighty pedestal of knowledge. Why don't you spit out what you're trying to say instead of beating around the bush?"

Jay-Jay stopped when he reached his seat, spinning on his heels to face her. "But that's the thing, isn't it?" His expression played on the corner of ornery and dangerous. "You already know what I know."

She stood there for a second, struggling to maintain her composure. It was clear whatever Jay-Jay was saying had gotten to her. Her voice cracked. "You smell like dead flowers, by the way." Turning, she marched out of sight.

Jay-Jay sniffed the sleeve of his shirt as he sat. "Dammit."

"What was that about?" I asked, thoroughly confused by their banter.

Jay-Jay shrugged, in line with his usual cryptic self. "I'm trying to keep her from making a huge mistake." He opened his notebook and began to doodle, ending the conversation.

Serena had made huge mistakes before. That had been the first time I saw Jay-Jay lose his cool. When he had discovered her involvement in bringing us to the neo-Nazis' attention, any friendliness he had displayed to her had disappeared. It hadn't stopped him from feeling bad for her after the fact, but he'd continued to ignore her. Did his sudden reentrance in her life mean he'd seen another mistake blow up in her face? Wait a minute. Was it not Savanna he'd seen die? Was it Serena instead?

When the bell rang, I ran to meet Serena in English class, hoping to uncover her side of the story. Maybe she would give me more information about her and Jay-Jay's weird spat. Instead, Serena was preoccupied with making her own cryptic side comments as her mother gave a lecture on *Romeo and Juliet*. Serena and I had the same school schedule, but for the next several hours, she refused to give me any straight answers, stewing in the terrible mood Jay-Jay had put her in.

At lunch, Jay-Jay hid behind a copy of a *Give Yourself Goosebumps* book, flipping back and forth among the pages as he chomped on his chicken tenders. I stared at the monkey on the flashy cover. Its sharp teeth were bared as it stared back at me, a ripped lab coat draped over its body. It was one of those choose-your-own-ending editions.

"Don't you know how that's going to end?" I asked. I could imagine that every choice he made led him to a vision that would spoil the ending.

Jay-Jay's grip tightened on the book, but he didn't answer. I waited until he flipped to a new page. Finally, he grumbled, "They should write one of these based on our lives, except no matter what choice we make, the ending is always the same." I couldn't see his face when he said this, but his voice was full of pointed anger. I got the sense I was still being blamed for his terrible vision.

I pushed myself from the table, stuffing the leftovers of my lunch into my backpack. As I made my way to algebra, I figured Mr. Lindt would let me sit at my desk until class started. I needed a break from Jay-Jay's toxicity.

Mr. Lindt wasn't in his classroom. Through the glass window of the door, I could see some old guy. He had a receding hairline and a sunspot and was fiddling with a remote, trying to rewind an outdated VHS tape. I didn't know what we could possibly be watching, but the guy looked like he needed some help. I opened the door.

"Mr. Lindt isn't here today," the old man croaked without glancing my way. He proceeded to bang the remote on the edge of the desk. "Damn piece of junk."

I stared at him for a second, silently debating whether to stay. He seemed kind of hostile. I'd left one angry person only to find another. "I was just gonna sit in here till class started," I mumbled.

The man snorted but didn't protest. As I took my seat, he turned to look at me. Recognition sparked in his eyes, his lip curling in amusement. "You're that troublemaker kid. The one who's got that officer tailing their every move." I internally cringed. How'd he know who I was? I hadn't seen him before in my life. He smirked, answering my unspoken question. "I've seen you in the substitute file. They act like you're public enemy number one around here. You don't strike me as dangerous, though. So, what'd they get you for?"

I quirked an eyebrow at the amusement in his tone. There wasn't a hint of accusation. Normally, people assumed the worst about me. There were no questions. His hostility had disappeared. Maybe I was still reeling from the effects of Savanna's heart, but I smiled. "Oh, you know me, I'm real dangerous," I said with a sarcastic edge to my voice. "They caught me shooting up heroin in the bathroom." I gestured to the insulin pump hooked onto my belt. When I was still using needles, I'd had to grab them from the nurse before slipping into the nearest bathroom. Any time someone caught me, the rumors of me being a drug addict would recirculate. I usually let people believe what they wanted. Believing I did drugs usually had people leaving me alone.

The man chuckled for a second but was interrupted by a loud commentary on Pythagoras booming through the speakers. He cursed, reached for the VCR, and punched the pause button. When he righted himself, he asked, "They got a cure for that yet?"

"If they did, you think I'd be sitting here with a tube attached to my stomach?"

"Touché." The man nodded. He was quiet for a moment as he sat in Mr. Lindt's swivel chair, his bushy dark gray brows furrowed in thought. "Had a buddy of mine die from type two."

I nodded. I wasn't sure how he expected me to respond to that. I knew that men with type one had an average life expectancy of sixty-six years, which is ten less than the usual. Type two isn't so drastic, probably 'cause it usually develops at a later age. People with type two still produce insulin. Their problem is that their bodies can't use insulin well.

"Fought in Nam together," the man went on, reminiscing over his dead friend. I really didn't want to hear the story, but I listened anyway. "Took a bullet for him. Still outlived that SOB." He shook his head. "Guy had himself a death wish or somethin'." Snapping his head up, he asked, "You don't go gettin' yourself shot at, do ya?" I grimaced. He had no idea.

I *had* been shot at several times, but it wasn't like I asked to be. "That's why you're in that file, ain't it?" The sub didn't pressure me on the details. Instead, he continued to fiddle with the tape. "This school could do with some updating," he grumbled at one point. I shrugged, a quick flash of my youngest brother lying on the ground with a bullet in his abdomen reappearing in my mind. My unwilling involvement in a school shooting had been the last straw before we moved to Indy. Mom had made sure Frank could keep an eye on me at school.

★

Serena didn't show up to class. I wondered if it had anything to do with her dad being gone. At first, I thought she had taken the rest of the day off, having left with her dad for an appointment or something. That theory died when she walked into world history as the late bell was ringing. Her dark brown hair was tousled, a few of the buttons of her blue-and-green-striped blouse off by one.

"The hell?" I muttered under my breath, my eyes following her as she took her usual seat near the back. Savanna and her two friends were staring at her too. Serena tried to hide her face as inconspicuously as she could, placing her arm on the table and letting her hair fill in the gaps. Her lips were pressed into a thin line, her light brown skin holding a tinge of red.

Mrs. Scar cleared her throat to gain everyone's attention, a pile of test booklets in her hand.

I glanced at Jay-Jay, gauging his reaction to Serena's entrance. He was staring straight ahead, the color draining from his face. When Mrs. Scar came by with his test, he asked if he could go to the bathroom.

"Class just started," Mrs. Scar pointed out, but she waved him on anyway. He looked like he was gonna puke. Jay-Jay nearly flung out of his seat as soon as she gave the okay. Savanna caught my gaze, questions clouding her blue eyes. I shrugged in response, stealing another glance at Serena, who hadn't seemed to notice Jay-Jay's exit.

"Eyes to the front, please," Mrs. Scar said as she continued to pass out tests. I faced forward, my brain running through all the possibilities. Something had changed between Jay-Jay and Serena in the last twenty-four hours. I had yet to find any answers.

I didn't see Jay-Jay again the rest of the class. Mrs. Scar didn't notice he hadn't come back until we were packing our stuff in anticipation of the bell. Concerned, she dialed the school nurse. I couldn't hear what was said on the other end, but whatever it was left Mrs. Scar in a state of disbelief. She gathered his things, tsk-tsking the entire time. Savanna and I caught each other's worried glances as the bell rang to dismiss us.

"If he's in the nurse's office, I can take this to him," I offered, gesturing to the backpack and textbook the teacher had gathered awkwardly in her arms. Mrs. Scar raised her eyebrows, tilting her head slightly. I hadn't yet gained her trust. I groaned internally.

"I'll go with him and make sure it gets there." Savanna popped up on the other side of Jay-Jay's desk. The teacher didn't object. It wasn't difficult to trust Savanna. I rolled my eyes.

Once we left the classroom, we raced each other to the nurse's office.

"What d'you think's wrong with him?" I asked as we pushed our way through the crowded hallways.

"Whatever it is, I bet it has something to do with Serena." Savanna scowled. The two girls hadn't gotten along since the day they officially met. To be fair, Serena had tried to apologize to her, but she was never the best at apologies.

I doubted Savanna knew what was going on between Serena and Jay-Jay, but I asked anyway. "Yeah, what's up with them? I thought Jay-Jay wasn't speaking to her. Then this morning, they were bickering like they were each other's exes." *As if Jay-Jay were Kase*, I thought. Despite being the one to pull the trigger, Kase was still bitter about the breakup.

As we rounded the last corner, the basketball player from this morning nearly rammed into us. His lip had a dried cut at the left corner.

"Oh, sorry," he apologized, moving back with a slight limp in his step. He caught sight of Savanna and held his arms out like he was presenting her at an awards show. "Savanna! You grew up *nice*!" He started to circle her, checking her out. "So very fine." I gritted my teeth as he moved his hand in the air in one fluid motion, mimicking the shape of her body. "Hourglass. You know, I prefer a little more ass myself." I wanted to punch this guy's lights out. *What a douchebag.*

Savanna dropped Jay-Jay's textbooks before slamming her foot on Aaron's, jumping and twisting in such a way that when she brought her right hook in to meet his jaw, she managed to knock him unsteady. My jaw dropped.

The basketball player caught himself from falling, his hand scraping the metal vents of a locker. Savanna spat at him. "That's for Marcie." I wondered what he had done to Savanna's friend to make her react like that. It had to be bad. Savanna started to walk away as he straightened himself, but then she spun to face him again. "If you're looking for an ass, take a look in the mirror."

Only a few other students were in this part of the hallway, but they all uttered a collective "Ooh." I caught a few exchanging high fives. Someone called him out for getting beaten up by a girl. Savanna's nostrils flared at the comment. She reminded me a little of Olga in that moment. Olga would have turned on the commenter, going off on a tangent about male fragility. I had a feeling Savanna wanted to. Her annoyance shifted inside her as she struggled to contain it. It strangely flickered up and down my arms like little sparks of electricity.

For a second, I forgot why we were in this section of the school until Savanna gathered the textbooks in one arm and grabbed my hand with the other.

"Say hello to Jones for me!" The basketball player spat, tenderly pressing his fingers against his jawline.

Savanna let go of me, jogging to the door of the nurse's office. Her gasp was probably loud enough for her foe to hear it down the hall. I hadn't made it in the room yet, but I could feel her horror, my legs trembling as I joined her. I wasn't sure I wanted to see what she was seeing. I stopped just shy of the threshold, my eyes on the floor, listening.

"It looks worse than it is," Jay-Jay mumbled as the late bell rang for our final class. Water and ice sloshed— the sound of a half-melted ice pack jiggling. He sucked in a sharp breath. Jay-Jay was still holding his breath when he added, "Still stings a little." I dared a peek. The entire left side of Jay-Jay's face was bruised, a few dried spots of blood speckled here and there. His nose looked like it had been reset, more dried blood surrounding his nostrils. His lip had split in two places.

Savanna was shaking as she took in his bruised and battered features. So was I. "What possessed you to challenge Aaron?" she screeched, sitting next to him on the bench. Tears streaked her cheeks. I stepped inside, trying to focus on disconnecting from Savanna's emotions, but they were too strong. My stomach churned as rage pressed into my shoulders. I tried to roll it away.

Jay-Jay kept his mouth shut.

"I want to hit you." Savanna groaned, throwing a soft fist toward Jay-Jay without actually touching him. I could feel her restraint burn through my tendons. I shook out my arms.

Jay-Jay barely looked at me. "Is something bothering you?" His left eye was almost sealed shut. I was surprised he could see much of my awkward stretching.

I tried not to look uncomfortable, but I didn't appreciate being tugged under someone else's skin. The emotional connection thing was going to be tough to get used to. I didn't feel like sharing the reason for my weird behavior. Jay-Jay had made his newfound disinterest in Savanna's and my relationship clear that morning when I had asked him about us being fated.

Savanna caught on to my behavior though. She propped her elbows on her knees and stared at the wall, trying to breathe evenly. Thank God.

Jay-Jay swung his head between the two of us. "You've been around each other too long. You're starting to pick up each other's weird mannerisms."

"You have no idea," I muttered.

Jay-Jay dropped the ice pack he was holding. The ice sloshed in the sea of water beneath the surface. He examined it, picking off specks of blood. "Aaron had it coming."

The anger in Savanna's expression re-flared. She lost her concentration, waving her hands in the air. "He's six-two! An *athletic* six-two! You're five-one with zero hand-eye coordination! Plus, it's been three years since that thing with Marcie. What were you thinking?"

My stomach continued to churn as I sat in a nearby chair.

Jay-Jay ground his teeth. "I was thinking somebody needed to look out for Serena."

8
JAY-JAY HAS TOO MANY SECRETS
BRADLEY

"Jay-Jay." Savanna groaned, pinching the skin between her closed eyes. "If this is about your guilt over what happened in the bunker—"

He interrupted her with a frustrated shout. "She's taunting me! Serena wants me to save her, to prove that I could have changed her future. I can't take it anymore!" Savanna shushed him as we looked for the nurse. She was tending to another student on the other side of the room. Luckily, it was a good-sized room. His hand flew to his ribcage as he bent. Savanna grabbed another icepack and handed it to him. This one was already melted, but Jay-Jay held it to his side anyway.

"What does beating up Aaron Krause have to do with Serena?" Savanna crossed her arms. Oh. Right. She hadn't seen them together earlier.

"You haven't heard?" Jay-Jay let out a breathy laugh. "I kinda thought it would be common gossip among the cheerleaders by now."

Savanna's eyes rolled to the ceiling. "The only thing the squad is gossiping about right now is Gabrielle's not-so-secret tattoo. Oh, and how everyone thinks I was hungover this morning."

Jay-Jay shot a questioning side glance at her but didn't ask for any of the details. He grimaced, ignoring the admittance. "Serena's been a hot topic in the locker room lately. I'd rather not repeat what was said."

Savanna looked to me as if I would know anything. I shrugged. Jay-Jay and I didn't have the same gym class, and I hardly listened to half the bull that came out of anyone's mouth in the locker room. The people in my class were usually making wisecracks about "the freak with the tubes and compact machinery," a.k.a. me.

Savanna shook her head, not buying his excuse. "Aaron's been talking trash since middle school, probably longer. Why would you let any of that gossip get to you?"

Jay-Jay ran his fingers through his dark hair, puffing his cheeks as he let out a gust of air. "Because it wasn't just him, and because… because…" he stuttered, wincing at whatever reason he had for nearly getting himself pummeled to death. He stared at his lap, letting his free hand fall into it. "I saw the truth and I couldn't do a thing about it." His voice grew quiet as he croaked, "I don't want to see things." It was almost the same thing he'd said to me the day before. He was still reeling from that vision, letting it torture him to the point where he didn't want his powers anymore.

Savanna tried to hug him, but he scooched away, his teeth bared. "Don't touch me!" Whatever he'd seen had scarred him.

The nurse looked from the wound of another student to shoot us a warning glance. She tapped her watch. I glimpsed the time on the clock and groaned. We were ten minutes late for class. Frank was probably looking for me. "Was that the vision you had yesterday in Frank's office?" I whispered, leaning forward. I didn't want to leave before asking Jay-Jay about the vision.

"No." He scowled. He didn't meet my gaze. Fear swept over me like a long-lost friend, my gut wrenching at what more he could have seen. This wasn't all about Serena then. Maybe my initial theory was right. It was Savanna. Jay-Jay groaned, covering his face with his hand as he shook his head. "I can't do or say anything that will impede fate. The universe won't let me." He let his hand drop so he could look me in the eye. Jay-Jay nearly growled the words. "Stop asking me."

I remembered the other piece to the puzzle—the thing that had sent me into a whirlwind of panic the night before. "You know my mom can't see Savanna anymore." I narrowed my eyes, trying to drag at least *some* information from him. I couldn't keep living my life not knowing who, when, or how one of us was going to drop dead. Savanna gasped.

Jay-Jay snorted, apathetic. "Yeah, well, tell her good luck with that." The muscles around his dark eyes tightened.

A cold chill sprouted from the base of my stomach, shooting through my chest, my heart, and back down my spine, my skin flaring with goosebumps. The feeling overpowered my frustration. I shot a look at Savanna. Her eyes were practically bulging out of their sockets, her mouth hanging slightly open. "It's me," she said breathily, stuck in a state of shock. "I'm the one who's going to die." I didn't have time to reassure her.

Our conversation was immediately interrupted by the click-clack of shoes against the tile, and a woman's vocal fry. "My baby." I leaned out of the way as she cut in front of me, her hands stretched to cup Jay-Jay's face. "Who did this to you?" Her accent was clean and crisp—typical Midwestern. I would've assumed differently by the looks of her. I'd never met Jay-Jay's mom before, but I had assumed she was white like my dad. She hadn't been the parent to pass the diviner gene to Jay-Jay, and in my mind, somehow, that meant she looked like my dad—white and northern European. Instead, her skin was a shade or two darker than her son's, her black hair falling in tight ringlets past her shoulders. Her face was round—not at all like Jay-Jay's—but she had the same dark eyes. I started to get mad at myself for wrongly assuming. Just because my undivine parent is white didn't mean Jay-Jay's had to be. I felt like a hypocrite, being angry at how

Romanies are treated when I wasn't any better than the rest. People can't look at me and automatically know anything about my ethnicity other than that I'm white. It wasn't the same for me. Even being a little over one-fourth Romani, I was still almost three-fourths white. I could walk down the street, and strangers usually wouldn't look at me funny or worry that I would steal or injure or misunderstand them. That was a privilege. That privilege disgusts me that it's even a privilege at all. Nobody looks at me and wonders what I am. So why was I wondering what she was? Was she Romani? Latina? Filipina? I shook my head. *It doesn't matter,* I told myself.

Ms. Jones's entrance had sidetracked my brain so effectively that the cold from Savanna's fear had subsided within me. It wasn't until Ms. Jones asked Savanna what was wrong when the cold returned. I shivered.

"I should have known you were in here." Frank's relieved voice came out of nowhere, his hand clamping the back of my chair. I didn't turn to look at him. Instead, I leaned forward, staring intently at Savanna, willing the cold to go away.

Ms. Jones redirected her attention to Frank, stepping away from her son. "I want that boy suspended."

"He's had a stern talking-to—" Frank started before being interrupted by Jay-Jay's mom.

"A *stern talking-to?*"

Frank sighed. "There's not much I can do when your son was the one who initiated the fight."

"He *what?*" She spun to face Jay-Jay, letting out a string of Spanish, interrupted occasionally with words of a different language I couldn't quite pinpoint.

I tried not to let their conversation distract me, closing my eyes to shut them out. I held my hands for Savanna to take, focusing all my energy into being calm, attempting to mimic the feeling of warmth her love had shown me the night before.

Her hands trembled in mine, cold to the touch. I could feel her fear and her sadness try to take over my emotions. I knew how to handle fear. I'd been handling fear my whole life. Hers felt different, presented different, but I didn't let that get to me. It was still fear, all the same. I could diminish it, compartmentalize it—I knew that for certain. For once in my life, I had faith. She wouldn't die. I wouldn't let her. It was too cruel of the universe to define us as fated if one or the other wasn't going to survive much longer.

"Uh…" Jay-Jay's voice crackled distractedly. "You guys know your hands are glowing, right?" I heard feet shuffle, felt their warm bodies closer to ours. I hoped they were creating a human shield to hide us from sight. I pushed their voices away, fought to ignore them. This was important. More important than revealing ourselves to the undivine.

The ice melted inside Savanna, her quick beating heart slowing to a softer rhythm.

"Where did they go?" Ms. Jones asked nervously.

Frank's voice was strained. "You can't see them?"

I could feel the heat of the glow over my hands like the warm flames of a nearby bonfire. The warmth spread down my arms, slowly at first, and then all at once as it rushed over the rest of my body. That was when I heard it—a string of words clear as day. Savanna's high-pitched worries, strung together into one long, never-ending web of insecurities, sang in my head. Everything she would lose was laid out for me to hear.

Stop, stop, stop, stop, stop, I thought as I forced myself to swallow a lump in my throat. I pulled her toward me, hugging her tightly to my chest. The second my hands left hers, Savanna's irrational thoughts disappeared. I buried my face in her soft hair. I couldn't calm myself enough to calm her, and it frustrated me. I thought I could do it. I thought I was strong like she was, but I wasn't. I let her fears take over my own. She could no longer contain the sound of her cries as she shook in my arms. I cried with her. There was nothing else I could do.

"What's going on?" The nurse asked. My eyes flew open, my sight blurred by the tears. I didn't see the glow Jay-Jay had mentioned. It must have disappeared when I let go of Savanna's hands.

Ms. Jones turned to address the nurse, who was craning her neck to see in between the three of them. "Oh, you know teenagers. Everything's always the end of the world when you're young."

The nurse appraised us with her eyes. "Your friend's going to be fine." I knew she was talking about Jay-Jay, but this wasn't about him anymore. This was about Savanna. This was about our entwined fates. I couldn't tell her that, so I nodded, sniffling, as I pretended to go along with the only logical outside explanation for our behavior. I couldn't pull away from Savanna though. I couldn't let her go.

"Bradley." Frank beckoned me, but I hugged Savanna tighter.

Ms. Jones waved us toward the door. "Come on, you two." We walked awkwardly to the hallway, following Frank. She thanked the nurse as we left, her arm looping around Jay-Jay's.

When we reached a spot out of sight and out of earshot, Ms. Jones let go of her son and reached out to Savanna and me, placing a comforting hand on each of our shoulders. "What's going on?"

I opened my mouth to answer before clamping it shut. No. She wasn't going to die. That was the problem. Savanna couldn't believe me, and Jay-Jay's silence wasn't helping. It angered me. Why wasn't Jay-Jay saying anything to reassure her? Why did he have to torture her like this? My eyes met Jay-Jay's, my voice husky. "Tell her it's not true."

Jay-Jay shook his head, stepping back and averting his eyes. I shook, fury building like a red-hot fire in my bones. I started to loosen my grip on Savanna. He took a few more quick steps back. "Tell her!" I shouted, pulling almost completely away.

Ms. Jones stepped away. "Okay, what am I missing?"

Frank held his hand in front of me, ready to stop me from bolting toward Jay-Jay.

I gritted my teeth. "Savanna thinks she's going to die."

Ms. Jones gasped, and Savanna's cries grew louder. Jay-Jay's mom gathered Savanna into her arms as I finally let go. "Jay-Jay, you have this poor girl terrified. Tell her she's not going to die."

We all stared at Jay-Jay as his eyes flickered frantically. "I can't say anything. You have to believe me."

"Why not?" I shouted.

"I told you, the universe doesn't want me to say anything that could stop the future from happening. I literally cannot say. If I try to open my mouth to say the words, my mouth will not open. I can't say it, I can't write it, and I can't act it out. Savanna's going to die whether I have a say in it or not! And it's your fault!" He said it. He said the words. But the second he did, he dropped to the floor. His eyes rolled into the back of his head, his body convulsing.

"Jay-Jay?" I stepped forward as Frank ran to his side. Ms. Jones gasped again, instantly letting go of Savanna, running to her son's aid.

Savanna turned, her eyes barely open enough to see Jay-Jay writhing. She stopped crying at the sight, a new worry causing her to wipe away her tears. "What did he say?" Her voice was laced with anxiety. He said she was going to die. I wasn't going to repeat that. If she didn't hear it, that would be a good thing. She could be free of the knowledge, of her fear… at least, some of it. Her wide blue eyes stared at me, horrified. I knew then that she had heard. My heart jolted inside my chest. If she had heard that, she'd also heard the part where it would be my fault. I would be the cause of her death.

It sickened me—the realization I had been right all along. I hadn't wanted to date her. I knew this was going to happen. Death and destruction follow me wherever I go. I hadn't wanted to put her in harm's way. So, really, this was Jay-Jay's fault. He'd been the one who had pushed us to be together. Him and his stupid visions. Now I couldn't leave her. I knew it was selfish, but the feat seemed entirely impossible. We were connected on so many levels. We needed each other. We were fated… and I hoped that meant there was a way out of this death sentence.

9
THE INVASION OF THE SAD GIRL
BRADLEY

The ambulance came to take Jay-Jay before school let out. He was coming to when the paramedics got to the school, but he was still pretty out of it. Ms. Jones cussed out the nurse in Spanish for not checking to see if he had a concussion. I had a feeling the seizure had little to do with his fight with Aaron. The "universe," as Jay-Jay called it, was trying to stop him.

It was strange—the whole universe theory. I had never once heard my mother mention this rule. I mean, she didn't always share what she saw, but I always thought it was because nothing she could do would change the outcome. Jay-Jay was the first to make a big deal about it. My mom's seen people die in her visions, even if she wouldn't be physically there to witness it. I wondered if Jay-Jay knew how much time Savanna had left. After all, my mom had known how much time Mr. Burnett had.

I thought I had more time. It had been a day since Jay-Jay was joking around about not wanting to embarrass us because of some unknown vision. I thought that meant we had a chance. Had that vision already sailed? Was that what Jay-Jay meant when he said that vision hadn't meant anything yesterday in Frank's office? Was it because the timeline was unclear?

I couldn't believe it had only been a day since everyone was worried about *my* life. A lot had happened since then.

Dad was forty-five minutes late picking me up. He was arguing with someone on the phone as I climbed into the car. Rebecca had her hand on Blake's shoulder as he tried to tell Dad a story about some kid in his class who celebrates the Day of the Dead, but Dad had his pinky shoved in his other ear, straining to hear the voice on the other end of the line.

"Maybe 'cause they're not your grandchildren!" Dad vociferated.

"…and that's why I think we should celebrate the Day of the Dead." Blake ended his appeal, having completely ignored the fact that Dad wasn't paying attention. "Dad?" He leaned forward, tapping Dad's shoulder.

Dad squirmed from Blake's hands, putting the car back in drive. "They have a mother, and they'll go back to her when she's ready to care for them." He pulled the car from the curb before slamming the breaks. I stopped myself from hitting the dashboard. "What d'you mean that's not what Rin said?" He paused, listening to the other person. "Why would she tell you that and not me?"

Another pause, this time longer. Dad groaned. "Even if that were true, you don't have the space. How do you expect to feed nine of us?

"I'm sorry, *sixteen*. Don't want to leave Mindy out of this nonsense." As soon as he said Aunt Mindy's name, I knew he was talking to either Grandma or Grandpa—the ones who liked us. "No." Dad shook his head. A car behind us honked. Dad had stopped the car in the middle of the pickup lane. "Because Mindy's kids can't keep a secret." He pulled us back to the curb so the aggravated driver could pass. The guy gave us the finger as he sped through. "It didn't stop us before because our kids didn't have their powers then." Dad's fingers tapped the steering wheel. "Okay, so, they *did*, but you came to *us* last time."

Dad paused to listen before responding. "No, we don't have room, Dad." Oh. So, it was Grandpa. "We'd have it if we weren't taking in three more kids, apparently permanently, according to you."

Dad's face clouded over. "Well, I would if she'd pick up the damn phone." He hung up and tossed his cell onto the dashboard while muttering under his breath.

As he pulled the car out of the parking lot, Blake poked him again. "What d'you say about the Day of the Dead, huh?"

"What? Oh." Dad rubbed his forehead distractedly. "Maybe next year, bud."

Blake slumped in his seat, pouting.

"That wasn't a no," Rebecca said, teasing him.

"You don't even think we should celebrate it." Blake kicked at the back of Dad's chair.

"That's because it's not *our* holiday," Rebecca tried to explain.

"What was that about?" I asked Dad, gesturing to the phone on the dash.

"Thanksgiving," he grumbled. I didn't ask him to elaborate.

Holidays were always a mess. Whenever we were with Dad's family, we had to hide our powers from our cousins. This was easy for me, but we had to work extra hard to stay on Paige's good side. She still struggled with controlling her telekinesis to the point where I was surprised she hadn't exposed herself at school. Mom had kept her home a lot near the end of her fourth-grade year, fearful that her powers would act up. This year we also had Rebecca to worry about. My youngest sister was pretty chill, but she had her moments. She had completely redecorated the front room in a fit of rage back in August. Besides that, she was always trying to make other people's lives easier. Sometimes, like Mom, she would say mysterious things that suggested she, too, could see fragments of the future. Rebecca claimed it was some kind of inner knowledge or intuition and not an additional ability, but it was still disconcerting.

I'm not sure why we choose to lie to them. Grandma, Grandpa, and Aunt Mindy all knew about us. It sounded like Dad was worried our cousins wouldn't be able to keep the secret. After all, it would be pretty cool for them to find out their cousins had powers. Who wouldn't want to share that secret?

Mom's family was even more stressful. Whenever we were around Grandma and Grandpa Anderson, we had to live as they did, which involved a lot of rules we all struggled to remember. Some of them were easy because Mom hadn't stopped practicing them, like washing our clothes with the tops and bottoms separate or cleaning the cups first when washing dishes. It was the other things we struggled with, like remembering not to use soap or towels that had touched the floor or—the women in my family especially—not to step over specific objects. If a shadow passed over our food, we were ordered not to eat it. We couldn't take food from strangers who didn't practice Rromanija when preparing it, which meant we couldn't eat out. If Mom or Paige were on their periods, they had to eat separate from us. Mom never let us have a dog because she worried we wouldn't be able to hide the evidence. Animals that licked themselves were considered unclean. Mom was glad when her parents didn't show at Jesse's funeral. We would have had to burn all his stuff. I wondered if they would be burning all Mr. Burnett's stuff.

It started raining by the time we got to the house. It was hard to see out the windshield. "We're going to have to make a run for it," Dad said as he stepped out of the car. Then he mumbled, "What are we, an orphanage?" He grumbled something about taking in strays before tossing his keys to someone I couldn't see. "Go on, get inside before you catch pneumonia."

I hurried out of the car to see who he was talking to. Serena was shivering, completely soaked from the sudden change in weather. A small gym bag dangled from her shoulder. She snatched the keys from the sidewalk before hurdling toward the front door.

"You're not going to ask why she's here?" I slammed the passenger door shut, jogging to catch up with the rest of my family.

"I suppose it's about her father leavin'," Dad answered grimly as Serena ran inside.

My heart stopped for a split second before sputtering back to life. "What?" Mr. Lindt wouldn't leave his family, would he? No way. I refused to believe it. There had to be another explanation for his temporary absence. Maybe he was attending a conference.

Dad sighed, following Rebecca and Blake inside. "I don't have time to deal with this. I have to call your mother."

I closed the door behind us as he jogged up the stairs. Serena stood awkwardly in the entryway for a moment, wiping tears I hadn't noticed through the rain. Her nose and cheeks had a pinkish hue to them. Rebecca offered to make her hot chocolate before dashing into the kitchen. Blake ambled into the living room, not bothering to ask why Serena was here. After a minute of us standing there, she finally explained through her sniffling. "My mom and I got in a fight."

I placed my backpack against the wall and sat on the steps. "I guess it's been a day of fighting for you, hasn't it?"

She stiffened. "What d'you mean by that?"

I narrowed my eyes. "Well, first, there was that thing with Jay-Jay this morning—"

She interrupted me. "Oh, you mean when he called me a whore in front of everyone?" She laughed spitefully as she said this, her lips twisting as if she'd tasted something bitter.

I tried to recall their conversation. I would've remembered if he had called her that. It wasn't exactly a word I'd heard him use. My confused silence seemed to irritate Serena. She groaned. "Tristesssa?"

I shrugged. My Spanish was a little rusty, but I knew enough to know that *triste* meant sad. Jay-Jay had used English to call her "the sad girl." I didn't see how that equated to being called a whore.

She tried to lead the gears of my mind in the right direction. "Jack Kerouac?"

I shook my head. *Was he another student?*

She huffed, coming to sit next to me on the stairs. "Well, maybe I can hope that most people didn't get the reference then. Not everybody has an English teacher for a mother."

I nodded, still not quite understanding. Then I remembered what Jay-Jay had told Savanna and me earlier today. "Uh…" I tensed, anticipating her reaction. "You know there are rumors going around—"

I leaned away before the back of her hand could hit my arm. "What did you hear?"

"I didn't hear anything." I held both my hands up, my palms facing away from me. "Jay-Jay mentioned there was some talk in the locker room."

She narrowed her eyes. "I hope the stomach flu is treating him well." Her voice dripped with sarcasm.

I did a double take. *Did she not know?* "Jay-Jay's not sick," I corrected her. "He went looking for Aaron."

I heard her breath catch in her throat. Her eyes widened, her mouth dropping open. She hopped to her feet and paced. "I'm going to kill him," she threatened in a high-pitched voice. "I'm really going to kill him."

"You think Aaron didn't already try?" I sputtered.

She stopped pacing. "He saw something, didn't he?"

I rolled my eyes. "In case you haven't noticed, Jay-Jay doesn't exactly tell me what he sees." I wasn't entirely sure I wanted to know the details before, but Serena's anxiety was making me curious. I leaned over to grab my water bottle from my backpack while she stewed.

As I took a sip, she threw her hands up in exasperation. "That's it! He knows I slept with Aaron. It's the only explanation."

I spat out my drink, water and saliva decorating the wood floor. I don't know how I didn't connect the dots before, not that I thought about what Serena did in her free time. Maybe it's because I know half the stuff that's said in the locker room is complete bull, so I assumed whatever nonsense Jay-Jay overheard was false. Well, except for the fact that he'd said he'd had a vision confirming its validity. *Ugh.* I gagged at the thought. Had Jay-Jay seen that? I immediately felt bad for him. No wonder he hated his gift.

I capped my water bottle, shaking my head to rid the mental image.

"Don't be such a prude, Bradley." Serena scoffed.

"I'm not a prude," I argued. Trust me. I censor myself. I just didn't want to picture a girl who was practically my sister doing… that. But then I remembered who she was doing it with. Aaron was a junior. "Serena, he's two years older than you."

"So? It still fits in the half-age-plus-seven rule."

Ugh. She's making me do math, I groaned internally. *Aaron was probably no older than seventeen… seventeen divided by two was eight and a half… plus seven was… fifteen and a half.* I cringed. "You only turned fifteen a month ago."

She shrugged. "Technicalities."

I glared at her.

"What? It's not like it's illegal."

"He's a terrible person." I crossed my arms against my chest, remembering Savanna's encounter with him earlier. "I don't know what he did to Marcie Thomas in middle school, but whatever it was must've been bad." Why else would Savanna, of all people, throw a punch at him? She could have been picking up on my desire to punch his lights out, but still, it had seemed like a conscious choice on her part.

Serena squinted, her arms crossed. She snorted. "You talked to your girlfriend. Awesome. You love gossiping about me behind my back, don't you? I'm sure Savanna appreciates all the dirty little secrets you have on me. It will make excellent ammunition someday." She would know all about ammunition, not that she had much on me anymore. She didn't know that though, but what did she know about Marcie?

"Savanna doesn't have time to care about your petty problems!" I shouted, grabbing the rail to pull myself to my feet. "You know what? Jay-Jay's been busting his butt trying to keep you safe, and all you do is ignore his advice. Now you're ignoring mine. I get it. You run your life. But don't say we didn't all warn you about Aaron." She had to know *something* about Marcie. Why wasn't she considering it a cautionary tale?

I was caught off guard when her chin started to tremble. Serena wasn't usually an easy person to make cry. She loved a good argument. "No, no, no. Don't cry," I begged. She held the back of her hand to her mouth, but it didn't stop the sobs. "I'm sorry, I didn't mean it." I did mean it, but I'd say anything to keep the tears away.

"Yes, you did!" she screamed, the sobs growing louder as she backed away. Her head fell into her hands.

Rebecca appeared around the corner with a mug of warm cocoa, perplexed by the scene in front of her. She quietly set the mug on the built-in bookshelf.

"I hear crying. What's going on down there?" Dad's voice floated from upstairs.

Serena shook her head, sucking in a deep breath to try to quench the emotion. "My problems are nothing, right?" she asked. "Because having rods rip through your body is a flipping breeze. Because the scars from my surgery that will never fade are just the most beautiful sights. Because the organs in my body that I never wanted to lose were just cannon fodder for the cause. I'm expendable. Even my dad couldn't stand to look at me anymore!" She sniffled, pausing to catch her breath. "You can tell Jay-Jay that he can stop trying to save me because nothing he can do can make up for what I've lost."

I stared at her, my heart sinking with every word she said because, it turned out, I knew nothing. I knew nothing of the rods or the scars. I didn't know that there were more organs besides the one kidney she had lost. I didn't believe a word she said about her dad, but everything else? How could she still be standing here, alive? A small glimmer of hope flickered below my left shoulder. Against all odds, Serena had survived the impossible. She was living proof. Could Savanna do that? Survive when Jay-Jay believed her to die?

Rebecca approached Serena carefully, holding out her arms in such a way that Serena would recognize the incoming hug. My sister wrapped her arms around Serena as she cried. Rebecca was only an inch or two shorter despite the five-year age difference. Serena wasn't exactly the tallest girl in the ninth grade.

"You're not going to grow up and betray me, are you?" Serena sniffled.

A funny expression flickered across Rebecca's face before correcting itself to its normal collectiveness. She answered in her small, sweet voice. "I would never."

Dad wasn't much of a cook, so he ordered pizza for dinner. We mostly sat in silence as we ate, except for when Dad tried to unsuccessfully convince Serena that her dad leaving wasn't her fault.

"Really? 'Cause that's not what my mom said," she shot back as she sat in front of her empty plate. I think Dad had forgotten that Serena's family lived Rromanija more consistently than we did.

"I'm sure she didn't mean it," Dad said reassuringly.

"Oh yeah, I'm sure she didn't mean to call me a whore." Serena plopped a slice of pizza on her plate. She stared at the slice for a second. "Might as well break all the other rules too."

10
DAD TRIES TO GIVE US THE TALK
BRADLEY

Because of Serena's comment Friday night, Dad took it upon himself to make Saturday afternoon as awkward and uncomfortable as possible. We were all lounging in the living room, marathoning some boring show Rebecca had picked when Dad suddenly grabbed the remote and shut the TV off.

He gestured to Rebecca and Blake. "Go get some sunshine." They glanced at the back door then back at him. Blake narrowed his eyes while Rebecca raised her brows. We could hear the storm from inside, thunder booming at uneven intervals. It took a moment for Dad to realize the ridiculousness of his command. "Upstairs then." He pointed to the ceiling. They scrambled away without a complaint, much to my surprise. Blake usually put up more of a fight.

Serena and I sat at opposite ends of the couch scrutinizing him warily. He cleared his throat, tugging nervously at his collar. Sweat perspired on his forehead, his skin shining like it did whenever Mom put too much cayenne in his food. He rubbed the palms of his hands together. My heart thumped in my chest, always ready for bad news. Dad didn't look at us as he spoke, his words coming out slow and calculated. "I think you kids are old enough for this conversation now that you're in high school." He swallowed. Serena and I glanced at each other, trying to figure out from the other what this was all about. He cleared his throat. "I know there are certain expectations that you feel you have to meet. But I want you two to know that meeting them is unnecessary. In fact, they may deter your success." His brown eyes kept narrowing in concentration at the corner of the coffee table.

Serena groaned with impatience. "Just spit it out, Mr. C."

Dad squirmed a little in his chair. "I think we need to have a talk about sex." *Oh. Dear. Lord.* I let my forehead hit the arm of the couch.

Serena exploded into a fit of maniacal laughter. "What makes you think I have to be a part of this ludicrous conversation?"

Dad glanced from the coffee table to hold her gaze, stepping into his usual authoritativeness. "Because you're my goddaughter, and you will listen to what I have to say, so zip it." He motioned his hand over his mouth like he was zipping an invisible zipper. Her laughter subsided. So did Dad's nervousness. "Look, I know the pressures of being in a relationship and how they can get out of hand, especially when it seems like everybody else is doing it."

He pointed to the blank television. "Nowadays, you kids seem to be bombarded with all kinds of this nonsense in everything you watch. You know what I call that?" He paused, waiting for us to answer. I slumped lower into the couch. Serena didn't say a word.

Dad answered his own question. "Pressure." He stared at each of us pointedly for a few seconds to let the word sink in. "Here's the thing. If you let what you see on television influence what you do in real life, then guess what? You don't control yourselves anymore. The media does." Great. There he went with his conspiracy theories.

Serena dared to challenge him. "But, as teenagers, don't *we* control the media? I mean, there has to be some truth in there, or else they wouldn't write it."

Dad's face grew red. I could practically see the vein in his forehead pop. He jabbed a shaky finger at her, but his mouth remained closed.

Serena continued to defend her stance. "It's not just television either—it's books too. It's in the books they give us to read for class, and it's in the books we pick out at the library or the bookstores. I think you're just going to have to admit that teenagers have sex." I wanted to ask her what the hell kind of books she was reading because, so far, the books her mom had assigned us didn't include sex unless you counted the false rape accusation in *To Kill a Mockingbird* and in *Of Mice and Men*. It was all potential violence against women, and it was not the same.

"This is your mother's fault," Dad accused, wagging his finger in Serena's direction. "She's always had an obsession with those banned books." He scowled, shaking his head in disgust. "Listen to me. I'm starting to sound like my parents." He shook the thought away, returning to his point. "The point is you kids are too young to have sex. It takes a lot of maturity, trust, and commitment to be able to have that kind of relationship with a person."

I wondered what that meant for couples who were fated. Not that Savanna and I would have the chance since she was apparently going to die.

"That's total bull, and you know it," Serena scoffed. "And why do you keep looking at *me*? What about him?" She waved her arm in my direction. Dad looked like he was ready to yell at me.

I held my hands up in defense. "I don't know what she's talking about." Seriously. Savanna and I hadn't come close to discussing anything like this.

"Oh, come on." Serena narrowed her eyes accusingly. "I see the way you two look at each other. *Everybody* sees it."

"Savanna isn't even allowed to be around me outside of school," I argued. Of course, that was a new rule, but I wasn't going to give her any more ammunition.

Serena rolled her eyes. "I'm sure you find ways."

Dad's angry jabbing finger refocused on me. "I wouldn't do anything to piss Savanna's father off if I were you. I have no doubt that man would find a way to kill you and make it look like an accident."

I rolled my eyes. Death threats weren't exactly uncommon for me. He knew that. How would Mr. Huckleberry find out anyway?

My lack of a reaction seemed to anger Dad more, his face growing red again. "Got it?" he said through gritted teeth. I nodded reluctantly. He opened his mouth to say more, but Serena interrupted him.

"I'm curious, Mr. C—you and Clarinda dated all through high school. That's four whole years. Do you honestly expect me to believe that you two waited until marriage?"

Dad chuckled nervously, tilting his head. I never thought about the possibility before. Rromanija strictly prohibited premarital sex, and so did Dad's Southern Baptist background, but for a second, I thought he was going to admit she was right. That was before he leaned forward, his smile devilish. He looked too proud for her to be right. "My father-in-law's a mind reader. He's not like *your* father, Serena. He's not a telepath. He can't choose to listen. He hears *all.*" Dad tapped his forehead for emphasis. I shuddered at the reminder. Grandpa knew us living Rromanija was all an act whenever we visited his house, but it still pleased him to hear us learning about his culture. Of course, Dad was never with us during those times. On the rare occasions when Dad visited with us,

Grandpa would ramble on about how Dad's insistence on not adopting the Romani way of life had ruined us.

Serena winced at the mention of her father before slumping further into her corner of the couch. She was quiet for a few seconds as her eyes unfocused. Finally, she muttered unhappily, "You dated longer than my parents." She bit her lip, her fingers clawing at her arms.

Dad huffed, shaking his head. "Your parents courted. It wasn't the same. Their marriage was arranged. Still, they love each other as good as anyone. I was extremely jealous of them at our double wedding. Most of the guests were there for them. Clarinda's dad wouldn't even walk her down the aisle. He showed up, though, with *Trent*." He said Trent's name with so much disgust that it pulled me out of my embarrassment slump. I'd overheard pieces of this story. It always sounded like something from a sitcom. Ex-boyfriend shows up at the wedding to try to win the bride's heart—definite TV trope. The difference was Trent wasn't an ex-boyfriend of Mom's. He was an older—I don't know how much older—Rom and lived outside Nashville. Trent wasn't a diviner, but that didn't seem to matter to Grandpa as long as he lived Rromanija. Grandpa's marriage wasn't arranged, but he was glad when Trent's family approached him. He liked the idea of knowing exactly what kind of man his daughter would marry. He didn't count on my father interrupting his fantasy.

"I don't know how much you kids understand about arranged marriages," Dad said. "They're not all bad. Your parents turned out alright. They may be having issues now, but so does every married couple. I really believe your father will come back." He assessed Serena as he said this, watching her body language. She squirmed a little before he moved on, addressing us both. "The problem with arranged marriages is that they can potentially open a whole can of worms. There is a dark history of parents—either knowingly or unknowingly—selling their daughters into abusive marriages or even into prostitution rings. Nonprofit organizations have tried to diminish that possibility by pushing lawmakers to create laws against child marriages, hence why state laws prevent anyone below a certain age to marry. That bar is low in Indiana." He said that last line darkly, glancing between us as if he were waiting for a reaction. We didn't give him one. He frowned. "There are several states where marriage is legal at your age"—he nodded to Serena, who was nine months older than me—"with a parent's consent. Indiana is one of those states."

"So?" Serena shrugged. "My parents agreed not to set us up with anybody unless we asked to be."

Dad nodded approvingly. "I know that, but I thought you should know that it's not illegal here. A lot of people here in the US believe that things like that don't happen in this country, but they are wrong. I want you to be worried. If not for yourself, then for others."

He turned to me. "I want you to know because I suspect it is those laws that scare Savanna's dad the most about your relationship. If a boy showed up on our doorstep and told me he was fated to be with Paige, especially one who had, even accidentally, put her in danger, I would have shouted as Mr. Huckleberry had Thursday night. He and I were not raised to believe in arranged marriages. I think he might be equating your situation to all the bad things that could come from an arranged child marriage because, though you two are fourteen, you are *still* children under the law." I swallowed hard. Who said anything about marriage? Savanna and I had only known each other for three months.

Serena's round eyes widened as she stared at me. "You're fated?" Her tone was shrouded in shock and disbelief.

It was my turn to squirm uncomfortably. "Yeah, but we're not getting *married*." Even *if* Savanna somehow survived whatever was coming, marriage was not my intention. I loved her, sure, but marriage seemed so formal and old people-ish. Besides, it was gonna take a while to get used to the emotional connection. I couldn't imagine how much worse that would be if we lived together.

A teasing smile slowly danced on Serena's lips. "Oh, so you *are* the reason we're getting the sex talk."

I huffed, trying to ignore her accusation. "What do you know about the fated?"

She shrugged, still smiling. "Just that you can feel each other's inner desires." She wiggled her fingers like she was tickling the air before bursting into laughter.

Heat flooded my face as I returned to my slumping. Dad snapped his fingers at her. "Enough. I'm still not done talking to you. I want to say something about your dad."

Serena clamped her jaw shut.

"I think your dad needed a break so he could work through his guilt without any distractions."

"Guilt? What guilt?" Serena's body shook with anger, her eyes blazing. "He has nothing to feel sorry for. Mom was the one who shouldn't have let him leave. She knew he was going to. She could have stopped him."

Dad shook his head, opened his mouth, then closed it. Clearing his throat, he readjusted his sitting position. Finally, he said, "No, I don't think this is about their relationship. I think he's racked with guilt over what happened to you."

I lifted my head. This sounded familiar, except it was Jay-Jay who couldn't let go of his guilt. What did Mr. Lindt have to feel guilty for?

Serena blinked, her mind faster than mine. "What happened in Terre Haute wasn't his fault." Oh. Right. The whole ordeal with the New Order hadn't technically started and ended back in August. It had started on Serena's tenth birthday. Mr. Lindt took her to the hospital because she wasn't transitioning into her powers well. It happens sometimes. Some diviners experience painful side effects on the day their powers come in. Mr. Lindt had thought something was seriously wrong. He couldn't stand to do nothing. But instead of helping his daughter, he'd exposed them to the undivine—one in particular who was a member of a neo-Nazi regime. If Mr. Lindt had kept Serena at home that day, everything that happened in August wouldn't have gone down. Serena had been blaming the wrong person the entire time. The exposure wasn't her fault.

Dad's response was grim. "Even if it wasn't, he blames himself for what happened with you kids in that bunker." He shook his head. "You shouldn't have been there in the first place."

"I went on my own." Serena's voice cracked with the reminder.

"Then why have you been blaming Jay-Jay?" I asked.

She closed her eyes, a couple of tears slipping through. "I thought my death would be quick." Her eyes flew open, fury burning in their depths. "Jay-Jay lied to me by omission to my face! I should have died—because now, what's the point?" She cried. "What's the point of this entire conversation anyway?" Serena sprung from her seat on the couch. "Mr. C, you want to have the sex talk with *me*? Why? What d'you think's gonna happen if you don't? You think I'm gonna get pregnant?" She grabbed the box of tissues, slamming it on the coffee table with every frustrated word. "That's a real funny story!" She chucked the box to the floor before running out of the room. Her footsteps pounded up the stairs.

We sat there for a moment in stunned silence until we heard a door slam shut. I blinked. "Wow. It's like Paige never left."

Dad groaned as he left his chair to fetch the beat-up tissue box. "Don't tell your mother these were on the floor." He returned the box to its spot on the coffee table. "That's what I get for taking advice from her mom."

"This was Mrs. Lindt's idea?" I snorted.

"Only after I accused her of bad parenting. She tried to turn it on me, asking if *I* ever spoke with *you* about sex, and I realized I hadn't. I don't have to worry, do I?"

I shrugged, wishing he'd leave the subject alone. "You haven't heard about Jay-Jay's new vision?" I laughed, trying to hide my fear. "Apparently Savanna's going to die soon, so no worries here."

Dad narrowed his eyes, probably trying to figure out if I was kidding. He leaned his weight on the table for support as he stood. "You do anything to hurt that girl, and you know we'll be forced to move again. Milo Huckleberry will slaughter us if we don't."

Jay-Jay had said Savanna's death would be my fault. Would Mr. Huckleberry really slaughter us? He had the gift of quantity manipulation and multiplication. He could multiply himself to match our numbers and slice all our throats in a quick, simultaneous fashion. It wouldn't be difficult for him—if he doesn't have an aversion to murder. I'd seen him shoot Nazis, but that was different. Or was it? I shuddered at the possibility.

Dad raised an eyebrow. "Makes you think twice now, doesn't it?" He pointed to the ceiling. "Tell Serena to watch for STIs when you get the chance." He lumbered into the kitchen, no doubt searching for a snack.

I sat there for a second, the gravity of our conversation taking its sweet time sinking in. It's not like I've ever thought about Savanna in that way—maybe that was a lie. But it wasn't something I ever thought had to happen for us… not yet anyway. And Dad was right. Mr. Huckleberry would knock my block off if he ever found out. But who's to say he would find out in the first place? He wasn't a mind reader or a telepath. I know lots of people think we're too young to have sex, but Chad and Olga did it when they were fourteen. Not that it ended well. But see, that was the difference between them and us. Savanna and I are fated. We belong to each other like two pieces of a puzzle. So did it matter if we took that jump?

Dad slammed a can of diet coke on the counter, the sound making me jump, pulling me out of my thoughts. "Damn Rebecca," he muttered. He popped the tab, taking a large gulp. He exhaled, putting down the drink and pointing at me. "Maybe it's a good thing Milo banned you from seeing each other. Two teenagers who can literally feel each other's emotions does not sound like a good move on your sister's part."

He had no idea. If I focused enough, I could feel what Savanna was feeling across the street, but it wasn't as intense as when we were in the same room with each other. The farther apart we were, the less it felt like there were two sets of souls inside me. I wondered what the distance limit was. Could we get far enough apart that it would cut the bond?

The bond was the only reason I could let her out of my sight. As long as I could still feel her emotions, I had a guarantee that she was still alive. If Jay-Jay turned out to be right about her death—I winced at the thought—I'd immediately feel it. In theory. That didn't sound fun. Not that any of this emotional sharing stuff was. In fact, it all felt heavy, like a twenty-pound weight was tied onto my heart. I could still feel Savanna's fear churning away at my gut. In less than twenty-four hours, it had become familiar enough to me that it had stopped being too much of a nuisance. There was something else in my shoulders too. I stretched my arms, trying to loosen the joints. What was that? It seared through my muscles like it was trying to rip through my skin. It wanted to escape more than anything. That's what it was—determination. I smiled a little at the realization. That was the old Savanna I knew and loved. I knew from our experience with the New Order that once she got over her initial shock and fear, her determination to succeed would overshadow it all. The feeling was small, but I could feel it pulsing, threatening to grow.

11
SO I MIGHT HAVE GOTTEN INTO
A FIGHT
BRADLEY

It was two more days before Mom and Paige arrived with the Burnetts. Dad tried to make Serena go home to her mother after school, but she refused, so Rebecca made a makeshift fort out of blankets and pillows for Serena to sleep in. When we got home, Mom and Seth— one of the twins—were putting together an additional bunkbed in Paige's room while Paige and the other twin, Sage, were entertaining the toddler in the living room.

"You need help with the crib?" Dad asked when we found Mom and Seth. Mom nodded, her facial features layered with exhaustion. Ever since we moved, we had a spare bedroom. It had stayed empty for months after Mom moved Jesse's boxes to the basement. It was sad he never got to live here with us, although his premature death had been the determining factor in our parents' decision to move. Jesse lived in Itasca all six years of his existence. He knew no other place. Still, it felt weird to give the room to somebody else, even if that somebody else was a one-year-old named after a day of the week.

Though Sage and Seth were twins, they were very different people. If it wasn't for their father's death, Sage's extroverted personality could have easily brought Seth out of her introverted ways. I guess I couldn't blame them for being unusually quiet. They'd been through a lot that weekend. The energy in the house was tense and somber with them there. Seth had always been the more down-to-earth twin. It was rare to see her get emotional in any regard. Paige didn't seem to understand their gloom. She wanted to live life in her usual upbeat fashion. It didn't take long for Sage to snap at her. They were screaming at each other in the living room during dinner.

"Seth helped me cook. Isn't that nice?" Mom said, ignoring the argument as she lifted a forkful of whole-grain penne.

I took a bite. It crunched as I chewed. The dressing tasted like soap. Mom continued to eat, smiling at Seth every few seconds, who was idly moving her food around her plate in a daze.

There was a crash of sound in the living room. Everyone flinched except for Mom. Dad stood, but Mom shook her head. "Leave them be."

"I'm not gonna sit here and let them wreck our house," Dad protested.

"No offense, Mr. C, but I don't think you stand a chance against two raging telekinetics," Serena pointed out.

Tuesday threw a chunk of applesauce in Dad's direction, giggling in delight when it hit Dad's pastel dress shirt. Serena stifled a laugh.

"Forgot what it was like to have toddlers in the house," Dad grumbled, dabbing at his shirt with a napkin. There was another clang in the living room. Mom sighed, closing her eyes.

Seth pushed away from the table before stomping through the kitchen on her way to the living room. "Would you both just shut up?" Her screech managed to outmatch the argument. Sage and Paige's screaming ceased immediately. Seth padded back, plopped in her chair, and resumed staring at her uneaten food.

★

The rest of the week was uneventful, despite the extra people living in our house. Savanna calmed a little with every passing day, but I could still feel a certain level of anxiety rattling her bones. She was trying to stay focused on her cheer routine for state finals that weekend. I tried to give her space to do that. She could use the distraction. Besides, I couldn't stay in the same room with her without feeling shaky.

Jay-Jay was out the entire week because of his suspension, so I ate alone at our lunch table, listening to the mundane conversations of our nameless tablemates. It wasn't until Friday that life at school started to take a new and unfortunate turn.

It wasn't the almighty strike of death that Savanna and I had been waiting for. It was more like comeuppance for Serena. Maybe I shouldn't say that. Comeuppance isn't the term. Comeuppance implies that she deserved what was coming to her, and as Savanna tried to point out to me later, nobody, not even someone like Serena, deserved it. It was the first time I ever witnessed Savanna take her side.

It all started in gym class. Although Serena's and my schedules were the same, we were separated for gym. The girls always did their own thing in a separate gymnasium. Some of the guys were gathered in the locker room before class, gawking at something on someone's phone screen. They were asking if he could forward whatever it was to them. I didn't think anything of it at first, especially since I knew the guy was always taking snapshots of fancy sports cars at his uncle's auto shop.

I spent success time reading the beginning of act 3 of *Romeo and Juliet* for English class. I wasn't planning to get this far in the book, let alone read it, just as I hadn't planned to read the first two books she had assigned. Frank was adamant that I keep up on schoolwork, probably 'cause he knew he'd be blamed if I failed the semester. He thought if I kept my grades up this year, it would somehow keep me out of trouble. I wasn't sure I believed him, but it was either do homework or have awkward psychoanalytical conversations that usually ended with me wanting to break something.

It wasn't until my intro to business class when I learned what the guys in the locker room had been talking about. Kase slammed himself into the seat next to me. "Have you heard?" he asked, his voice low but seething with fury.

I glanced up from our class project notes. Kase wasn't one to gossip, so his question sent my head into a downward spiral. *Was something wrong? Did something happen? Was Savanna hurt?* I grasped for the emotional assurance of Savanna's liveliness. I could still feel her. I tried to relax, taking a deep breath before I responded. "What?"

Kase took his phone out, pulling up the last conversation in his text messages. The text was in all caps. "FWD: PROOF THAT SERENA LINDT IS A—" The photos attached were too tiny on his screen for me to make out, but the rest of the sentence, filled with sexual expletives, explained it all.

I pushed his phone away, looking around for Serena. She seemed to be oblivious to what was happening, writing something in her notebook. "Who sent that to you?" I hissed.

Kase frowned. "I got several of them from multiple sources. Some of the guys thought *I* took these." Kase always referred to his football teammates as the guys. He pocketed his phone, scowling. "They think I'm trying to get revenge." I had to admit, he did have a motive. Serena and Kase's relationship had ended on rough terms after

Serena returned to school. It wasn't like Kase to pull something like this though. If he had, why would he be showing me?

I tapped my pencil on the edge of my pile of textbooks, the name of another possible culprit popping into my head. "What do you know about Aaron Krause?"

He shrugged. "Haven't heard of him." I was surprised. Jay-Jay and Savanna seemed to know him pretty well. Then I remembered that Kase and Serena had attended a different middle school—one that did not have the "privilege" of educating the likes of Aaron. Though Aaron was two years older, he made an impression on my friends back then, probably because of whatever that whole ordeal with Marcie was. I wondered if this was what he'd done. Send nudes and risqué shots of Marcie Thomas, who would have been eleven or twelve at the time, right in between the ages of my two sisters. Could he have done that? Judging by Savanna and Jay-Jay's mutual hatred of the guy, maybe. The thought made me sick.

"He's your guy." I nodded with certainty. Who else could it have been? Serena had admitted to sleeping with him. Kase would definitely have better success with beating Aaron to a pulp than Jay-Jay.

We walked to lunch together—Kase wanted me to identify Aaron in the crowd for him. I wasn't entirely sure he had the same lunch period as us. I scanned the sea of students, pleased to see Aaron at a table of varsity players. He wasn't hard to spot.

All the guys sitting around him were skinnier than the football players but still looked like they could hold their own in a fight. I probably didn't stand a chance against a single one of them. There were a few girls who sat with them, and I hoped for their sakes that their boyfriends weren't absolute trash too. Serena hadn't yet arrived at the table when I pointed Aaron out to Kase.

Kase seemed to recognize him. "Oh, that douche," he muttered.

Aaron saw us coming. He looked up from his friends, smiling cockily. "Where's your girlfriend?" He was addressing me, his tongue dancing on his teeth. I didn't respond, trying to stare him down. I wanted to seem intimidating. If this were Itasca, maybe I would have. He winked. "She's such a feisty little tease." I clenched my fists, attempting to hold my anger back. I had promised Kase the first punch.

Kase leaned over the table between a few of Aaron's buddies, snarling. "Did you send those pictures of Serena?"

Aaron crossed his arms, his smile never wavering. "Incredible, aren't they? The whole school's taken a liking to the…" He hesitated, searching for the right word. "Exquisite uniqueness of her physique. The contrived artwork on her skin, malformed yet magnificent—"

Kase didn't let him finish whatever poetic idealism Aaron was concocting. He lunged over the table, reaching for Aaron's shoulders. I expected the varsity basketball team to step in as Kase tackled him onto the floor. I figured I'd have to be the one to fend them off so Kase could complete his mission. They all stared at the fight with their mouths hanging open, their eyes transfixed on the scene, fists reaching to block their mouths. "Oh!" several of them shouted in unison as Kase's fist collided with Aaron's nose. The basketball player cried in pain, blood dribbling from his nostrils.

Serena dropped her lunch when she saw the commotion. "Oh my God, get off him!" she screeched, flinging her arms over Kase. He pushed her away, and she looked at me, eyes wide, begging for me to intervene. I shook my head. One of Aaron's teammates nudged another, pointing at her when he got his attention. They nodded approvingly, surely undressing her with their eyes. I kneed one of them in the back, pushing their head forward into their food. The other lunged at me, tackling me to the ground. His fist collided with my cheek, my skin stinging with the sudden impact. I tried to push him off me but to no avail. More punches. I could hear Aaron threatening Kase. "You wait till my father hears about this!" He was one of *those* guys.

One of the other players pulled his teammate off me. He nodded to the other fistfight. "Listen, fool, we might have a chance at getting that dumbass off our backs."

I sat gingerly, my ribs sore. My hand flew to my pump, checking it for damage. Luckily, it hadn't been knocked loose.

A slew of teachers finally picked up on the altercation, running to break up the fight. "You do so much as look at her"—Kase spat as several teachers pulled him back—"and I'll kill you." Aaron moaned, rolling on the tile.

Serena ran to assess the damage Kase had done to him. "You broke his nose, you idiot!" she shouted.

Frank jogged into the cafeteria, spotting us immediately. He grabbed Kase by the arm. "I got him." He nodded to the teachers, yanking Kase a few more feet away. He nodded at me, jerking his head toward his office. I heard a teacher say something about getting the nurse as I followed Frank and Kase.

We were a few hallways back when I spotted Savanna outside a classroom, her face flushed with exertion. She was pacing rapidly in front of a door, occasionally jumping, clenching her hands in the air. Every time she did this, she'd grasp her hands, wringing them as she puffed out her cheeks. She did a cartwheel at one point, stopping at the end to stare at the floor with a hand on her hip. When she released a breath, she rolled her eyes, grinding her teeth. She was clearly agitated, as if she were having some kind of episode. My heart plummeted at the thought. Maybe she was. Maybe this whole impending death business had triggered a slew of erratic behavior. But, wait a minute, why wasn't I feeling her agitation?

Frank noticed too. He looked like he was going to say something to her but stopped himself, eyeing me suspiciously instead. "Take some breaths, Bradley," he ordered, as if I were the one freaking out. Sure, my blood was still boiling from the injustice, but I wasn't the one pacing the hallways in a frenzied panic. Savanna started to scratch at her skin. She was so absorbed in her anxieties that she hadn't noticed us staring at her. "Now," Frank commanded. I rolled my eyes, implementing a few of the breathing techniques I'd learned in anger management a while back. When I started to feel the anger slip away, I stopped. I needed that anger. Serena deserved nothing less, even if she didn't realize it yet.

"What the heck's wrong with your girlfriend?" Kase asked.

My eyes flew open. Savanna had her head resting against one of the lockers. She was still scratching at the skin on her arms, her shoulders shaking. It took me a moment to realize why I couldn't feel her. Not easily anyway. My emotions were clouding hers. Her fist hit the metal in frustration, sending a rattle of noise through the empty hallway. She still hadn't seen us.

"She thinks she's going to die," I muttered. Kase might as well know.

"No." Frank shook his head at me. "You need to control your anger."

"I don't need to do anything," I shot back.

Frank pointed at Savanna. "That's on you. Your anger is literally hurting her." Savanna's emotions had been overshadowing mine for so long that I didn't think about the impact mine had on hers. I stared at her, my heart aching. *I was doing this? I was hurting her?* The anger I felt toward Aaron suddenly turned inward on myself. I knew this would happen. I knew I would hurt her if I got too close to her. Why had I ignored my advice? Even Jay-Jay said her death would be my fault. Was this why?

Savanna sank to the floor, pulling her knees to her chin, and cried silently. I wanted to comfort her, but I was worried that by doing so, I would continue to hurt her more.

Kase's eyes moved between the two of us. "No way." His words were breathy with awe. He held his head in amazement. "Now I get how you two ended up together. You're fated." Kase always thought Savanna was out of my league. He shook his head. "Aw man, I know the legends but never thought…" Kase didn't finish his sentence.

For someone whose family rejected their diviner status, I was surprised they ever mentioned the legends to him. Not every diviner knew of the fated. If they did, they thought it was a far-fetched fairytale. Savanna had no clue. Serena only knew about the emotional connection. I didn't even know the full story, only what Rebecca had divulged to me the week before. I felt some of the anger dissipate as I mulled over Kase's comment. He knew something.

Looking back at Savanna, I noticed she had let her legs loose from her hold. She'd stopped crying but was still staring at her feet. I could feel her emotions now. Confusion swirled in my head like a gray cloud of smoke, a small pit of her usual fear weighing in my gut. I breathed some more, trying to get the anger to fade completely. My emotions weren't helping any of us.

Frank approached her cautiously, trying not to scare her. "Savanna?"

She still jumped at his voice, leaping to her feet. Quickly, she tried to wipe the tears away. "Oh my gosh, Frank, you scared me." Savanna forced a smile, trying to act normal, as if none of what we'd witnessed had happened. She looked beyond him at Kase and me, my heart feeling sorry for wrecking hers. Her smile wavered as she took in my appearance. I wondered if bruises were starting to form on my face. Her misty eyes met my own, hands flying to her mouth. "It was you." She ran past Frank, crashing into me. Burying her face in my chest, she lightly tapped her fist at my sore ribs. "Don't you ever do that to me," she said, crying.

I wrapped my arms around her, my mouth buried in her soft hair. "I'm sorry," I apologized.

"I almost punched a guy in French class," she murmured.

I stifled a laugh. "I'm sorry," I apologized again.

12
SERENA PROTECTS THE ENEMY
BRADLEY

"**W**hat the hell is wrong with you guys?" Serena stormed into Frank's office in the middle of his lecture. Her eyes darted between Kase and me before eventually zoning in on her ex-boyfriend. "What were you trying to do? Smash his entire face into his skull? His first game of the season is next week!"

"You think I should have cut off his balls instead?" Kase asked, scratching the back of his neck.

I thought Serena was going to strangle him. She stood there, fists clenching and unclenching, her whole body shaking like a volcano getting ready to erupt. For someone so tiny, Serena was freakishly strong. Even against Kase, I thought she could get a couple bruises in before he could stop her.

"Serena," Frank said in a warning tone, getting ready to stand if he had to. "What have we talked about?"

She stared at Frank for a second, teeth clenched, before closing her eyes. I recognized the breathing techniques. Funny how she used to make fun of *me* for it. When she reopened her round eyes, she was still glaring furiously at Kase, but the clenching and shaking had stopped. Frank relaxed slightly in his rolling chair.

"You and I aren't dating anymore," Serena said slowly, keeping eye contact with Kase. "I don't care if you're jealous—you don't have the right to go after anybody that I'm seeing."

"Jealous?" Kase asked, incredulous. "You think I'm jealous that you're tramping around with losers like Aaron and whoever else I don't know about? I dodged a bullet when I broke up with you."

Serena blanched. Her voice cracked with her next question. "Then why'd you pick a fight with Aaron?"

Kase shook his head, sneering. "I can't believe you don't know." I waited for him to tell her, but he didn't. He was the only one in the room who had the evidence.

"Show her the text," I said as if it were the obvious solution to their misunderstanding.

Kase bristled. "No."

"What d'you mean, no?" I asked. Kase looked at me like the answer was obvious. I shrugged. "What?"

He huffed. "If Savanna were in her position, would you show her?" My heart dropped into the pit of my stomach at the thought. He had a point. I'd be going out of my mind trying to keep Savanna from finding out. But that was different, wasn't it? Savanna would never be in this situation in the first place because she was with me. I didn't anticipate us breaking up anytime soon. I was sure Kase knew that, especially if he knew the legends.

"Show me what?" Serena demanded.

Frank cleared his throat, his voice serious. "Kase, give me your phone."

Kase glared at me. "Now look what you've done."

"I'm not gonna let Aaron get away with this. He'll do it again to some other girl," I argued.

"Aaron hasn't hurt me," Serena protested.

Kase rolled his eyes before digging his cell phone out of his pocket. He unlocked it, opening his text messages. As he set the phone on Frank's desk, he eyed the officer. "I don't want to get charged for this."

Charged? What was he talking about? It wasn't like he sent the messages.

Frank glanced quickly at one of the texts, keeping a straight face. He started scrolling. "How many of these did you get?"

"At least eight," Kase answered.

Serena tried to see, but Frank shut the screen off and laid it facedown on his desk. He gestured to Kase and me. "I'm gonna have Lisa at the front desk call your parents. You're still suspended for a week for initiating a fight." Frank tapped Kase's phone. "Kase, I have to keep this for evidence until the administration can get to the bottom of this. You're not in trouble for it. It doesn't appear like you forwarded the photographs to anybody nor did you ask for them. As for Aaron Krause, he was not one of the people who sent these photos to you, so unless I can find proof that they originated from him, I can't do anything about

Aaron. If you two could go sit in the main office until your parents come to pick you up, I need to speak to Serena alone."

I glanced at Serena before leaving. She was finally starting to look worried, a crease forming between her dark eyebrows, her nails between her teeth.

Kase and I sat in the main office for a while, neither of us speaking. I think we were listening, waiting for some kind of explosion from down the hall. There was nothing. Either Frank had soundproof walls or Serena was taking the news calmly. She wasn't one for calm and collected, though, so I was going with the soundproofed-wall theory.

The first sound besides the rhythmic calls to the front desk was the entrance door banging shut. A tall man in a suit with a briefcase angrily thumped to the desk, his blond hair slicked back. He looked familiar, but I couldn't place my finger on why. Kase stiffened. "Crap."

"What?" I whispered.

"You don't recognize him from his billboards?" he muttered.

Lisa, the front desk receptionist, was in the middle of a call when the man slammed his fist on her counter. She nearly dropped the phone. "Um, would you mind holding for a moment?" she asked whoever was on the other line. After she set the phone in its cradle, she addressed the man. "May I help you?"

"Yes," the man hissed, his icy blue gaze penetrating hers. "My wife and I entrusted the faculty and staff of this so-called administration with the health and safety of our son. But today, I received a call that some hoodlum broke my boy's nose! I want answers!"

Kase leaned over to me. "That guy is a powerful and successful criminal defense attorney. He has a ninety-eight percent success rate according to his ads. If that's who Aaron's dad is, we're toast."

Lisa frantically paged the principal.

I've met Principal Lewis once when he replaced Principal Brickmore mid-semester. I'd probably know him a lot better if all my punishments and progress meetings didn't go through Frank. In fact, I was practically on a first-name basis with my old principal in Itasca. When Principal Lewis emerged, the guy we assumed was Mr. Krause grew even more agitated.

"Who the hell is this?"

Principal Lewis held out his hand to shake. He continued to hold it in midair as Mr. Krause refused it. "I'm sorry if you were expecting somebody else. I was brought in a little over a month ago when my predecessor took a job elsewhere. I haven't been able to introduce myself to all the parents yet." He kept waiting for the completed handshake.

There was a long awkward pause before Mr. Krause responded. "Well, no wonder this school has gone to absolute crap! You know, I wanted our son to go to private school, but my wife thought we'd test the waters with the public schools. Hell, maybe he'd learn more valuable life lessons. But instead, our son gets stuck at a school with a bunch of hooligans. Tell me, how'd you trick the board into getting you this job?" Kase and I looked at each other, our jaws dropped.

Principal Lewis cocked his head, letting his outstretched hand fall to his side. "Mr. Krause, I can assure you that I am more than qualified for this job."

"Are you?" Mr. Krause asked. "Because if you were, you wouldn't have let your people act like savages toward my kid!" Kase and I cringed at his blatant racism.

Principal Lewis held his hands behind his back, flexing his jaw. What I would give for someone to smash Mr. Krause's face in. "This school prides itself on its zero-tolerance policy for violence. I assure you, we do everything in our power to keep the students safe. I apologize for your son being harmed today, but trust me, the student responsible for this act of violence has been punished." He didn't glance at us as he said this, keeping his eyes steadily focused on Mr. Krause.

Kase flexed his hand, showing his bruising knuckles. I was surprised they bruised at all. He must not have been using his powers. I couldn't decide whether that was a smart move on his end or not.

I caught sight of a flash of russet hair from the corner of my eye, spotting Marcie through the window. At the sight of Aaron's dad, her hazel eyes widened, and she quickly disappeared.

Mr. Krause's face transitioned to the color of Marcie's hair. "This is the second incident in less than a month. You call this safe? I call this negligent racism! Clearly, my boy is being targeted for being white!" I rolled my eyes at his statement. "I'm pulling my son out of this godforsaken institution. Obviously, you people are a bad influence."

"We won't miss him," Kase blurted.

Mr. Krause snarled in contempt before marching out of the office.

"Ugh. Good riddance," Kase spat. "I'm tired of these white supremacists in my face."

Principal Lewis ignored him, raising his eyebrows at Lisa. "Parents."

She nodded knowingly.

Mom arrived not too long after Mr. Krause's exit. She had Tuesday in her arms, trying to hold her away from her shoulder-length brown hair. The baby's fingers kept grasping at the strands like they were candy. Mom took a seat next to me, sighing. "You were doing so well."

I thought about her comment. I guess in her eyes I was. I'd made it all the way to November before being suspended. It used to be a regular event for me—that and detention. I felt like I had a good reason this time though. I wasn't being punished for something stupid. Kase could back me up on that. I turned to him, but he had resumed his staring down the hall, straining to hear anything from Frank's office. I turned back to Mom. "We just wanted to protect Serena."

Mom smiled a sad smile, stroking Tuesday's growing blond hair. "Serena's made it clear that she wants to make her own choices. I think she's feeling lost right now. Sometimes lost people need reminders that will back up the truths they once knew. Every choice has a consequence that can serve as a reminder. But as a general rule, it can be difficult to help someone who doesn't want your help. Fighting is most definitely not a way to help someone. If anything, it further escalates a situation."

"But Mom, you don't know—"

Mom shushed me, placing her hand on my arm. "You may have made an enemy in the process." Coming from anyone else, I may have argued further, but this was my mom—a psychic, no less—and that little fact sent an ominous wave of panic through my body. She was right. I did just make an enemy—Kase and I both did—and with the knowledge of Savanna's impending demise, it added to my anxiety. Knowing that I was the cause of her death and that I'd also made an enemy—those two events seemed to click together in an incomplete timeline. Would Aaron come after Savanna next?

★

Savanna had state finals the next day. Mom and I drove the forty-five minutes to New Castle to watch her compete. The school that hosted the competitions had the largest high school gymnasium in the world. It was easy to believe once I saw it.

Luckily, Mr. Huckleberry never attended her competitions, and Mrs. Huckleberry wasn't as strict with the rule he had established about Savanna and me seeing each other outside of school. I'm not sure why Savanna's mom bothers to attend anything. She's always on her phone. Savanna once told me that her mom is a social worker and always throws herself into the lives of the children and adults she helps. Savanna doesn't feel she can be angry with her because she's literally making the world a better place. But I could still feel her disappointment, and it ignited a certain level of frustration within me.

Her sister, Ursula, wasn't interested in cheerleading. She always looked bored out of her mind at the performances she got dragged to. Ursula was purely a martial artist. She didn't have the extra pep it took to be a cheerleader.

It was fascinating to me how I ended up fated to a cheerleader. Nobody would describe me as the optimistic type. Savanna's friend Angela had called me broody once, telling me I was harshing her vibe.

Savanna performed several flips in their routine, but nothing compared to the one she tried to pull off in our front yard the day Rebecca eradicated our fears. Apparently, she'd pulled it off only once at practice. Her coach was considering placing her on the varsity team next year because of it. Savanna didn't like the idea of being separated from Angela and Marcie, though. They'd been cheering together for three years.

After the competition, Marcie approached me in the crowd. She was chewing on her bottom lip so much she was breaking the skin. "I saw Aaron's dad in the office with you yesterday," she admitted, her eyes nervously darting around.

"I thought that was you," I said, trying to follow her gaze to see who she was looking for.

She shifted her feet. "Could you tell Serena to watch out? Mr. Krause would do anything to make Aaron look like the victim." She started to scratch at her arms like Savanna had. I hadn't seen Serena since Frank kicked Kase and me out of his office. Dad had taken her stuff back to her house. Since I was suspended for a week and Thanksgiving break followed immediately after, I didn't think I'd be seeing her for a while.

"You should tell her," I suggested.

She scratched harder, leaving marks on her skin. "Can't. She's probably not allowed to talk about the case, and I'm already in enough trouble with the Krauses."

Something or someone caught her eye in the crowd, and she inhaled a small gasp of air. "I wasn't here," she said, pleading with her glistening hazel eyes. She bolted toward the restrooms, nearly running into my mother on the way in. Their shoulders brushed as they passed each other in the doorway. Mom gasped and froze in place for a few seconds until the door swung back and tapped her from behind. I looked through the crowd to see if I could find who had scared Marcie, but no one stuck out to me. When I turned back to look at my mom, she was still standing in front of the bathroom door, her head swiveling between the closed door and me. I weaved my way through the crowd toward her. "Mom, what's wrong?" I asked when I reached her side.

She pointed toward the bathroom. "Do you know that girl?"

"That was Marcie. She's one of Savanna's friends."

Mom's eyebrows knitted. "I think she's in trouble."

13
MY PARENTS ARE CONSPIRACY THEORISTS
BRADLEY

Mom didn't elaborate. I was starting to get real sick of all the psychic vagueness going around. First, there was Jay-Jay, and then there was Mom. What was the universe not wanting me to know? And what was the point of allowing Mom and Jay-Jay to have these visions if they weren't supposed to say anything? I mean, our powers are supposed to serve some greater purpose, but how was this serving any of that? All it was doing was putting everyone on edge.

Last time Jay-Jay had a major vision, it was so we could prepare ourselves. We used it to form an army to save Serena. Rebecca even ended up destroying the place. But how were we supposed to prepare ourselves if we didn't know what we were preparing for? The only clues I'd gotten were, one, the cryptic phrase my mother and Jay-Jay asked me—"If there was a cure, would you take it?"—two, Savanna having a high probability of dying, and three, Marcie was in trouble. I wasn't sure if that last one had any connection to the other two, though.

Regardless, it was still another worry. Mom must not have thought Marcie's situation required an intervention because she rushed me to the parking lot.

"Mom, shouldn't we be following their bus home?" I asked, hurrying after her as she unlocked Dad's car. The whole point of us being in New Castle was to protect Savanna. She glanced around, like Marcie had, before ducking inside. I yanked the passenger door open, plopping into the seat. She motioned for me to shut the door. As I did, she turned the key in the ignition and changed the radio station to classic rock. The music blared through the speakers as she maneuvered the car out of our parking space. It wasn't until we hit the highway when she spoke, having to shout over the music to be heard.

"Your friend Marcie is being watched by some very powerful people!"

"What? Who?" I asked, reaching for the volume dial to turn the music down.

She caught my arm, stopping me. "The kind of people who could be listening to our conversation! Do not turn that dial!" Mom rolled the windows down so the cool air whipping around us would create turbulence. I wasn't sure how she expected us to talk to each other with all the noise. That's when I realized that was the whole point— it wasn't safe to talk.

"Are they watching *us*?" I asked, but the wind drowned my voice.

Mom stepped on the gas, the old car straining to reach eighty miles an hour. She didn't answer my question. The wind slapped harder at my face. Mom's hair flew in random directions, sometimes blocking her eyes. She spat at it a couple of times, trying to blow a few strands from her mouth. Every few seconds she would glance in the rearview mirror. I turned to see if there was somebody following us, but if they were, they weren't being obvious.

Mom didn't take our exit. She flew past it, taking the downtown exit instead. Using backstreets, she weaved through city traffic, taking a long and complicated route back to the east side. When she pulled up to the house, instead of parking in the driveway, she steered the car onto the grass. Snapping her fingers, Mom pointed to me and then to the gate blocking our way. "Can you make that disappear?"

My jaw dropped. It was still broad daylight outside. Somebody could see me. Her hand hit the steering wheel impatiently. "We don't have a garage, and I need to park this car out of sight. Do it now." She was starting to scare me. I stumbled out of the car and to the wooden fence. It wasn't difficult to will the cedar away. My powers of dematerialization had grown stronger since the bunker. As soon as the last trace of the planks disappeared, Mom hit the gas, lurching the car into our backyard. Now the problem was rematerializing the fence. I still hadn't mastered that ability. I couldn't create objects out of thin air like most materializers. I could only destroy them.

"Get your sister," Mom ordered as she leaped out of the car and headed toward the small shed in the corner of our yard. I knew which sister she was referring to. Rebecca could do pretty much anything.

I jogged to the sliding glass door at the back of the house and yanked it open. "Rebecca!" I called. Paige and her friends were gathered in the living room, eyes glued to the television, pieces of buttery popcorn in between their fingers. There was an extra girl with them. I froze. I didn't recognize her.

I heard Rebecca's feet as she practically flew down the stairs. She hopped over the last step, her socks hitting the wood floor with a slap. As she approached, her eyes narrowed at the sight behind me. "What is Mom doing?"

I glanced at Paige's extra friend. What were the chances that she was also a diviner? Grabbing Rebecca's arm, I led her outside. "I need you to fix the gate," I whispered, sliding the door shut behind us. She watched Mom unscrew the license plate from the car. I nudged her. "Now." Rebecca darted around the corner.

"You really think that's going to help?" I asked Mom, jogging toward her. "If they were watching us, they probably already ran the plate." *Or they would have at least written it down*, I thought. *Whoever they were.*

Mom stopped unscrewing, letting herself fall to the ground in defeat. "You're right." She sighed, tossing the screwdriver into the yellowing grass. She buried her face in her hands, moaning. "The second they see our last name…" Her voice drifted off as she shook her head.

"What's wrong with our last name?" I asked as Rebecca joined us. I'd never had to worry about my last name before. It was a simple English last name that left no real hint of our ethnicity other than the white English part that nobody cared about. It was inconspicuous. It wasn't a name that pointed to our Polish Romani ancestry or hinted at all to our divinity. Chambers was a safe name. It wasn't like Lindt or Schwartz, both of which were German.

Mom didn't answer my question. "Maybe I should tell your grandparents not to come next week," she murmured. Dad never did talk Grandpa and Grandma Chambers out of visiting us for Thanksgiving. They were too excited about meeting the Burnetts. Aunt Mindy and her family were supposed to be coming too. Dad had been panicking all week about where to put them up. That was seven extra mouths to feed. Not only that, but if another bad thing was about to happen, that was seven extra people to protect. They weren't diviners. They couldn't protect themselves.

I heard the glass door slide open, and I whirled around. Dad slid it back in place. "The girls said you were out here. What's going on?"

Mom lifted her head, her voice serious. "We have a problem." She groaned as she stood from the cold ground, brushing loose blades of grass from her jeans. "You know those people who were watching your father?"

Dad crossed his arms. "They're *still* watching him."

What? Wait. These people were watching Grandpa too? I shook my head. I was coming at this all wrong. Maybe this wasn't a diviner issue at all. Grandpa and Marcie were undivine. What could they possibly have in common that would place them on these people's watchlist?

"They're watching one of Savanna's friends too," Mom explained to Dad. "She knows something. I think whoever had their eye on her saw her talking to Bradley."

Dad looked at me warily, his eyes briefly flashing to the lump underneath the bottom hem of my shirt. "That couldn't've been good."

"I think they tried to follow us," Mom continued. "But if they pulled our name from these plates"—she tapped the aluminum still semi-attached to the back end of the car—"we may have put her in danger."

Dad's eyes widened. "That's *really* not good." He turned to me. "What did she say to you?"

I shrugged. "She was worried about Serena. She's had a run-in with Aaron Krause and his dad before and wanted to warn her that they may try to make her look like the victim."

Dad's eyes narrowed. "Krause?" he asked. "The guy who leaked those pictures—his last name is Krause?" I nodded. He and Mom shared a knowing look.

Mom shrugged. "It's a common name."

Dad raised his eyebrows. "Is it? We knew they moved that lab to Indiana." They stared at each other for several long seconds.

The lab? What lab? What were they talking about? Their silence was torturous. I glanced at my sister, hoping she could explain, but she shrugged and shook her head, perplexed. My nerves buzzed underneath my skin, my stomach churning.

Mom shook her head, her eyes glistening. "We shouldn't have moved here. We put that girl's life in danger." She shot a quick glance at me before returning her gaze to my father. A spark soared through my gut. I felt like I was being called out, but for what, I wasn't sure.

Dad tried to reassure her. "We see my dad every other year, and they've never once tried to kill him."

"That we know of," Mom pointed out. "You know your father. He never tells us anything that he thinks will worry us."

Dad considered her point of view, tilting his head back and forth as if weighing his theory against hers. He hesitated before asking his next question. "D-do you think they think we know?"

Mom glanced at me again, this time longer. My heart rate rose with every glance thrown my way. She sighed, her shoulders drooping. "If they didn't, they do now. Bradley has that pump now. If they saw it, which I'm sure they did, we may have made some already paranoid people extra paranoid."

I looked at my insulin pump. What did my being diabetic have anything to do with this? Actually, hold on. What was I thinking? Of course my diabetes played a role in this. Even the Nazis had used it to their advantage. Whoever these guys were, they weren't exactly original.

"People from the government control that lab, Rin." Dad's voice was low, sending an ominous chill down my spine. Did he say the *government?* I thought of Kase's parents, who were convinced the US government might find them and throw them in some kind of diviner concentration camp. I thought the whole thing was ridiculous. But if the government was behind this…

"You think I don't know that?" Mom's voice lifted an octave. "Ever since your dad found that cure, they've taken control of everything." Wait. The cure? What cure? "If that attorney general would have cared even a little about the inhumanity of his actions—"

"Rin, calm down." Dad waved his hands in surrender. "You're starting to sound like my father." He chuckled a little as he said this. "I know the story. I just think we shouldn't be jumping to conclusions. We need to think rationally about this." Boy, had my parents switched roles.

"What we need to do is get Marcie untangled from this mess," I piped in. Their conversation was hard to follow, so this was the only thing I had concluded.

Mom and Dad stared at me—Mom's jaw quivering, Dad scratching at the shadow of his mustache. Dad looked a little guilty. Mom looked like she had something to apologize for. Were they really going to stand there and tell me we couldn't save Marcie? Were they really going to leave her without protection? No. I wouldn't let them. I would protect her myself if I had to. Or I would at least let Frank know. Not Savanna, though. For all I knew, Savanna protecting Marcie could be the reason for her death. It would be my fault for letting her in on the conspiracy.

"Bradley," Mom said breathily, her chin wobbly. She was gonna tell me we couldn't save her. It was obvious. I stepped back, wanting to hold my hands over my ears like a child, but I forced myself to hold them steady. She continued, her voice shaky. "This lab was built on research your grandfather was doing with islet cell regeneration and immunotherapy." She smiled through her growing tears, but it was a wobbly smile that broke immediately after her next words. "He found a cure."

A cure for what? Seriously, people. Why wasn't anyone being specific? My head swiveled from her to my father, hoping he would give me a better answer.

"My dad cured type one diabetes eighteen years ago," he told me.

Eighteen years ago? For nearly *two decades*, there's been a cure? Why was I just now hearing about this? And why was I standing here with an insulin pump clipped to my jeans when I was the grandson of the man who apparently cured type one diabetes?

"Attorney General Krause had been sending him cease-and-desist orders for months." Mom shook her head. "One day, your father and I came to the house after a date, and the entire place was trashed. All your grandfather's notes he had brought home with him were either missing or burned. The lab was being patrolled by the National Guard. He wasn't allowed access anymore. They stripped him of his medical license." I'd always wondered how Grandpa lost his license to practice. I wasn't expecting that to be the answer, though.

Dad scowled. "The government thought they could make more money off those *living* with diabetes than those being cured by it. That's why insulin prices keep rising. People need it to survive. The government is banking on them paying anything to stay alive."

"And you went along with it?" I shouted, anger searing through my veins. "You knew there was a cure for me, but instead, you kept paying the big bucks, just like they wanted you too?" I couldn't believe what I was hearing. There was a cure, my parents knew about it, knew exactly where that cure was, and yet they chose every day to throw money into the black hole that was the insurance companies and insulin distributors.

"Please don't be angry," Mom cried.

Dad held out his hands. "Bradley, calm down. You have to let us explain."

I shook my head and paced.

"Even if we had the means at the time to break into the lab, we'd have been running for the rest of our lives," Dad said. "You have to understand that your disease is manageable. If it had given you a death sentence, I'd've broken into that facility myself. I'd be an enemy of these people, wasting away in a high-security prison for you. If the choice had been between watching you live or die, I'd've chosen life for you. I'd've chosen a lifetime of my own torture to keep you alive. But that wasn't a choice I could make."

"That's exactly what they want you to believe. They're doing this because this disease is 'manageable.' Never mind the millions of complications that could arise from it. When our organs shut down, do these people just laugh at us? Do they tell each other we should have taken better care of ourselves? Do they consider the *seventy-nine thousand* deaths that occur every year due to diabetic complications as a necessary expense? More people die from diabetes than of AIDS and breast cancer combined, Dad! World Diabetes Day is this Tuesday. This entire *month* is dedicated to diabetes awareness. Are you telling me that all those people who are raising money for a cure are wasting their time? Are you telling me that all those people are being lied to? That diabetes research organizations are taking their money and these people are, what? Letting them keep it if they *pretend* to be working on a cure?" I could hear my voice as it cracked and bent with every word. But my mind couldn't stop spiraling, trying to wrap its way around the complete and utter nonsense of reality. My stomach felt sick, acid churning away, threatening to shoot through my system like a geyser. This wasn't solely a cure for me that my parents had been standing in the way of. They were standing in the way of a cure for over a million lives in the US. And that was only counting those with type one.

14
BIG PHARMA HAS TO BE
STOPPED
BRADLEY

I dashed inside, grabbing the phone from its cradle on the kitchen wall. Mom, Dad, and Rebecca ran after me, stumbling over the threshold. I sprinted from the kitchen to the front room, having already pressed the speed dial for Savanna's cell. As much as I didn't want to involve her, she was the only person who had eyes on Marcie Thomas.

"Bradley, you say anything, and we're all as good as dead!" Dad warned, maneuvering around the dining table. I could hear more feet hitting the floor. His words had enticed the group of girls in the living room. I held the phone to my ear, jogging to the front door. This wasn't a cell phone. If I left the premises, it would stop working. I hesitated at the thought, the receiver to my ear.

"Hello?" Savanna's voice was on the other end. I could hear the other cheerleaders in the background. Good. She was still on the bus.

"Savanna, listen to me." I said the words quickly, starting to pace in the entryway.

"Rebecca, stop him," Mom ordered. My sister looked from me to her, not sure what she was supposed to do. The phone suddenly flew out of my hand and into Sage's.

I glared at her. "Give it back," I growled, holding out my hand. Their guest gawked at Sage, eyes wide, her mouth hanging open. I didn't have time to worry about the implications of exposing ourselves. This was about saving Marcie. Actually, no. It was about saving millions. I wondered how far Savanna's bus was. They had to be at least halfway home.

Mom held her arm in front of Sage. "Don't give him the phone." Sage handed the receiver to Mom, who ended the call.

"Listen to me, Bradley." Dad stepped in front of me, reaching, his hands ready to grab my shoulder. I stepped back. "Do you want to get Savanna killed?"

My breath caught in my throat, angry tears sprouting from my tear ducts. *Oh man.* The back of my legs hit the bottom step as I stumbled, catching myself as I grabbed the railing. In one sudden rush of fear, it was like the air had left the room. I couldn't breathe. My lungs heaved, searching for sustenance. Lowering myself on the stairs, I tried to focus on staying calm, but I couldn't. Because Savanna *was* going to die. And I *was* going to be the cause of it. All according to Jay-Jay. He was right. This was proof enough. I now made Savanna a target. All because I was trying to protect her friend.

"There can be no contact," Dad continued, his voice low. "These people will not be afraid to take out anyone who they perceive as a threat to the system."

I dipped my head into my lap.

Rebecca's voice stuck out among the stunned silence. "Then why is Grandpa still alive?"

"They've done everything in their power to discredit your grandfather," Mom answered. "They also aren't afraid to make threats. I wouldn't be surprised if his silence is because they've threatened to kill those whom he loves."

"Wouldn't that have already made us targets?" I cried into my lap between gulps of air.

"For a different reason," Dad answered. "They may have been using us for leverage. I'm sure we weren't a part of their threat assessment until they saw Marcie talking to you. They probably think she's let you in on their secret. As soon as they connect you to my dad…" He paused, sighing. I was still confused about how Marcie had anything to do with the lab. As far as I knew, she was a victim of Aaron's and nothing more. What exactly had Mom seen? Dad continued. "They'll think we're plotting some kind of coup."

A coup? Now there was an idea. I lifted my head, my breathing becoming a little easier as I mulled it over. These people had been threatening the undivine. They lacked the power to fight back. What they didn't know was that their new targets could. We had the power to lash out—all of us diviners did. I mean, in our house alone we had three telekinetics, a psychic, and two materializers—one of which happened to be the Chosen One. Rebecca could probably knock 'em all out in her sleep.

"No." Dad answered my unspoken thoughts, his tone final. "This isn't worth exposing you all. If they find out about the existence of diviners—"

"What if we're careful?" Rebecca interjected. Dad swung around to meet her gaze. "What if we could find a way to not get caught?" she asked. "I'm sure with all our powers there's a way to do it."

"It's too dangerous," he responded, but he'd lost his superior tone. We'd gone against as much.

Rebecca crossed her arms, raising an eyebrow. "We've fought Nazis before. Lots of them. We all made it out alive."

"Tell that to Serena," Paige snorted, shuffling her feet. "I'm not about to take a risk that could get my insides hacked to pieces. I want kids in the future, thank you very much."

"What?" I asked, squinting at my sister, who was standing at the end of the line of girls.

Paige shrugged. "She can't have children." She looked around the room at everyone. "I thought you all knew this." Mom and Rebecca were the only people who didn't look surprised, but that was normal. Almost nothing surprised them.

I looked at my shoes, my fingers playing with the laces. "I guess that explains a lot of the weird comments she was making last week," I mumbled. Serena had gone on about missing organs. She'd also abruptly left the room at the end of Dad's speech, saying something about how she thought it was funny he was worried she'd get pregnant. Realization swept over me with a cold chill. Serena couldn't get pregnant. Was that why she didn't seem to care too much about sleeping with guys? The repercussions for her weren't the same.

I shook my head, trying to dispel the thoughts. We needed to get back to the problem at hand. We could worry about Serena later. Not that there was much that could be done for her. Not unless there was some magical cure at the lab we were planning to expose or pilfer or destroy. I wasn't sure what the best course of action was. Were we robbing the place? Exposing their lies? Or were we going to bring the entire lab to the ground?

Dad slumped his shoulders, resigned. He looked at Mom. "Vision?" he asked. She nodded. Vision? What vision? And it hit me. *If there was a cure, would you take it?* She knew all this time. She and Jay-Jay.

"The cure," I said, staring at her. "You asked about it last week."

Mom half smiled, but she looked sad. "I saw you with the cure in your hand. You were talking with your grandfather. I wasn't sure how you got it. I thought maybe he found a way to recreate it and was going to bring it here for you next week, but after everything that happened today, I'm not so sure."

I glanced at Rebecca. Mom's vision was reassuring. We would win this. If we didn't, she wouldn't have seen me holding the cure. "Any bright ideas?"

A devious smile crept up my sister's face. She cocked her head to the side, tongue in cheek, as she studied me. "Can you and Savanna hear each other's thoughts yet?"

I shook my head. Was that another cool thing the fated could do? Then I remembered. "Wait, yeah, once." In the nurse's office last Friday, I could hear her fears racing through her mind. I didn't think much of it at first. I thought it had to do with being able to detect each other's emotions. But it only happened that one time. Jay-Jay had said we were glowing, but I hadn't seen it myself. What were we doing to bring it on? Holding hands? We've held hands since, and nothing's happened. Maybe it required a certain level of focus or concentration. What I'd been trying to do was dismiss Savanna's fears. Actually, I was trying to talk to her, trying to force my assurance on her. I wasn't sure why Rebecca wanted to know. It seemed kind of personal. "Why?"

"If you could figure out how to communicate with each other telepathically and from a distance, you could be like silent walkie-talkies," Rebecca explained.

I shook my head immediately at the idea, my hands in the air. "No, no. Savanna is *not* going anywhere near this." Our parents were right. I couldn't risk her dying.

Rebecca's smile disappeared, replaced with a look of urgency. "Bradley, we *need* her. I'll keep her safe, I promise. I've done it before."

I stared at her. "You almost buried us all alive in the process, remember?"

Rebecca bit her lip, tapping her foot. "But I didn't," she argued, her voice pitchy and apologetic.

"What's plan B?" I asked.

She thought about it for a moment, her foot tapping even faster. She reminded me a little of Bugs Bunny. She turned to Paige and her friends. "Are you in or are you out?"

"I'm in," Seth answered immediately, smiling for the first time since God knows when. Paige shifted her feet nervously, mulling it over. Sage shook her head at her twin sister, her brown eyes wide with worry.

Their nameless friend swiveled her head among us all. "I don't think I have a say," she said, pulling at a loose strand of her brown hair. "I'm just a mere mortal." She didn't seem too freaked by what she'd seen Sage do or by our conversation. I shot an accusatory glance at Paige. Had she told her friend about us?

"What?" Paige defended. "Robin's boyfriend's a psychic." This was the first time I'd heard Paige mention other diviners. For some reason, I thought I knew all the ones in the area.

"He has brothers who go to your school," Robin piped up. "Calvin's a telepath and Liam's a pyro." I didn't think I knew them, but I couldn't be sure. My school was huge. We had psychics and telepaths already on our side if we needed them, but a pyro—that was a new one. Pyros could create and manipulate fire. I didn't know anybody who could do that. It might be useful for us to have one on our team.

I turned to Rebecca. "You thinkin' what I'm thinkin'?"

Her smile returned. "We do need someone to destroy the lab."

"Wait, hold on," Dad cut in. "Why are we destroying anything? That building houses important research. If you destroy it, how do you plan to administer the cure to everybody who needs it?" My heart sank. He had a point. If our ultimate goal was to rid the world of diabetes, how were we going to produce enough of the cure for every single person living with the disease, and how did we plan to administer it? Dad noticed my excitement dwindle. "This is exactly what I was afraid of," he explained. "You can't blackmail these people, and they'd know it was you if you tried to expose them. I think the best you kids can do here is steal a few vials, maybe some notes while you're at it, but the lab's gonna notice if suddenly a bunch of people are cured."

"Anything we do is going to have to be discreet," Seth said, piggybacking into the conversation.

"This is ridiculous," I said. What was the point then? What was the point of breaking into the lab if the only person we'd be able to cure was me? It all seemed selfish. I didn't want to be cured if it meant nobody else would be. There were people in the world a lot worse off than I was. It also didn't feel right to let the lab continue to let people think there wasn't a cure. I wasn't sure how we could expose them without sacrificing ourselves for the cause. I thought of Savanna in Jay-Jay's vision and shuddered. I was beginning to fully realize the danger we were all in. All because of... wait, who? *Ugh.* This was getting confusing. Was this because of Grandpa? Marcie? Me? The Krauses? *The Krauses.* I'd forgotten about their potential connection to all this. Marcie had told me she was in enough trouble with the Krauses as it was. Were they the real reason for her fear? And what about Serena? Was she at all safe from them now that the scandal had broken out? Or had she also become a target—an enemy of the Krause family?

"Mom?" I asked, swallowing. "You said the attorney general's last name was Krause?"

She glanced at Dad, who was the one to answer. "It might be a stretch, but there could be a relation to that boy at your school."

I nodded. "His dad's a criminal defense attorney. How much you wanna bet being an attorney runs in the family?"

Dad shrugged. "I'm not gonna lie, it does seem plausible."

I hoisted myself from the stairs, my hand gripping the banister. "I think I know where we need to start then."

15
THE CURSE OF STAR-CROSSED LOVERS
BRADLEY

"**S**uspended means off the school premises, Bradley," Frank said gruffly as he meandered his way across the parking lot on Monday. School hadn't started yet. I had woken up early to catch a bus.

I squinted at the line of parents in cars dropping off their teenagers. A yellow Porsche stuck out among the less colorful sedans and minivans. It swerved around the line, turning into the lot. The car screeched to a halt in an empty space near the front, several lanes ahead of where I stood. I watched as Aaron stepped out, rapped his knuckles on a nearby bright green muscle car, and laughed with the friend who escaped its trappings.

Our school was financially diverse, to say the least. That's how it was living on the outskirts of a city. There were rich kids like Aaron and his friend, middle-class kids like me and Savanna, lower-middle-class kids like Kase and Serena, and tons of poor kids—kids who qualified for free school lunches and whatnot. Marcie was one of those kids. Well, sort of. I remembered Savanna mentioning that Marcie's mom made next to nothing, working odd jobs to pay their rent. She ran some kind of jewelry-making business during state fair season. Marcie's dad made good money before he was arrested for embezzlement when she was eight, but he only served five years before they released him on good behavior. He lived elsewhere but would occasionally reappear in her life with a wad of cash offering to buy her whatever she wanted.

"These uniforms aren't cheap," Savanna had told me when her sister managed to spill a few drops of red Kool-Aid on the white fabric. "Marcie cried for weeks one time in the sixth grade when a boy threw his chocolate milk at her." My jaw tightened at the memory. She hadn't said the name of the boy, but after what I'd learned since, I was willing to bet it was Aaron.

I watched as Aaron, his dark sunglasses barely hiding the bruising around his nose, darted across the slow-moving traffic toward the school. "I thought his dad was gonna pull him out of this place," I muttered, leaning against the back of a dark-colored sedan. Both the front and passenger doors opened as I said this. I quickly shifted on my feet, pretending to be shocked that the car wasn't empty. Two heavyset guys stepped out—one with curly thick brown hair and dark thick eyebrows, the other with too much gel in his blond hair. Frank pulled me out of their way as they approached the building, doing their best to ignore us.

I'll let you know what I find out, the older one with the dark hair noted, his thought echoing in my head.

I had to do my best not to nod back. *Thanks.*

Paige's friend Robin had come through when it came to getting a message to her boyfriend's brothers. That was the whole reason I was at the school. I needed to be within a certain range for Calvin and me to communicate telepathically. I couldn't risk anyone seeing us talk.

Frank responded to my comment about Aaron. "Private schools have waitlists that not even guys like Jeremiah Krause can crack in the middle of November. Aaron's got basketball games starting this week too. Between you and me, his dad paid a lot of money to get him on the team. Coach Curry has coached quite a few students who have gone on to play in NCAA Division I schools and the NBA, which is why his father wanted him here in the first place." That wasn't at all the story Mr. Krause told on Friday, but I guess he was too smart to admit the real reason Aaron was enrolled at our school.

"How's the investigation going?" I asked.

Frank scratched at a spot behind his ear. "Serena doesn't want to press charges." Before I could react to the ridiculousness of that statement, he held his hands to stop me. "Her mom does, though. Serena's still a minor, so she can do that. Aaron gave them a sob story about how someone stole the photos off his phone, which Serena claims she took herself. I don't believe any of this for a second, but until we can prove otherwise, we're just going to have to sit tight."

I shook my head, my voice full of disgust. "Why would she lie for him?" Hopefully, Calvin would be able to dig up a legitimate answer to my question.

Frank cleared his throat, gazing out at the parking lot. "Probably doesn't want to end up like Marcie Thomas."

I glanced at him questioningly. At this point, whatever Aaron did to her wasn't hard to guess, but I didn't remember ever mentioning anything about Marcie to Frank. Somebody else must have brought her to his attention. Either that or... "You pulled Aaron's file."

Frank shook his head, exasperatingly. "That file is full of nonsense. Not that I should be discussing another student with you."

"You gonna talk to Marcie about it?" I wasn't sure she would talk, but maybe...

He shrugged. "I might." He turned to face me, his expression wrinkled in authoritative seriousness. "Do I need to escort you off the premises or are you going to leave on your own?"

I held my hands up, stepping toward the street. "I'm going." I turned, feeling his eyes on me as I headed toward the parking lot's exit. I stopped at the street, gazing across it for an idea of how to spend my day. There was a library past the football field. I only knew about it because Serena spent a lot of her free time there. I headed in that direction. Maybe I could do some digging. Library computers weren't completely untraceable. That was how Serena had fallen into the New Order's trap.

I'd never been inside a library that wasn't a school library. I'd also never owned a library card in my life. So I was a little overwhelmed by the massive amounts of bookshelves divided by rows of genres and the scattered tables of bulky computer monitors. There were several small rooms off to one side, all empty. The only sounds were coming from a couple in their twenties behind the front desk, catching each other up on their last twelve hours. There were only a few visitors that early in the morning. An older guy dressed in dirty clothes was reading a biography on a beanbag in one of the corners. A girl who looked maybe a year-or-so older than me was hiding between rows of shelves, crouching in the young adult section, her eyes glued to a manga. I glanced at the guy sitting at one of the computers, immediately recognizing him. Apparently, my idea of spending the day at the library wasn't original because Kase Schwartz was studying the screen, his forehead wrinkled with analytical effort.

I popped up behind him. He was reading a Wikipedia page on the French Revolution. He glanced at me casually after noticing my shadow. "Do you know anything about this?" He gestured to the screen. "Serena used to help me with this stuff."

I shook my head, taking the seat next to him. My class recently started this unit last week, and I wasn't exactly paying too much attention to it. The one fun fact that stuck with me was that King Louis XVI and Marie Antoinette married at our age. The French hated the marriage and also made obscene comments about their sex lives. I mentioned this to Kase, and he laughed. I was relieved by his reaction. If I had told this to any of the girls, they probably would have hit me, mocking me for "only thinking about sex." Like, how do you forget something like that? Who goes to history class and expects to learn about historical figures' sex lives?

Kase shook his head, his smile sticking. "Dude, all I know about Marie Antoinette is 'let them eat cake.' If Serena were here, she would probably be telling me all this nonsense about how she never actually said that. She was always pointing out flaws in our textbooks. Who would have thought half the stuff in there isn't legit?"

I shrugged. "Now you know why I hate school."

Kase smirked. "My parents told me I had to do something productive with my time, so they dropped me off here." He looked around, noticing my lack of cargo. "Why did you come to a library if you didn't have any homework?"

I hesitated, glancing at the entrance as a woman in her forties entered. "I was in the area." I wasn't sure I wanted to let Kase in on the plan. He would be an asset and would go along with whatever, but the fewer people who knew, the better. This wasn't a strategy for the numbers. At least, not yet. We hadn't quite sorted all the details. Besides, I wasn't sure who could be listening. Despite the library being practically empty, I still thought it wise to assume any of these people could be in on the insulin agenda. We probably shouldn't have been talking, but I knew if I did incidentally get Kase dragged into this, he could take care of himself.

I looked around the room at the large nonfiction section of bookshelves, trying to change the subject. "Do you think there're any books over there about Romanies?" If I had a whole day to kill, I thought maybe I'd use it to learn more about Romani history and culture. With my dad the way he was, I always felt I was more out of the loop than others.

Kase puffed his cheeks before releasing his breath. "If there are, they're probably not accurate. If you want to know anything, it's best to ask an actual Romani."

I returned my attention to him. "I guess I can ask you what you know about the fated."

Kase quickly clicked out of his internet browser and turned to me, suddenly serious. "That's not a Romani question. That's a diviner question. All diviners may be Romani, but not all Romanies are diviners. Don't confuse the two."

I held up my hands in defense. "Geez, sorry."

Kase huffed, shaking his head. He turned to his computer but didn't click anything, just stared at it for a few seconds. Finally, he spoke again, his voice lower. "We're not considered true Romani by the others. Most of us live a watered-down version of Rromanija if we follow it at all. As you know, my family doesn't, so I'm not the great source of knowledge you think I am."

"Okay," I said, dragging the word out. I was rethinking the possibility that he knew anything more about the legends of the fated. "But what about—?"

He stopped me. "You know it's a curse, right?"

I frowned, the lining of my stomach doing a weird flip. I tried not to be bothered by his question. "Me being cursed isn't exactly a new thing." I've always been cursed. That's why bad things keep happening to me. And Kase knew that.

His heavyset eyebrows knitted. "Right. Well, you know my maternal great-grandparents were killed in Auschwitz?"

I shook my head, confused. "Serena told me your ancestors survived World War II."

"My *paternal* great-grandparents survived, and so did my maternal grandmother when she was a little kid. They were able to escape the death camp. But my *maternal* great-grandparents didn't make it. You wanna know why?" I swallowed, waiting for him to answer his question. I wasn't sure I wanted to know. He practically spat the words like they were slurs. "They were fated."

My heart stopped, feeling like a solid weight in my chest.

He chuckled a little to himself, a nasty, bitter chuckle. "My mom is named after a member of the most fated couple in literature, except in that story, they were called 'star-crossed lovers.'"

I started to feel sick. I knew what he was getting at. I recognized that phrase from the prologue of Shakespeare's *Romeo and Juliet.* "A pair of star-crossed lovers take their life." Like Louis XVI and Marie Antoinette, they were another famous couple around our age, but unlike them, they actually liked each other, becoming so infatuated with the other that they killed themselves when they realized they couldn't be together. Suddenly the story seemed all too familiar because I knew if I lost Savanna, I wouldn't know what to do with myself. According to Jay-Jay. Savanna would be dead because of me. Well, not simply because of me but because we were fated, which was beyond my control and in the hands of destiny and the universe or whatever.

"That kind of infatuation isn't healthy," Kase explained. "People like to romanticize the story of Romeo and Juliet, but to be so attached to a person that you couldn't possibly live without them is incredibly dangerous. The entire play glorifies suicide, making it sound romantic. The whole 'I will die for you' business is completely blown out of proportion." He shook his head. "It may be fiction, but it holds pieces of truth in it and clues to the unhappy ending of fated diviners. It's not a happy thing to be fated. It's not some kind of special added superpower. It's a curse, and it should be treated as such." He looked me square in the eyes. "I know you can already feel each other's feelings. That's not a good sign. The closer you get to each other, the closer you get to death."

It took me too long to respond. I knew my voice would come out strangled, and I was trying to keep from embarrassing myself with too much emotion. "Jay-Jay saw Savanna die."

Kase nodded, not showing any sympathy for our situation. "I'm not surprised."

"How do I fix it?" I couldn't help the childish whine in my voice.

"You can't," Kase answered sharply. "All you can do is try to postpone it."

I shoved away from the computers, leaving the library and taking a bus to the outskirts of my neighborhood. Kase's warning wasn't at all what I expected him to say, not after the way he reacted when he first discovered Savanna and I were fated. I guess sometimes certain ideas take a while to sink in, and this one was tough for me to accept. I was already doing all I could think to do to keep Savanna safe, but was that enough? The only thing left was to leave her, but where would I go? Would my parents let me live with my grandparents in Tennessee? Would that be far enough to dull our connection? I still had a few loose ends to tie up with the lab, but afterward, I could leave town and never see her again.

Mom was home with Tuesday when I arrived back at the house. I could hear her gushing in the living room as the toddler babbled, repeatedly slamming her small pale hand on a rubber block. She was starting to say short two-letter words like no and da, but that was it. The rest was utter nonsense.

When Mom saw me, her smile immediately subsided, her forehead creasing with worry. "What's wrong? Did you find anything?" Tuesday screamed from the sudden lack of attention, tossing the rubber block. Mom lifted her onto her lap.

The lump in my throat wasn't swallowable, so the words were strained and slightly muted. "It's a curse, isn't it?" Mom stared at me, her expression blank. "Me and Savanna!" I shouted, the lump dissolving.

She frowned, hugging Tuesday tighter to her chest. "No, not at all. Who told you that?"

She stood as I explained. "Kase Schwartz. His great-grandparents were fated, and they died in Auschwitz."

"Honey, wait." Mom shifted her weight so she was balancing Tuesday on her hip. "An untold number of other Romanies and diviners died in that camp. Just because two of them happened to be fated doesn't mean they were cursed. You have to have a little faith that everything will work out for the better."

My hands squeezed the back of the armchair, my words menacing. "Faith? You want me to have faith?

How am I supposed to have faith when Jay-Jay has literally seen her death?"

A small smile played on Mom's lips. Her reaction confused me. How could she smile at a time like this? Her words were soft, gentle as she spoke. "Because he didn't see yours."

I shook, anger taking over my frame. How could she not understand that Savanna's life wasn't less important than my own? How selfish was she to only care about *my* life, as if Savanna's death wouldn't completely wreck me? How could she not understand that my life didn't matter if Savanna's didn't?

"Bradley, wait, listen to me," Mom begged, placing Tuesday on the floor. She stepped toward me, her hands outstretched. Her next words were slow, each one distinct. "You. Are. Connected." I closed my eyes. I knew that. I've known that for a while. Why was she telling me this again? Her hands gripped mine. "If she dies, you die. And I know you don't die."

My eyes snapped open to meet her warm, caramel gaze.

Why didn't anyone tell me this earlier? If I die, she dies and vise-versa? Come on. They could have saved us all this worry. Savanna wasn't going to die. But what was the point of Jay-Jay's vision? Visions can't change, but the minor details in the visions can. Did that mean Savanna was a minor detail? What else had Jay-Jay seen?

I shook my head. It didn't matter. Savanna would live. That was the important part. The "universe" must've changed its mind on letting me in the loop.

Mom sighed, stepping away. Still speaking to me, she returned her attention to Tuesday. "Your father told me he spoke with you and Serena while I was gone."

I froze. She wasn't gonna try to give me the same speech, was she?

Mom continued. "I'm glad he isn't afraid to talk to you about certain things. I have a hard time with all that. It was taboo to speak of it in my family growing up. However, I'm worried your father may have said some things about my parents' culture that might have come across in a negative way." She took a deep breath, tapping Tuesday on the nose as the toddler tried to grab at her finger. Mom smiled. "Do you know what ethnocentrism is?"

Ethno-what? I shook my head. Big words were Serena's thing.

Mom didn't turn to witness my movement. She interpreted my silence correctly. "Ethnocentrism is when a person looks at another culture through the lens of their own. It's difficult, if not impossible, to not do that. We all have our own worldviews, brought on by our own beliefs and our own experiences. We tend to think of our own culture to be superior because it is the only culture we know. Your father's relationship with my father is a true example of that. They each see the world through very different lenses and those lenses show them how wrong the other is. There have been moments when your father and I have had little spats because it sometimes seems as though your father treats me as some sort of rescue mission. I'm afraid that his opinions on the Romani way of life have instilled a similar point of view in you and your siblings. Your father has shown your grandfather how a little knowledge can be a bad thing. It showed him why many Romanies stay silent."

I found myself drawn to her words, making my way to the living room floor to sit across from her and Tuesday. Mom rarely spoke like this. Through the years, she'd been fading it out, her culture hidden in more subtle ways. An outsider who had no knowledge of Rromanija would be hard-pressed to notice. Dad dominated our way of life.

"After New Mexico, I let your father take over the belief system we taught you. I'm afraid, because of that, your knowledge of your ethnic history on my side of the family is… skewed. The image of your grandfather is one of hatred. He hears it, you know, in your thoughts when we visit. That's why he rants about your father. He's trying to change your mind—see things his way. It's hard to do that, though, when I've been passive in the way I've raised you. It might be too late now." She frowned, her hands occupied with Tuesday's light baby hairs.

I shook my head. "No, Mom. Tell me. I'm sick of people keeping things from me."

Mom didn't look away from Tuesday. "Women hold a lot of power in the Romani culture. It's hard to see it that way from the outside. *Gadje* may see us as suppressed because in some of their varying cultures, our rituals would have no other significance but to diminish the power of women—to keep them on lower ground. Our rituals, however, harness that power. If we wanted to—although it would be ill-advised—we could easily transform something or someone from pure to impure, like Midas and his golden touch. Being impure is so feared in the Romani culture that a man might easily fear a woman. Women look after the well-being of their community. They guard the moral code and pass the legacy to future generations.

"When a girl reaches puberty and gains that power, she is often—at least in some of the more conservative Romani cultures—arranged to be married. I was raised to believe that it was my duty to be married as soon as I could so that I could bring the next generation into our family. I did kind of do that, but not in the way it was expected of me. The pressure for me to be married was very high because I'm an only child and therefore the only person capable of continuing our family's legacy. I needed to be able to preserve our culture, especially after our family line was almost wiped out. My father was adamant that I marry a Romani man for those reasons. I don't blame him for wanting that. Your grandfather was born after the war to a single mother who had been orphaned because white men who believed they were the superior race murdered her entire village."

I swallowed, remembering the story my great-grandmother had relayed in August. Mom's lower lip began to wobble, a tear slipping before she had a chance to hide it. "There is an untrusting darkness that erupted in our history, a darkness that feeds my father's desperate attempts to preserve our culture for future generations."

"If you understood Grandpa's intentions, then why did you marry Dad?" Even as the words left my mouth I realized I was afraid of the answer.

Mom didn't hesitate. "Because I loved him. I still love him. That doesn't mean there aren't challenges, but I don't regret that decision. I don't regret having you and your sisters and your brothers. Marrying your father was the easiest decision I ever made, but leaving my family over it was the hardest."

Tuesday let out a shriek at the same time a stack of magazines slipped from the coffee table. I hadn't noticed her leave Mom's lap. Mom turned, scooping the toddler onto her lap and examining the papercut near her eye. She stopped crying as soon as Mom paid attention to her. Mom handed a stuffed giraffe to Tuesday before continuing her story.

"If I would have married Trent, I would have gone to live with his family. I don't know how that would have turned out. Maybe it would have been fine. Maybe we would have learned to love each other. My father liked the idea because there was safety in numbers. He knew Trent's mother would look after me and help me since we would be living with them. The marriage wouldn't have been legal by this country's standards. It would have gone through the *Kris*, or the Romani court. If something were to happen like, let's say, infidelity or—God forbid—abuse, I wouldn't have had a way to leave the marriage. Our legal system doesn't work the same way as the one in the *jado*, or the outside world. When I married your father and we moved into a tiny apartment for just the two of us, your grandfather feared that no one would be there to watch over me. He would constantly drop in unannounced, which is part of the reason we moved so far away."

I thought about that for a moment. It all vaguely resembled sense. But Dad had said something else, too, in his speech. "Dad thinks Mr. Huckleberry's afraid I'll try to marry Savanna." I snorted. It had been irrelevant then. At that point, I had thought Savanna wouldn't live long enough for us to get that far in our relationship. We were still nowhere near that level of commitment. We were *fourteen*. Still, I wanted to hear Mom's opinion.

A smile danced on her lips. "I'll have to explain to Savanna's father that we are not in the business of arranging marriages." Thank God. "Neither of our families should be pulling that card. We are both in the *jado*, the world of the *gadje*. You two have way too much to learn. You have three and a half more years of high school left, then college if that's something either of you want to pursue. And…" She reached over to give my shoulder a gentle shake. She had barely touched me before I flinched. Her eyes lost focus for a brief second. "This business with the lab," she added slowly. Her eyes flicked back to mine, her smile suddenly nervous. "I think you and she both know someone who could help."

I snorted. "Yeah, right. Jay-Jay's not exactly in the helping mood."

Mom shrugged, letting Tuesday struggle out of her lap. "Maybe someone else, then."

16
REBECCA FEELS A LITTLE STABBY
BRADLEY

I paced the front yard for twenty minutes before Calvin's black sedan pulled to the curb a few houses away. He practically flew out of the vehicle before jogging along the opposing sidewalk. He had a thick band pulling his hair back, a few others on his wrists. He looked like a complete dork trying to pretend to be somebody he wasn't.

"You know I can hear you, right?" Calvin's thoughts invaded my brainwaves.

"You know they can see you, right?" I retorted in my thoughts.

"Do you want to know what I found or not?" he asked.

"Sorry," I apologized. "What did you find?"

"You're not going to believe this." Calvin's thoughts were loud in my head. "Your friend isn't as stupid as you give her credit for. Chick's a freaking mastermind. I wouldn't get in her way if I were you. It might destroy her entire operation." I wasn't sure what he was talking about, but I let him continue to ramble anyway. He'd answer my unspoken confusion in time. "Getting rid of Jones was her biggest challenge. She knew he was watching her like a hawk. Him being nonconfrontational and all, she didn't expect him to go after Aaron, but the oversight worked to her advantage. It gave her enough time to bait Aaron into being the slimeball that he is."

"Hold on," I interrupted. "Serena did all this on purpose?"

Calvin's inner voice was full of admiration. "That girl is way too smart to be a ninth grader. She had me worried there for a second when her nudes leaked all over school. Who would have thought *she* was the one in the relationship with the hidden agenda? Not me. I wasn't expecting to spend too much time analyzing her thoughts, but it turns out she knows as much as any of you. She spent all last month trying to find a cause to bring to justice and who did she stumble upon but good ole Jeremiah Krause, the son of an ex–attorney general and the husband of the vice president and spokesperson of Priori Labs here in Indianapolis. Priori is known to conspiracy theorists as part of Big Pharma. Mila Walker-Krause is a big name in the type one diabetes research and fundraising community. She's the one who organizes the local walk every fall that garners millions of dollars to aid in the funding for a cure. Guess when this year's walk—" His voice cut out. I looked to see him jogging past the last house on the block—out of range. He turned at the corner, heading back in my direction. "Sorry about that. Anyway, this year's walk is—"

"Tomorrow," I finished his thought. That wasn't hard to guess. Tomorrow was World Diabetes Day. "What's her plan for that?" I asked. Tomorrow was also Tuesday. She'd have to miss school if she was gonna crash the walk. I wouldn't be surprised if Frank was watching her attendance as closely as he did mine.

"It's iffy," Calvin replied. "Jones was back in school today. She's got that guy's mind all warped and confused—considers it payback. But his presence complicates matters, especially with you and Schwartz out of the picture. Guy's a loose cannon.

"I couldn't get a clear read on Marcie. Whatever she knows, she's signed some kind of nondisclosure agreement. You know how the CIA can't say shit without having to kill you? Yeah, those things are legit. I think she's scared to think of the things she can't say. The reason she ran from you Saturday? There was a woman following her."

Calvin stopped jogging when he reached his car. He drummed his fingers on the hood. "By the way, your girlfriend's getting suspicious. If she starts pestering Marcie for answers, she's going to find herself smack-dab in the middle of this mess. I don't think it's going to take much for Marcie to crack under all the pressure."

I glanced across the street at Savanna's house. I wasn't as nervous about pulling her into this as I *had* been. Her involvement seemed to be inevitable anyway.

Calvin heard my thoughts shift to her. He jogged to the front of her driveway. "Should I have not kept my thoughts to myself? I thought you wanted me to be discreet."

I jerked my head to the side before catching myself. "No, you did the right thing. I need to get a message to Savanna, though. Do you know if she's already planning to be at the walk?"

"I don't know. I didn't have time to dig too much in her head. I was too busy with the others," Calvin explained. The storm door of Savanna's house clattered shut. Calvin looked like he was going to lose his balance. "Woah." He teetered on his feet for a second, his hands on each side of his forehead. Correcting himself, he shook his head. "Three-way call alert."

Savanna stepped off the porch, her blue eyes flashing to the high school senior on the sidewalk. Her thoughts echoed in my head, and I jumped in surprise. "He's a telepath. You're a telepath? What-why is Bradley talking to a telepath?" This was weird. I'd never known a telepath to be able to read more than one mind at a time, let alone have a three-way conversation with their thoughts.

"Are you guys connected or something?" Calvin asked, rubbing his head.

"We're fated," I answered before addressing Savanna. I was getting tired of having to explain that to people. "Are you going to the diabetes walk tomorrow?"

"I was thinking about it." She stopped walking halfway down her driveway. "I don't think my parents will let me out of school. Why? Do you want me to go? If that's important to you, I'll find a way to go. Maybe I can catch a ride with Marcie. Her mom has a jewelry booth along the route…" Her thoughts went on as she planned it all in her head.

Mom pulled the van into the driveway.

"Yeah, I'm going to have to let you go," Calvin interrupted, heading toward his car.

Blake and the girls exited the van.

"Are you gonna meet us at the walk?" I asked him, but he must have broken the connection. I couldn't hear Savanna's thoughts anymore. Her eyes met mine. Great. I had no way of telling her not to speak to me. Wow. Even in my head, that sounded rude. I mean, eventually we were gonna have to communicate face-to-face, but I was hoping not to do that outside, where we could easily be watched.

She headed down the rest of her driveway, her face full of questions.

Mom's voice pulled my focus. "Do you mind explaining to me why your godmother seems to think you're about to put her daughter in danger?" She had a stern edge to her voice. It was no secret to her that

Rebecca, Seth, and I were plotting to steal a few things from the lab, but I guess Serena's involvement had apparently been decided by the adults to be a bad idea. They were probably right. Serena was still healing from her close brush with death.

I held out my hands in defense, taking a few steps back. "It was her idea. I didn't know about it until a few minutes ago."

Mom glanced in the direction of Calvin's vehicle as it took off. She waved to the front door. "Get inside. All of you."

Savanna reached our driveway. Her voice was soft, innocent, as she wondered aloud, "What's going on?"

Rebecca grabbed her hand and steered her toward the front door. We all gathered in the safety of the house. Mom made a point of locking the door before turning to the group. "What else did Robin's... boyfriend's... brother"—Mom rubbed her forehead, struggling to remember the relation—"learn?"

I reiterated the conversation I had with Calvin, painfully aware of Savanna's confused gaze. I could feel the clouds rolling in her mind, and it was making it difficult to focus. She grew more frustrated the more I delved into the story. By the time I mentioned Marcie's possible involvement, I thought her head was going to explode.

"What?" She stomped her foot, waving her hands in the air. I stopped talking, cringing as I turned to her. She was staring at me with incredulity, her blue eyes both somehow wide with wonder and burning with ferocity. Her upper lip curved at a slight grimace, her hands frozen in midair as her fingers curled in, as if preparing to claw.

"Later," Seth said, stepping out of the room, dragging her twin with her. Paige was too enthralled by the impending drama to leave, her brown eyes wide and darting between the two of us, her lips pulled over her teeth. Rebecca and Mom watched us warily.

"What the hell, Bradley?" Savanna growled, but it was a pretty growl. She didn't have a deep enough voice to pull it off. Her anger rang in her pitch. She took a step toward me. I tried to back away, but she already had me pressed against the wall. "When were you planning to tell me any of this?" she shouted.

"He was actually trying to keep you out of it," Paige chimed in, adding to Savanna's hurt.

I shot my sister a death glare, but she just waved back, enjoying the confrontation. I could feel Savanna's anger subside slightly, tugging at my gut as it made room for a fresh wave of sadness. I realized she still thought she would soon meet her end. I reached to grab her hand as it slowly lowered to her side. "You're not going to die," I said with more confidence than I ever had before. I remembered the conversation I had with my mom earlier that day and as I did so, I saw what Jay-Jay had been talking about in the nurse's office. A faint yellow glow emanated around our entwined hands. She stared at me as the rest of her anger faded away, her sadness ebbing slower. Her inner voice was clear as day in my head as she contemplated my sincerity. Her eyes widened, her entire body racked with relief, as she listened to my memory. After several seconds she turned to my mother, tears in her blue eyes. "You knew I wasn't going to die?" She pulled her hand from mine, breaking the connection, the strange glow disappearing with it. I caught Rebecca staring at our free hands, her head cocked to the side as she mulled silently.

Mom smiled, nodding. "You're not going to die."

"But Jay-Jay…?" Savanna turned to me, searching my face for an answer. I shrugged, preoccupied with whatever crazy ideas Rebecca was clearly conjuring. As I was watching my sister, I felt Savanna's anger flare once again. "I'm tired of everyone thinking I can't handle the truth!"

"Savanna, honey, I want to explain something here," Mom said delicately, reaching for my girlfriend's shoulder. "Did you do anything out of the ordinary this past week because you thought you might pass on?" I scrutinized Rebecca's sudden smile, a mischievous glint sparking in her brown eyes.

Savanna sputtered. "What? No… well." She shifted her feet. "I didn't do anything different because I thought I would die. It was more like I did things to *keep* from dying."

"Like what?" Mom asked.

Savanna crossed her arms, her eyes on the bottom step instead of focusing on anyone. "I trained harder—both with my powers and without."

Mom nodded. "Sometimes the reason psychics can't say everything they know is because their visions put into motion certain events that wouldn't occur if the person in their vision knew what they knew. It's complicated, like time travel. The common rule is not to disclose too much of the future in the past."

"So, basically"—Savanna looked up irritably, untangling her arms—"I'm being emotionally manipulated."

"I wouldn't say that." Mom shook her head.

"I would." I jumped in, stripping my gaze from Rebecca. Stepping from the wall, my annoyance matched Savanna's. "That's what the whole last week and a half has been like. You and Jay-Jay and, heck, even Rebecca have been pulling us along on strings like we're your puppets."

Rebecca finally spoke, still staring at Savanna with a ridiculous grin consuming half her face. "You can do it now, can't you?" I didn't know what she was talking about. It didn't look like Savanna knew either.

"Do what?" she asked, rolling her eyes.

"This," Rebecca said as quickly as a large butcher knife appeared in her hands. In one swift movement, the weapon was flying at Savanna. Paige screamed, and I lunged forward, trying to reach my girlfriend before the knife did. In the same second, Savanna was gone, disappearing from sight. I hit the floor, the knife gliding over me and lodging itself in the wall. Savanna reappeared inches from my fingers.

"Are you trying to kill me?!" Savanna screamed, rushing at my sister. Mom slid in between them. Savanna skidded to a stop, glaring at Mom. "Your daughter just tried to kill me, and you're defending her?" I leaped to my feet.

Rebecca was still grinning. "Most materializers never learn to do what you did. That's an upper-level skill. That's like me turning the carpet red." She gestured to the carpet in the front room, which had once been a bright crimson color for a solid month before Rebecca changed it back to its original boring tan.

"What exactly was that?" I sputtered as I walked to the wall, my legs trembling from the scare. Wrapping my fingers around the handle of the knife, I tried to yank it out, but it disappeared as soon as I had my full grip on it. I leaned my head against the wall, needing to take a second to breathe.

"It's called self-materialization," Savanna answered. "I basically dematerialized myself for a second or two."

My fist hit the plaster above me, shaking a few picture frames. "You didn't need to throw a knife at her to prove your point," I growled at my sister. I'd never known Rebecca to be violent. Flying weapons were usually Paige's thing.

"Yes, I did." Rebecca crossed her arms. "If she didn't think she was going to die, then she wouldn't have disappeared."

"Your point being?" I asked, still staring at the wall.

"My point being that—"

Savanna interrupted. "I've only done that once before."

I felt a cold chill run along our spines, the hairs on my neck standing up. I pushed away from the wall to get a better look at her. She was calming down, shifting her emotions, her right eyelid fluttering like she had something stuck in her eye.

Mom relaxed, stepping from between the two girls. "That's probably what's going to save your life—both of yours," she added, her eyes briefly flickering to me. "You needed to believe you were going to die to learn that skill."

Savanna slowly turned her head to meet my gaze. "If I'm in that much danger, how much danger is Marcie in if she's involved in all this?"

"It depends," I answered. "You said her mom will have a jewelry booth at the walk. Judging by the fact that she seems to be afraid of the Krauses, I'm not sure what to think."

17
PRIORI LABS IS LYING TO YOU
BRADLEY

I had to reexplain the entire conspiracy to Savanna, this time with more than just Calvin's new details. She had missed the entire reason we were interested in the lab in the first place. When I mentioned there was a cure for type one diabetes, her blue eyes widened. I thought I sensed a small glimmer of pity in her stomach, but it was soon outmatched by the same sickening feeling I had felt when I first learned what the Krause family had done to my grandfather's research.

"So, this walk they do every year is just for show?" Savanna had asked, her voice rising an octave. "My parents and Angela's parents have been donating for as long as we've known the Thomases. Marcie's dad used to work at the lab before he was arrested. He was chairman of the board." I didn't want to tell her they'd been contributing to one of the nation's largest scams, but it was true. The only thing their money had been doing was feeding the families of Priori's already wealthy employees. Her hands gripped her head as she processed this fact. "Do you think the Thomases have known all this time? One of my best friends has known this entire time?"

We were sitting on the two-person couch in the front room as the sun set. I was surprised her parents weren't looking for her. Maybe they hadn't noticed she was gone. Or maybe Mr. Huckleberry wasn't home yet to care. Unlike ours, their house had a two-car garage, so it was difficult sometimes to know who was home and who wasn't. I didn't ask her though. Whatever the reason for the lack of angry parents at our front door, I was glad.

Savanna was practically shaking by that point in the conversation. I could feel her distrust growing with every question, swirling in her neck and shoulders, marred with frustration. "I know my friends don't like you, but I can't believe Marcie knew there was a cure for you and didn't say anything."

Marcie and Angela didn't like me? I thought about that for a second. It would explain why they rarely spoke to me. Angela would ignore me whenever we were around each other, but Marcie didn't seem that way. Whatever. Marcie must have changed her mind about me, or she wouldn't have tried to warn me about the Krauses. "Calvin said she'd signed a nondisclosure agreement. They've probably been threatening her. Maybe they told her they would kill her dad." I couldn't believe I was the one defending Marcie instead of the other way around. She was Savanna's friend, not mine.

"She still could have told me," Savanna wailed.

I didn't say anything, but she was making this about herself.

"Bradley." She sniffled after a long pause. "We've been looking at this all wrong. We know I don't die soon because *you* don't. But even if we weren't diviners, if we were regular people who didn't attract all kinds of trouble, you still have a shorter life expectancy than I do. But since we're fated, you having this disease is slowly killing me too." I froze, my heart beating quicker. I hadn't thought of that. If my disease killed me, it would kill her too. She shook her head, wiping away a few stray tears. "I get it. Marcie doesn't know. She's not a diviner. She doesn't know anything about us being fated and our lives being connected, but you have to understand what her betrayal feels like to me. Her withholding information regarding a cure for you directly affects my life too."

Her point of view left my mind reeling for hours, long after she'd gone home. It was unsettling for someone to claim my disease as *their* problem. Even with our emotional connection, she couldn't know what it was like for me to live with diabetes. She wasn't the one who spent countless hours in their early childhood hiding their symptoms so their parents wouldn't have to pin them down to inject more insulin. She wasn't the one who spent every day of their life having to prick their finger. She wasn't the one who had to obsessively count carbs every day. If I could live fifty more years with the threat that diabetes would kill me but live without symptoms, without needles, without insulin and glucose tablets, life would be a breeze. I wouldn't be complaining.

I get that she was worried, but she was making me feel like my existence was a burden. That my illness made my life less worth it. She had to be sensing that. Or was her own selfishness masking my hurt?

I was hoping she'd sleep away her ridiculous feelings. Her getting into an argument with Marcie wasn't going to help us. Unfortunately, she still seemed on edge Tuesday morning when Rebecca, Seth, and I met her in a parking garage downtown. She'd pretended to go to school, knowing her parents wouldn't approve of her entangling herself in another mess, and convinced Calvin and Liam to give her a ride.

"Marcie's mom's booth is in Monument Circle," Savanna said without stopping to greet any of us. She marched straight to the exit.

I shot a side glance at Calvin, who shrugged. "Don't look at me, bruh. I'm not reading either of your minds unless it's absolutely necessary. It's not worth the migraine." Savanna and I still hadn't learned how to communicate telepathically from a distance. Calvin could only connect us if we were both within his telepathic range. Rebecca's walkie-talkie idea wouldn't be able to help us.

We followed Savanna as she led us northwest. Most of the streets in Mile Square were cut off to traffic, so as soon as we hit the corner of Delaware and Maryland, we were free from having to dodge frustrated drivers. It was still early enough in the morning that the crowd hadn't hit its peak yet, so it wasn't too difficult to weave through the masses. Several vendors were still setting up their booths as we passed. The closer to the circle we got, the heavier the foot traffic.

Savanna spotted Marcie's red hair before any of us. I grabbed her arm at the outskirts of the circle to keep her from moving forward. "Wait."

Savanna pointed toward Marcie. "We need to get to her before—"

"If anyone sees us, it could cause trouble," I said, my eyes scanning the crowd.

"We're practically in the belly of the whale." Liam snorted, but his eyes were also studying the masses. "They would have spotted us by now if they were paying attention. They have to know we're here."

"They at least have to know *I'm* here," I said, my eyes stopping on two people on the other side of the circle. Their lips were locked. The guy was too tall for her, having to bend to kiss the girl with the dark shoulder-length hair. She stood on her tiptoes, her hands wrapped around his forearms. I nodded to them. "They most definitely know Serena's here."

Seth's eyes widened at the sight. She stepped forward instinctively, but Rebecca caught her arm, shaking her head tersely.

"This would be a lot easier if I were a mind reader," Calvin muttered, his eyes focusing on one random person and then another. "You know, lots of these people have diabetes. Why would they be worried about Marcie telling *you* about the cure if she were around all these other people?"

I clenched my jaw. "I have a personal connection to the lab. They probably thought I knew already and that I was using Marcie as my way in."

Seth bit her nails. "You mean to tell me they've been expecting us this whole time?"

"We need a distraction," Rebecca said, her eyes landing on the unbelievably tall monument in the center of the circle. She cocked her head to the side. Before she could devise a plan though, Seth had pulled from Rebecca's grip, darting across the crowded space toward Serena and Aaron.

Savanna pulled me in the direction of Marcie's booth. "That's our cue. Go!" I followed her, unsure who the others would choose to trail. I didn't look to check.

Marcie was unpacking a cardboard box full of jewelry sets while her mother hung a few T-shirts on a wire in the back. Marcie froze when she saw us, her hands on a pair of blue and gray ribbon earrings. "Savanna," she said, forcing a smile. She didn't move. "I didn't know you would be here."

"You mean you didn't think I would be at one of the nation's largest events for diabetes awareness when my boyfriend is a type one diabetic?" Savanna asked. Her voice held an unusual snippiness. I flinched at her use of my disease as a noun. I didn't mind being called diabetic, but that pesky *a* before the word made it sound like that was my entire identity. I wasn't Bradley anymore. I was the diabetic.

Marcie's smile faltered, but she kept at it. "Did you want to buy a necklace? All the proceeds go to finding a cure."

"Oh, you mean the cure that's been around since before we were born? That cure?" Savanna pressed, leaning forward, her hand on the table.

Marcie shrank back, her smile disappearing. "What?"

Her mom turned to see what was going on, her eyebrows knit. She didn't say anything but watched us with a certain level of suspicion.

Savanna waved her hand in the air. "That's what you've been so upset about lately, hasn't it? That Serena Lindt's being threatened by Aaron's father, who, as it turns out, is still threatening you?"

Marcie was shaking. Her mother finally closed in on us. Mrs. Thomas's voice was stern. "You and your friend need to leave."

I glanced behind us. The others must have followed Seth. I tugged on Savanna's elbow. It wasn't smart of us to throw accusations when we didn't have backup. Not that it would have helped anyway considering we were standing in a public space.

Savanna yanked her elbow from my grasp. "How empty is the lab right now, anyway? I mean, if this is their largest event of the year, then surely, it's like a holiday for them or something. What? Are all the employees hovering around here somewhere?"

Mrs. Thomas spoke through her teeth. "I've never known you to be a social activist, Savanna, so why don't you stop harassing us before I call security."

Savanna scoffed, stepping back, her arms crossed. "Why? Scared we'll all be killed? If that isn't an admission of guilt, I don't know what is." She and Mrs. Thomas stared at each other for several seconds before their contest was interrupted by mass hysteria.

Screams rang out from all around us. People ran through the roads that led out of Monument Circle. Savanna and I spun in a circle in search of the culprit. It took me a minute to realize the cause of people's terror wasn't *in* the crowd—it was above us. The large monument was shifting and reshaping like it was soft clay, the attached statues melding into the large gray form as it transformed into an oversized message. The phrase "Priori Labs is lying to you," loomed over us. I stared, stunned into silence.

Savanna's hand gripped my arm, her voice full of urgency. "Where's your sister?"

I blinked, unable to answer. My sister? Why ask about her suddenly? Did she not see the giant sign in the middle of the circle? *What was happening?*

She yanked me sideways. "Your sister!" she shouted. "She's the only one who can do something like that!" The form froze, solidifying to its aging, hardened rock form.

It took me a while to process what Savanna was saying. *Oh God. My sister.* Was this Rebecca's idea of a distraction? I ran with Savanna through the terrified crowd. There were several people as stunned as I had been, staring at the figure with fascination. We rounded the monument to the other side, calling my sister's name. There was a small crowd at the base, murmuring to each other. We pushed through it.

"She's still breathing," I heard Calvin say as we reached the center. Rebecca was unconscious in his arms, a streak of blood running from her nose. He looked at me, asking through his telepathy, "Does she normally do this?" Savanna's inner voice flooded my thoughts. I tried to ignore her, focusing on Calvin's question.

"What, fainting after she does something big, like manipulating the design of a century-old statue?" I would have gestured at the statue, but we were being watched by a small crowd of onlookers. "Yes. Did people see?" I gazed at the crowd. Half of them had their eyes on the statue, the other half worried about Rebecca's limp body.

"People weren't paying attention to her. It's kind of tough to do that, you know, when a three-hundred-foot statue is changing before your eyes," Calvin responded. "Most of them think she fainted from the sight. It *was* a little shocking." He stood, keeping her in his arms. "How long does it usually take for her to wake up?"

I shrugged. I wasn't sure. The last time she had fainted was after she destroyed the bunker, and I was out for that as well.

"She was unconscious for maybe five minutes last time," Savanna answered.

I looked around. "Where are the others?"

Calvin scanned the crowd. Most people had moved on from us and were rounding the circumference of the monument to get a better look at the statue. He bobbed his head forward, angling it toward Meridian Street. "Liam and Seth followed Serena and Aaron that way."

A gunshot rang through the crowd, causing another wave of mass panic. It echoed throughout the circle, making it impossible to judge the direction the sound came from. Calvin ducked slightly at the sound as I yanked Savanna's arm, knocking her to the ground. My heart rate quickened, listening to the screams coming in all directions. I waited for another shot, but if there was more than one, it was masked by the screams. Reaching for Savanna's hand, I met her wide, terrified eyes. For a second, our hands glowed until I let go. We didn't need to add to the hysteria. I did hear a single thought scream from Savanna's mind before I dropped her hand. "Marcie!"

We leaped to our feet, racing back the way we had come. When Marcie's booth reappeared in our sights, I couldn't see the Thomases through the panic. Shirts flapped in the cold breeze—a few of the displays were knocked over. The table stopped our momentum as we reached it, our hearts tightening at the sight. A small pool of blood had decorated the concrete where Mrs. Thomas had been standing minutes before. A few droplets ran from the back of the booth to the wall of the theater behind it. I felt guilt claw its way through Savanna's body, and I grabbed her hand.

"Maybe they're fine. We don't know yet," I thought as I twisted my body, this way and that, to see if I could catch a glimpse of them. "Maybe they had run."

"Or they were captured." Savanna's fears countered my theory. The circle had mostly cleared.

We stood debating the possibilities for several minutes before Calvin caught up to us. "What's with the glowing arms?" He asked as he set Rebecca gently on the concrete. I let go of Savanna. We had to stop doing that.

Rebecca stirred, blinking rapidly as she came to, wiping her hand underneath her nose. Most of the blood had dried, so she started to scratch aimlessly at it. Sitting, she stretched, cracking her neck, followed by her knuckles. She squinted at Calvin. "That ought to keep them busy for a while, don't ya think?"

"They have Marcie," Savanna told her, practically spitting the words.

Rebecca looked at us but didn't seem too concerned. I wasn't sure if that was because she knew better or because she was still waking up. Finally, she cracked a smile. "Yes, but we have Aaron."

I looked across the circle where Calvin had said the others had gone. I couldn't see anything past the monument. Aaron would be the perfect collateral, but something about this part of the plan was bothering me. By taking Aaron, were we not any better than the Krauses? "How can you be sure we have him?" She'd been out cold for the last several minutes.

"Because we just gave Serena enough backup to execute her plan," Rebecca answered, gesturing for someone to help her to her feet. *Oh. So that part was Serena's plan. Of course it was.* Despite what Calvin thought about Serena being a genius, I wasn't sure I trusted my godsister's plan. Last time she'd gone rogue, we wound up having to save her. This couldn't end well.

18
AARON IS A SLIMEBALL AND SERENA KNOWS IT
BRADLEY

Serena smirked as she circled Aaron in a nearby hotel room. She had zip-tied his hands and feet to a chair, but it didn't stop Aaron from trying to break free. I didn't remember this being a part of the plan Calvin had shared with me. Aaron seethed, a bit of saliva foaming at the mouth. I was surprised he wasn't making a lot of noise. We didn't exactly have the building to ourselves. His eyes narrowed, occupied with Serena. Maybe she'd scared him into submission. It wouldn't be hard. People were normally afraid of those with superhuman abilities. We could probably take over the world if we wanted. Keyword: *If.*

"They'll call it self-defense—me killing you," Serena said, circling him. "Everyone loves a good story about rapists being murdered." She stepped a few inches back, assessing him. "Well, actually, they like stories about pedophiles being murdered, but hey, it shouldn't be too hard to accuse you of something you've actually done."

I tried to assess her body language from the other side of the room. *Was she serious? Murder?* Sure, Aaron was a slimeball, but I wasn't gonna be an accomplice in his death. And what did she mean by "pedophiles"?

"What are you talking about?" Aaron spat, but I could see the nervousness in the whites of his eyes.

Rebecca had led Calvin and me there. She and Savanna were in the hall. Seth and Liam were keeping watch near the hotel entrance.

Serena leaned over the couch, Aaron's laptop lying open on a cushion. She swiped a finger over the touchpad to wake it, and an encrypted file folder appeared on the screen. I had to lean forward to read its title. It was something vague like "new folder" or "untitled." Nothing too peculiar. She straightened, shooting Calvin a look as if to ask, "Are you ready?"

Calvin smirked, unfolding his arms.

Serena introduced him. "I met Calvin today. Guess what his special talent is?" She leaned forward, her nose nearly brushing Aaron's. "He is excellent at guessing passwords."

And Serena was excellent at hacking, I thought. *Why did she need Calvin to tell her Aaron's password?*

Aaron squirmed slightly in his seat. "Yeah, right."

Serena stepped away, raising her eyebrows at Calvin. The telepath didn't pause to reconsider. "007aaronisabeast."

I couldn't help but laugh. Aaron's face grew red. He watched with horror as Serena typed his password, revealing hundreds of images.

My laughter died in my throat, a sharp pang slicing through my heart. Serena wasn't kidding. She had unlocked hundreds of photographs—some of girls our age, others of kids younger than my siblings. I looked away as my mind was being hijacked by flashbacks. My stomach flipped. Serena slammed the laptop closed. Regardless, I couldn't stay in the room anymore.

Bang! I flinched at the sound in my memory—a bullet soaring above my head. Garrett's tight grip around my body loosened, and I dove forward onto the cold, hard ground of the Sangre de Cristo mountains. I blinked rapidly, shaking my head as I made my way to the door of the hotel room.

"Either I turn over these files to the Indianapolis Police Department, or you start talking," Serena said threateningly as I fumbled with the doorknob. I knew it was a bluff. Even if Aaron did talk, she would still turn him in. If she wouldn't, I would. Aaron's dad was good, but I doubted he was good enough to win a case with that much hard evidence. Maybe Aaron would be tried as an adult. I slammed the door shut behind me, gasping in a lungful of air. The least Serena could have done was warn me beforehand. I'd been doing so well—not having to deal with the flashbacks.

"Are you okay?" Savanna's voice lilted with concern. Her hand rested on my arm, but I automatically pulled away. A cop had run to me in the memory, hoisting me from the safety of the ground. "Bradley." Savanna's soprano was sad, frantic as she continued to reach for me. I slid against the opposing wall, my face covered by my hands, fingernails clawing at the skin around my eyes.

"He's gone. You're safe," the cop tried to assure me, but I knew that I'd never be safe. What was safe anyway? Gretta had said the same thing—"We saved you." *Safe* wasn't real anymore. Safe meant *wuhzo*—pure. This wasn't pure. This was hell.

Rebecca suggested Savanna trade places with Seth, concerned the emotional connection would be too much for her. Savanna refused to leave my side though, her soft hair tickling my arm. "I can handle it. I'm fine." She was crying as she said this, her arms wrapped tightly around me. She buried her face in the crook of my neck as she clung to me, shaking nearly as much as I was.

"You're fine. You're safe." Her inner voice broke through my rage of memories, a mantra in the background of the flashes. I'm sure her words were well-intentioned, but they caused my mind to reel backward, bringing Gretta and the RV to the forefront of my memories. "You're fine. You're safe," Gretta had cooed, her bony fingers combing my short hair. I jerked my folded arm forward, trying to pry Savanna away. She released for a split second before returning her grip.

"I'm sorry, I'm sorry, I'm sorry," she whispered in my ear. The images began to blur, becoming opaque as random other memories tried to occupy the same space. My sixth birthday party—I couldn't get the last candle blown out. My best friend, Justin, leaned in to blow it instead, said it helped the wish come true if somebody else joined in. My wish did come true, thanks to him. I got to tag along on his family vacation to Disney World that next spring. It would have been a happy memory if the car hadn't hit a wrong-way driver on the way home. That was the last time I saw Justin alive.

The memory switched abruptly to a time when Chad and I were playing on the school playground. This was back before he lost his mind. I was maybe seven or eight. It shifted again to the day Jesse was born. I was around that same age. It was Memorial weekend, so flags decorated the hospital wing. Paige and I got to hold him in the hospital. We were so little—*he* was so little. Why do all my good memories end with sad stories?

And then… Savanna. The first time I saw her floored me. The first time she kissed me. The first time *I* kissed *her*.

"I'm not a sad story," she whispered softly, holding me close. *She* was doing this. She was picking and choosing the memories I saw. Dropping my hands from my face, the memories disappeared from my sight. I could see now that we were glowing brighter than before, the light encompassing our entire bodies.

A door opened further down the hallway, a couple walking out. I ripped myself from Savanna to make the glowing stop. She reluctantly let me go as the couple walked away, turning the corner. As soon as they were out of sight and earshot, Rebecca turned from the emergency evacuation plan she was pretending to study. "They couldn't see you."

I blinked. "What?" My voice was raspy.

Rebecca stepped toward us. "When you glow like that, you become invisible to the undivine. You're lucky they were heading the opposite direction when you popped in from out of nowhere." Savanna and I exchanged a wide-eyed glance. We'd been doing that all day—even in the square. Did someone see us disappear? I mean, the gunshot and the statue were distracting enough, but still. That would have been important to know beforehand.

"Ms. Jones couldn't see us," Savanna said, the memory dawning on her. She grabbed my hand to replay it—the memory of the nurse's office.

"Where did they go?" Ms. Jones asked nervously.

My hands were wrapped tightly around Savanna's, my eyes closed and focusing on her thoughts.

"You can't see them?" Frank had asked.

The memory ended and I blinked. We needed to pay more attention to that stuff.

The door in front of us opened, Calvin stepping out before closing it behind him. "Dude, you missed the best part," he said, addressing me. For someone who could read minds, he clearly wasn't great at reading a room. I wasn't sure what my face looked like. It felt sticky from all the panic breathing I had blown into my hands, which had circulated the moisture from my breath back into my face. I tried to casually hide my face from his, not wanting him to think I was a wuss.

"Dude sang like a canary." Calvin went on. "Although he didn't have to." He smiled, tapping his temple with his index finger.

Seth appeared around the corner, slightly out of breath. She leaned against the wall for support. "There are cops everywhere." Savanna and I scrambled to our feet.

Calvin smirked. "Good. They can haul Aaron's ass off to prison."

"No." Seth shook her head. "I mean, like, they've flooded the square. There's SWAT, there's guys in suits, there's state police, US Marshals, the National Guard—it's like they called everybody, like they found somebody featured on *America's Most Wanted*."

Savanna squeezed my hand. "They're not looking for us, are they?"

"I don't know," Seth answered. "They haven't come in the hotel yet, but it's only a matter of time."

"We need to warn Serena," I muttered.

Liam bounded down the hallway from the opposite direction. He pointed at the door behind Calvin. "Get in," he hissed, practically pushing Savanna and me into it. We all quickly scrambled into the room, Liam grabbing the chain on the door, sliding it into the holster when we were all through.

"What are you guys, like fuckin' mind readers or some shit?" Aaron asked loudly.

Savanna let go of my hand. "Or some shit," she hissed as she rushed forward. Rebecca beat her to him, reaching to place her small hand on his head. Immediately, he lost consciousness.

Serena stared at the group of us, her eyes wide open, her mouth hanging slightly ajar. "What are you guys doing?"

Liam peered through the peephole, waving at us to keep quiet. In the silence we listened, our breathing making up most of the sound. We heard knocking and shouting from down the hall. "Indy PD!"

We all exchanged frantic looks. Serena grabbed a pen and paper and began scribbling furiously. When she was done, she somehow managed to pin it to Aaron's shirt using a bobby pin.

Daintily, Savanna pulled the curtain of the window just enough to study the view. We were in the back hall of the first floor. She gasped and jumped, returning the thick green curtain to its place. "We're surrounded," she mouthed.

Seth locked eyes with Serena. "Can't you walk through walls?"

Serena shook her head in one swift, tight motion, her eyes wide. She wrapped her arms across her chest and stomach, seemingly self-conscious. I hadn't seen her use her powers since she was captured by the New Order, but I thought that was because she'd had no reason to use them. I was pretty sure she hadn't lost her ability. It wasn't something physical the Nazis could have ripped from her. Serena wasn't one to scare easy, but the mention of her powers seemed to have her stuck in the headlights. Her eyes flickered to Calvin, who was studying her with intense concentration. She shook her head at him, the only indicator of their telepathic conversation. The shouting and knocking were getting closer.

Rebecca shoved me toward Savanna. "Invisible," she whispered, barely audible. I wasn't sure what she was getting at.

Rebecca grabbed Serena's hand and closed her eyes, bowing her head as if she were praying. Serena's shoulders dropped, and Rebecca let go. Serena shot a look of wonder at my sister before gesturing to the far wall. Placing her hand on the wallpaper, Serena squinted at the design as if she were trying to decipher what was on the other side. She reached for the closest hand—Seth's— pulling her into the next room.

"Indy PD!" The knocking shook our door. The rest of our group scattered to the wall, impatiently waiting for their turn. The pounding grew heavier and more constant, accompanied by the deep voices of the police officers.

Rebecca went through, then Calvin, Liam… I stepped toward the wall, but Savanna jumped into me as the door crashed open. She had me pinned against the corner, her hand covering my mouth. Her other hand was entwined in mine. "Invisible," she mouthed as the glow encompassed our bodies.

Oh. That's what Rebecca meant. I tried not to move.

"What the hell?" an officer asked, waving away the small cloud of free-floating dust the door bust had caused. He squinted at Aaron's body tied to the chair.

Two other officers followed the first officer in, their guns at the ready. One of them peered into the bathroom and shouted, "Clear!" The other did the same with the closet.

The first officer holstered his gun, bending to read the note Serena had left. "Well, I'll be damned," he shook his head, checking Aaron's pulse. He pressed the button of his radio attached to the shoulder of his uniform, leaning his head to speak into it. "We're gonna need an EMT and CSI at the hotel off Meridian and Ohio—room one-thirteen."

"EMT heading your way," a feminine voice crackled through the radio. A few seconds later the voice confirmed the crime scene unit. One of the other cops asked the first one if he thought this was related to the "deal with the statue." The first cop flicked a finger at the note pinned to Aaron's chest. "Note says his name is Aaron *Krause,* so what d'you think?"

The second cop raised his eyebrows, his hands on his belt. "I think someone went through an awful lot of trouble to frame him."

I tensed, looking at Savanna, who was facing away from the scene. Although she couldn't see what was happening, I knew she could hear my brain analyzing the events. *Frame him?*

Her thoughts shot back at me. "Give them a minute to process the scene. Serena seemed to have compelling evidence." I heard a second thought float in her background thoughts before she had time to catch it. "Or else you wouldn't have reacted so badly." She heard my thoughts latch on to hers and quickly tried to change the subject. "Do you think there's a way to walk out of here without them seeing us?"

I eyed the doorway. There was a clear shot from us to it. "Won't know unless we try," I answered.

Savanna smiled, letting her hand drop from my mouth. Slowly, she stepped back, keeping her fingers entwined in mine. The glow snapped to our hands. I glanced nervously at the cops, but they all seemed preoccupied with the scene. She tugged on my arm, the glow returning to encompass our full bodies. I stumbled, freezing in place as the third cop looked my way.

"Did you hear that?" the cop asked his buddies as he stepped toward us. *Holy crap, they could hear us.* I held my breath.

Savanna let out a laugh, waving her free hand in the air, her fingers wriggling, "Ooh, I'm a ghost. A floating voice with no body."

I stared at her, my hand gripping her hand so tightly, I was surprised she was still smiling. I tried to make my thoughts loud inside hers. "What are you doing? Stop!" She ignored me, continuing to tease the police officers. I wasn't looking at them anymore, but I knew what was about to go down. "Run!" I shoved her toward the open door as bullets started flying. We were out in seconds, racing through the hallway in the direction that the others had fled.

"What the hell was that?" I asked, gripping her arm to keep the glow. "Cops shoot first and ask questions later. Were you trying to get us killed?"

Savanna shrugged. "Frank doesn't shoot first," she argued as we hit the end of the hall.

"Frank isn't 'cops'!"

"He is too. He has a badge and a uniform and everything," Savanna said.

I glanced down the adjacent hallway. I wasn't sure where we were supposed to be meeting the group. We stopped running. "I mean cops as in the plural. Frank is a singular person. Most cops only have a twenty-four-week-long training program and some field training that prepares them for duty. Frank has a four-year bachelor's degree in psychology. He's literally trained to ask questions."

I could hear her processing what I was saying. She pointed down the hallway. The cops hadn't followed us. They probably thought we were still in the room. "So that's normal?" Her voice was pitchy. It was another fact to add to her new growing list of realities. She heard me think the word "sheltered," and turned back to me.

"I'm not sheltered," she defended.

I shrugged.

In some ways, she was. I was surprised she hadn't come across the issue before. Her skin was the darkest of all ours. She'd experienced persecution and prejudice because of it. Sure, this was modern times, but cops hadn't seemed to evolve that much. If they couldn't see people of color as people, they wouldn't see invisible, disembodied voices as people. They couldn't feel bad for shooting someone they couldn't see.

A hand poked out of the wall behind her, and I pointed to it. "You better take her hand."

She scowled, annoyed with me. "Don't tell me what to do."

19
A DRAGON TAKES ON MILE SQUARE
BRADLEY

Savanna was still upset with me when Serena pulled us through. We were in the last room on the hall, trapped on all sides with a high probability of being caught. If we tried to walk through the back walls to the outside autumn air, we would be greeted by two people with machine guns. If we tried to leave like normal undivine teenagers, we ran the risk of being detained by whoever was guarding the front entrance.

"We heard gunshots," Serena noted as she pulled me through. "What happened?"

I glanced at Savanna, who was purposefully putting distance between the two of us. "Savanna thought it'd be funny to tease the cops."

"I didn't know they were going to shoot at us!" Savanna defended herself.

Seth rolled her eyes, deciding to change the subject. "We need to find a way out of here."

"Who's going to suspect seven teenagers?" Calvin asked. "I say we try to walk right through the front door."

"*Five* teenagers," Seth muttered a correction. She and Rebecca hadn't reached that milestone.

Serena crossed her arms, swaying on her feet. "I'd rather take my chances with the armed guards. I'm never going to get past any security at the entrance. If they learn my name, I'm toast, especially with Aaron's body down the hall. It's too easy a connection."

Liam snapped his fingers with one hand and grabbed his wallet from his back pocket with the other. "Who has their school IDs on them?" He fished his out of his wallet, along with a driver's permit. "Anything with our names on it we should burn." He held his cards between his fingers and, within seconds, flames licked the edges.

I searched the ceiling for a fire alarm. We didn't need to bring any more attention to ourselves. One was not too far from where Liam and his flames were. I grabbed a chair and stood on it to reach. My fingertips grazed the object. I closed my eyes, willing it to disappear before Liam inevitably set it off. Within seconds it was gone. I leaped to the ground.

Liam's ID cards were replaced with a pile of ash. Everyone was staring at him, some with their mouths agape and others who seemed reluctant to give in to his idea.

Calvin was the most against it. "Do you know how long I had to stand in line at the DMV to get my license? How am I supposed to explain what happened to it? Am I supposed to just tell them, 'My brother burned it with his hands'?"

"You don't have to say it like that." Liam scowled.

I grabbed my school ID from my back pocket. It wasn't like I used it much for anything anyway. I could have dematerialized it myself, but Liam's way was much cooler to watch. Serena did the same with hers. Seth didn't have hers on her. Rebecca didn't have one at all. They didn't issue them at the elementary level.

Calvin and Liam had a staring contest with each other until the older brother finally caved, slapping his IDs into Liam's open palm. "Fine, but you're holding my place in line at the DMV."

I glanced at Savanna, who was standing in the far corner with her arms crossed. She had her nose and mouth twisted and her eyebrows scrunched together. Her emotions were heavily mixed, but she had been on edge ever since she agreed to join our mission. A heavy mixture of frustration, sadness, anger, and... what was that buzzing in the background? Doubt? Mistrust? I cocked my head to the side, concentrating on that one small glimmer in her emotions. It was familiar to me, but not an emotion I had felt from Savanna.

Seth reached, poking her in the arm with a single finger, and in a millisecond, Savanna was gone. Seth jumped back. "Woah! Is that what you two meant when you said she could—"

Savanna reappeared, gasping for breath. She grabbed hold of an end table for balance.

"—self-materialize?" Seth finished, dragging her words.

"Don't"—Savanna paused to catch her breath—"do that." She held a hand over her racing heart.

Serena stared at her with her usual wide eyes. "You're not gonna randomly disappear and reappear in front of witnesses in a sec, are you?"

Savanna shook her head, closing her eyes. She tried to level her breathing. "I'm not usually that jumpy. Just give me a second."

I froze at her choice of words. Savanna wasn't normally jumpy. That's not a word anybody would use to describe her, but I had felt the emotions that usually went along with jumpiness swirling inside her. She was dampening them as we all stood there watching, trying to hide her sudden mistrust… her doubt… her fear. *Wait a minute.*

Rebecca eyed me suspiciously. "Bradley is," she murmured, tagging onto Savanna's claim. My sister was right. Jumpiness was *my* thing. But I didn't feel that scared at all. I was feeling weirdly calm, ready for the next step in our plan to commence. We needed to escape from the hotel. We needed to get to the lab before they destroyed all the evidence. We needed to find Marcie and Mrs. Thomas.

"Whatever happens to one, happens to the other," Rebecca clarified for anyone who didn't already know. She turned to Savanna. "You probably shouldn't spend so much time shifting through Bradley's memories. It's not going to help you."

Savanna wasn't looking at any of us when she answered quietly. "I just wanted to understand." Her eyebrows creased before she studied me with her blue eyes. "You know Olga." I felt my usual guard rush back to me. It wasn't a question. I wasn't sure which memory she had been looking at, but whatever one it was, she had recognized Olga. I'd never mentioned her in all the times I'd spoken to Savanna, but I had assumed she'd seen it all a couple weeks ago on the night she witnessed my past flash before her eyes.

"I didn't know how to bring it up. I didn't want to trigger any bad memories for you. But I feel like I need to tell you this." She chewed on her lip. "I called her last night after I left your house. I wanted to ask her for a favor."

She called her? How? I still hadn't dug up Olga's number. I hadn't called her since May.

Savanna tried to explain. "My mom's a licensed counselor for social services as well as a licensed foster parent. It's rare, but sometimes she takes in diviners who land in the system so they don't have to hide their powers."

"Olga's not a foster kid," Seth interrupted.

Savanna glanced at Paige's friend. "Yeah, but she was in some sort of troubled teens program." She turned back to me. "She stayed with us practically the whole summer. She went back to Illinois the day before you moved across the street."

I wasn't sure what to say nor was I sure what Olga had to do with our plan. What kind of favor had she asked for?

Savanna's face wrinkled with worry. "I asked her to fly here."

Olga would have jumped at the chance to take her words literally. "Savanna, there are thousands of armed uniforms out there!" I shouted.

"So what? Nobody's gonna shoot a bird." She didn't sound convinced of her own statement, though. The cops shooting at us must've affected her confidence.

Suddenly, Seth moaned, "Oh no." She pointed her thumb to the wall behind Savanna. If the walls were clear, we could've seen part of the statue from there. "Do you think that thing Rebecca did made the news?"

"It most certainly did," Rebecca answered, unsmiling.

Seth shifted her feet but didn't elaborate.

Calvin shook his head in frustration. "I can't follow all your minds. What is going on?"

"Bradley's friend Olga is a shapeshifter," Seth explained. "And she loves to escalate chaos."

As if on cue, the walls of the hotel began to tremble. It sounded like a helicopter was above us—a very large helicopter. The sound was joined by an unmistakably deep reptilian roar. I felt the blood drain from my face as Seth and Rebecca ran to the window.

"Holy smokes!" Seth shouted. I caught sight of the armed guards, machine guns in hand, abandoning their posts. If the monstrous beast I was hearing was really Olga, she stood zero chance of surviving.

Serena joined them at the window. "The heck?" The creature screeched. "There goes another government conspiracy reveal," Serena muttered. "Now everyone's going to think dragons actually exist."

Holy crap. She flew in as a dragon? I didn't join them at the window. I didn't want to watch another one of Olga's impulsive plans fail, especially not one that would end in her death.

"They'll probably write it off as mass hallucinations and hysteria," Calvin said. "You won't believe the lengths the undivine will go to prove they're hallucinating. They'd much rather think their eyes are playing tricks on them than deal with the truth."

"That monsters exist?" Serena asked.

"No," said Calvin as he shook his head, then joined the crowd near the window. "That they're the monsters."

Bullets flew in the distance as he said this, my heart sinking with every new sound. They were shooting at Olga. All of them. And some were bound to hit her.

Savanna ran to the door and flung it open. The police who were in with Aaron were running, shouting into their radios. They didn't pause to give her a second look. There was a giant dragon in Mile Square. Who would have thought?

I joined Savanna at her side, peering into the empty hallway. "They're going to kill Olga," I worried aloud.

Savanna gripped the doorframe. "She'll be fine." She nodded, anxiety clouding her voice. "Unless you know more about how far bullets can travel?" She eyed me questioningly, one eyebrow raised. I shook my head. Maybe if Olga stayed in the air, she'd be fine. But of course, these guys had military-grade weapons, so who knew how far the bullets could reach. The freaking air force could come after her.

Liam whined from behind us, "Aw man! I burned all those IDs for nothing. My brother's going to kill me."

Savanna glanced at him. "They could still catch us." She dug in her back jeans pocket, procuring her school ID. "You can burn this one if you like. I can always rematerialize a new one."

Liam snatched it, eyeballing the photograph. "Even in photos, you look good." I threw him a nasty look. He didn't catch it. The tenth grader was too busy burning the evidence.

The rest of the crowd soon joined us in the hallway.

"We need to get to that lab," I said, attempting to steer us back on the right track. Olga continued to screech in the background.

"Any bright ideas on how we do that?" Seth asked.

"If only we had a teleporter," Calvin murmured.

Seth flinched. The one teleporter I knew was her mother, and she was currently pregnant and admitted to a psych hospital.

"The lab's not too far from here," Serena said. "We might be able to walk."

"And risk people seeing us? No way." Savanna shook her head.

Serena blinked. She leaned back, crossing her arms in the process as her brown eyes flickered between Savanna and me. "They won't see you and Bradley."

Savanna bristled. Anger boiled inside her. "You're not suggesting we go in there alone?" She was right. This wasn't going to work with just the two of us. That's why we assembled a team in the first place. Everybody had a role to play.

Serena narrowed her eyes. "All eyes are on Priori right now, thanks to *Rebecca*." She uttered my sister's name with a snarl of contempt. Another roar blew overhead from Olga. I was pretty sure all eyes were on the dragon. "Nobody's getting in or out of that lab unless they're invisible to the undivine."

"And to security cameras," Seth tacked on. "If only there was a way we could sneak in that didn't involve walking through the front door."

The front door. Last time we had to infiltrate a building, it was completely underground. There *was* no front door. Instead, there was a hatch that led into a pit. We didn't use the hatch because we had Kase—he had mass manipulated our bodies through the floor. It somehow drew less attention that way.

This time, we didn't have Kase—but we had Serena. Maybe we could do the opposite this time—come up from underground. "What about the sewers?" I asked. I'd seen people do it enough times in movies that it seemed plausible. Unlike them, we wouldn't need a laser to cut any conspicuous holes through the floors or walls.

Serena scoffed. "This isn't New York, Bradley. We don't have an elaborate underground system. So unless you want to wait twenty more years for the city to invest billions of dollars into your plan, you and Savanna are going to have to enter through the front door alone."

"Or we could hitch a ride on your friend," Calvin joked. "She could drop us off on the roof."

Another screech filled the air, followed by a loud thump. The building shook. My heart stopped, sputtering for a second before restarting. "How much you want to bet there are snipers on the roof with Olga?" My voice shook as I said this, my hand doing the same as I tried to run it through my hair. We all stood, quiet, listening for the sounds of the dragon, but there were none. The gunfire had ceased as well.

I bolted through the hallway, grabbing the wall for support as I turned to take the carpeted stairs two at a time. The others raced behind me as I ran up and around, up and around, from the stairs to the landings, until I saw a sign that read Roof Access. The door to the roof was propped open with a metal folding chair. I leaped over it, without thinking, into the cloudy November light.

A storm was beginning to brew. The air was chillier than before, nipping at my sweat-soaked skin. I stared ahead at the wall of armed men in their black attire—a small militia with bullet-proof vests, helmets, and machine guns. They all stood facing away from me, their heads directed at something or someone I couldn't see. I stopped cold in my tracks, my heart beating rapidly against my ribcage. Someone grabbed my shoulders from behind but didn't pull. I felt the warm glow on my skin, a rush of extra emotion flowing through me. It must have been Savanna, making sure we stayed invisible. Her thoughts, which were basically an echo of my fears, pounded in my head.

If Olga had landed on the roof, there was no way she was still an oversized mythical creature. There wasn't room for her. She had to be human. They had to have shot her. That's who they were all staring at. I could imagine her body, riddled with bullets. All that time with Chad and not once had a bullet pierced her porcelain skin, but of course, she had to be a dragon surrounded by trigger-happy heathens. Her death was practically a suicide. She wasn't a hero. She never was. Stupid, impulsive Olga, never knowing what was good for her. I didn't want to step forward, to try to see around the uniformed men. I didn't want to see her dead body. I'd seen enough of those in my fourteen years.

Savanna's shallow breathing tickled my neck, her hands trembling as they struggled to keep their grip on my shoulders. "Maybe she's not dead," she thought, running through all the positive possible scenarios in her head. I didn't let myself believe any of her hopes. It wouldn't have been worth the fall when we confirmed Olga's death.

"What the…" a man deep in the small crowd sputtered in surprise. A small squawk came from behind the crowd. My heart leaped, my breath catching in my throat, as the sound pulled me toward Savanna's hopes.

A small creature emerged above them—a much smaller dragon than the one I had imagined. It was the size of a raven, flying overhead in circles, chasing its three-point tail like a dog. It paused when it saw us, smiling wide to show its pointed row of pearly white teeth. Its green eyes were Olga's, sparkling with relief before sharpening with sudden determination. She dove straight for us. The change was so fast, I barely had time to register it as her upper body bloomed from the tiny creature, her human arms extended. Her dragon wings quadrupled in size from her back as her claw-like fingers dug into our shoulders. She pushed us, our legs knocking over the metal chair with our momentum. Her wings disappeared as she threw us to the floor amid the rest of our posse, who had been waiting at the top of the staircase for us to return. Her human feet landed firmly on the carpet, her body twisting to grab the door handle and pull it shut. Bullets flew at the metal but failed to penetrate it, the door acting as our shield.

"Great calling card, Bex." Olga held her thumb up as she appraised my sister, a little winded from the exertion. "Like the bat signal."

Rebecca narrowed her eyes but didn't say anything.

Olga studied the group of us as Savanna and I scrambled to our feet, rubbing at the aches around our shoulders and legs. She smiled at the sound of the men banging their fists on the door behind her, failing to break in. Chuckling to herself, she flicked her platinum blonde hair over her shoulder. "Oh, please. I'm not afraid of those boneheads. One of my boyfriend's alter egos is a misguided protector with a history of violence. Nothing terrifies me."

Calvin and Liam's jaws practically dropped to the floor. Liam glanced at me, exasperated. "Seriously, bro, how do you find these women?"

I ignored him, annoyed with Olga's comment. I hated how she excused Chad's violence by claiming it was due to his mental illness. She wore him like a badge of honor, thinking it made her seem tough. But I knew

Olga. I knew her attitude was a facade. She wasn't as resilient as she made herself seem. Her black choker necklace and dark purple lipstick said nothing of her true nature. She always wore too much eyeliner underneath her eyelids because she thought it made her look tough. The tattoos all along her right arm were a skin-colored piece of fabric—like pantyhose with elaborate design work. Olga was always a faker. But I knew the real Olga. I knew all her usual lies.

20
OLGA PICKS A FIGHT WITH THE CHOSEN ONE
BRADLEY

"You're right. I fell from heaven, blah blah blah. What a beautiful fallen angel. What a disgrace it was to be pushed from that Godly place. Forbidden! Can you believe it? For plucking an apple from a tree. A regular Eve. Ugh. That tramp!" Olga rambled on as we descended the staircase. She loved this bit. Olga was fiercely anti-fundamentalist—a strange belief for someone madly in love with a preacher's kid. Raised in Chad's father's church, she understood all the biblical references and used them like poetry every time a guy tried to hit on her.

I turned, trying hard not to trip backward down the staircase. "Do you have a point to being here?"

She stopped midstep, her smile growing wider. "I'm offended, Brad. As I understand it, this is *your* coup, so why did it take a call from Miss Goody Two Shoes to invite me?" She turned to the oldest of our posse. "Calvin, right?" He nodded wordlessly. She beckoned him with her finger as if she wanted to tell him a secret. He bent his head, and Olga craned her neck, brushing away her hair. She tapped the side of her throat with a long, bright crimson fingernail. "Do me a favor and give me a kiss." I watched in disgust as he mindlessly obeyed. The second his lips touched her skin, he was gone. She cupped her hands just in time to catch a toad dropping from her neck.

Serena quickly backtracked a few steps, grabbing the railing in shock. "What the hell kind of witchcraft—?"

"Oh, please," Olga said, bending to release the confused creature.

Calvin hopped onto the carpet, his eyes and throat bulging. "*Ribbit?*"

Olga chuckled to herself as she bit a perfectly manicured nail. "I've always enjoyed the fairytales."

I pointed at the toad. "When did you learn to do that?"

"Spend a while at Savanna's house and you get to learn a few things, huh, Brad?" she winked, her lips curling suggestively. I rolled my eyes. She gasped theatrically, staring at the toad. "You don't have to do that." Olga crouched, tapping an index finger on the toad's head. "I can understand you perfectly fine. I speak fluent toad."

Serena crossed her arms, coming down a step. "Okay, Tiana. What's your plan for getting us out of here?" As she asked this, heavy footsteps pounded along the stairs, soldiers barking orders from the first flight.

Olga eyed the wall at our next turn, and I followed her gaze. I saw a small air vent. Snapping my gaze back to her cunning smile, I gritted my teeth. "No."

Olga glanced at her wrist like she was checking her watch—she wasn't wearing one. "You have about twenty seconds to agree with me. And that's not me making the threat." She dropped her wrist. "That's the frickin' SWAT team's threat." Olga reached a hand to Serena. "You with me, sister?"

Serena tentatively grabbed Olga's hand, squeezing her eyes shut in the process. In a half second, she was gone, replaced as a small white mouse in Olga's cupped palms. I stepped back, tripping over the next step as Olga reached for Liam. Grabbing the railing to keep from falling, I stuttered, "T-turn her back!" Liam shrank to Serena's size—another furry white mouse. I yelped, losing my grip on the rail. Savanna reached to stop me from falling. The footsteps and shouts were growing closer. My heartbeat sputtered sporadically in my chest, my stomach churning as Olga turned to grip Seth's outstretched hand.

Olga rolled her eyes, addressing me. "Ugh. You need to get over your stupid fear of mice." Seth shifted into another mouse. It was Rebecca's turn. I squeezed my eyes shut, trying not to imagine a hoard of tiny white mice staring at me with their hungry red eyes. My skin crawled at the thought. I'd seen mice chew the skin off bones of decaying children. Heck, I'd seen them chew the skin off *each other.* They weren't friendly animals.

"Bradley and I can escape by ourselves. Don't worry about us. We'll meet you at the corner of Ohio and Delaware. Calvin knows the way," Savanna said as she tugged me down the last few steps and into a corner. "Don't make a sound," she thought to me, her sweet breath on my face. I tried to stay still, but I could feel my hands trembling. SWAT was close, maybe a flight below us. Savanna covered my mouth with her hand. My breathing must have been too loud. I wasn't focused on it, though. I couldn't get the image of the demon mice out of my head. She tensed in front of me as I heard the men pass us. The floor shook as their heavy footsteps trampled the staircase. When they were gone, Savanna let go, stepping back to let me catch my breath. "Are you alright?" she whispered.

I nodded, blinking and sputtering. I swallowed a ball of excess saliva. "I-I'm fine. I-I'm sorry."

Savanna shook her head. "Why are you sorry? You don't have to apologize. She could have made them literally anything else."

I shook my head. "Expecting Olga to be considerate is like expecting Serena to stop digging into the personal lives of terrible people. It's not gonna happen."

"That's no excuse."

I reached for her hand. "Let's get out of here."

It was easy to walk out the front door without anyone spotting us. It was the outside world that was pure chaos. When Seth had mentioned Mile Square being filled with law enforcement, she wasn't exaggerating. It was tough for the two of us to walk hand-in-hand without the threat of being bumped into or separated. I thought for sure we'd be caught when I spotted a few K-9 units, but the dogs ignored us as they did every other human. Maybe if we had explosives or drugs, it would have been different.

Uniformed men and women were barking into their radios, asking for an update on the dragon. One suggested it had been a light show or trick of mirrors, but they weren't finding any evidence of either.

"Maybe we should leave some evidence for them," I suggested to Savanna.

She shook her head. "Ask your sister to do it. I really just want to get out of this square."

We walked three blocks to the roadblocks where Savanna told them we'd meet. We waited in front of the corner liquor store, invisible to most people. Curious and terrified civilians crammed together in hopes of receiving answers. Some only wanted to see the dragon again. Others were complaining about the walk being canceled. Apparently, it was an annual family event for several out-of-towners. One family said they had traveled all the way from Louisiana to help fundraise. Most people were concerned by how many military and law enforcement personnel had commandeered the area. News crews were swarming the boundaries, interviewing people on the street. Savanna and I tried to stay clear of the cameras. We didn't want to lose each other's grip and expose ourselves on live television.

We waited ten minutes before Rebecca calmly walked out of the liquor store, followed by the rest of the gang. She and Olga were the only ones not busy stretching their limbs. Seth twisted her neck as she cracked her knuckles. "That was so not as fun as it looked."

Olga swung her arm around my sister, squeezing her tight to her side like they'd suddenly become best friends. "Bex really knows how to have some fun with these losers. I can't wait to tell everyone back home that I know the Chosen One."

Rebecca scowled, attempting to squirm free of her grip. "I'm not a celebrity you can casually name drop. Besides, who's going to believe *you*?" She broke free of Olga's grasp, stomping toward Savanna and me.

Olga's light eyebrows twisted, her lips curving in disapproval before snapping her expression back to her usual nonchalance. She cocked an eyebrow, eyeing my sister. "Every diviner watching the news knows the Chosen One is in Indianapolis. Who else could have transformed that monument? Our entire race is either going to be flocking here for protection or fleeing for their lives. You exposed our existence on an international scale. And all for what? To cure your brother of a disease that isn't currently threatening his life? You're lucky I got here when I did or you would all be in some secret government lab, your identities wiped away as if you never existed. I don't think you can even imagine what they would do to you, *ĉhaj*. After all, this life is new to you, and you've always been a bit naive."

My hands shook, fire ripping through the veins of my arms, gurgling in my chest. I yanked my sister behind me, gearing for a fight. Savanna tried to hold me back, but I could tell my anger was affecting her too. She was debating the consequences of letting me go in her head.

"I trust Rebecca with my life," Serena announced, stalking to my terrified sister and reaching for her hand. "You don't know what some of us have been through here," she explained, her round brown eyes focused on Olga, who had taken a few quick steps from me, nearly bumping into Calvin. With a shaky hand, Serena lifted her shirt to reveal a small portion of her skin near her lower right abdomen. A thick dark scar protruded from her otherwise flawless light brown skin. Her voice shook, tears gathering in her eyes. "We *can* imagine what they'll do to us because they've already tried."

"Damn," Calvin whispered. "I thought those photos were doctored."

Olga was silent, her jaw slack.

I took a deep breath, trying to steady my anger.

Serena tugged her shirt back down. "We didn't decide to do this lightly. At least, *I* didn't." Her eyes flickered to Savanna and me. "I know more than anybody the dangers of what this operation could bring. I should be dead right now, but I'm not, and honestly, I don't have that much more to lose if this all goes south. But I don't think it will because we have something nobody else in the world has. We have Rebecca."

I could feel my anger dwindling as Olga accepted her words.

Savanna nodded in agreement. "Bradley and I wouldn't be standing here if it wasn't for Rebecca." She buried her head in my shoulder, wrapping her arms around my arm. "She saved me."

I staggered as the flashes from her memory played in my mind. Savanna had never shared with me what had happened during the time we were separated in the bunker. Rebecca reached for my other hand, squeezing it tight as I watched in horror. Why would she show this to me when it was Olga we were trying to prove a point to? Their memories filled my vision.

A man ran a finger at Savanna's hairline, brushing her dark hair from her face. He smiled, his white teeth perfect, licking his lips hungrily. "Such a pretty girl."

Savanna jerked forward, failing to free herself from the chains that tightly bound her to the concrete wall. Across the dimly lit room, Rebecca whimpered on a cot, her feet bound by loose chains. I wondered why they were restrained differently. Had they seen Rebecca as less of a threat? My sister had always come off meek. Savanna was the fighter in their duo.

The door to the room opened, and the man in charge strolled in. Another man who was standing inside the entrance greeted him with a salute. The one in front of Savanna did the same, pulling away as he did so.

The man in charge chuckled—low, throaty, and condescending—as he approached Savanna. He gripped her chin tightly, holding her face so they could see the whites of each other's eyes. "Your little boyfriend is dead, and soon, so will all your friends. Your daddy can't hold my brothers off much longer. We will defeat every last diviner who enters this facility, sweetheart. Our job is to send you all back to your cursed underworld, and we will *not* fail."

Savanna spat in his face. "I think you're a little confused on which one of us is the devil incarnate."

The man slapped her—her head banged against the wall. He grabbed her hair, holding her head against the concrete. "You listen here, little girl. The brethren I have you in this room with have orders to do whatever the hell they want with you. I've let them know to be extra unkind to you." He planted a kiss on her neck before letting her go and headed to the exit.

"Savanna!" Mr. Huckleberry's voice rang in the distance.

Savanna tried to shout back, but the first man clamped his hand over her mouth. His other hand swept greedily over her body. The distant shouting ceased.

"He'll never find you in this maze." The man breathed into her face as he unhooked the button of her jeans.

Savanna's eyes met my sister's. "Don't look." She kept her voice calm though her heart beat furiously, trying to escape. "I'll be fine."

Rebecca's innocent brown eyes shifted from terror to fury, her eyebrows furrowing, her fists shaking. She let out a bloodcurdling scream. The chains from Savanna's wrists and ankles disappeared. She dropped to the floor as the opposite wall exploded into dust, burying the third man with its blocks of concrete.

I blinked in the daylight, returning to reality.

Rebecca squeezed my hand a little tighter before loosening her grip. She stared at Olga as she said, "I'm the only one who can get us out of this mess if it all goes south. I practically control the outcome." She cocked her head to the side. "That doesn't seem so naive at all, does it?"

Liam nudged Olga with his elbow. "I wouldn't get on her bad side if I were you."

Olga's green eyes bored into my sister's. "You're just a little she-devil, aren't you?"

Rebecca grinned.

21
SERENA FINALLY CRACKS
BRADLEY

We walked along Delaware Street in the direction of the lab as the blades of helicopters churned overhead. The outdoor temperature continued to drop. Savanna and I attempted to use each other's body heat to keep warm. I tried not to think about the memory Savanna had played me, especially since she could hear me when I did. My mind kept brooding over what could have happened if Rebecca hadn't been there—if my sister hadn't lost her cool in the bunker. At ten years old, she had something the rest of us didn't. It wasn't her powers either, or whatever extra knowledge and skills she possessed as the Chosen One. She had a history far more terrifying than being able to move the earth underneath our feet. She had killed. Not in the indirect way that I had caused, but in the direct and deliberate way. Pounds of concrete crushed the bones and organs of an untold number of neo-Nazis underneath Fort Ben, creating a grave of bodies in the soil of a state park. As much as I wanted those men dead, and as much as I was glad they weren't around to do more harm, I couldn't help but think we weren't any better than they were. An eye for an eye— it was them or us, I tried to remind myself. They nearly killed Serena. They tried to kill me. They would have probably killed Savanna. And yet, I was bothered by the fact that my little sister was technically a murderer.

Seth squinted at the darkening sky, her breath barely visible as she spoke. "Do you think we'll get snow?"

"Not much," Serena answered, wincing as she held her side.

"Are you okay?" I asked.

"I'm fine," she breathed, wincing again. Her pace slowed. "When Olga turned me into a mouse, she undid whatever voodoo magic Rebecca put on me."

My sister apologized. "Sorry. I'd do it again, but the pain's only going to feel worse when it wears off."

"What are you, like a walking Vicodin?" Liam asked her.

Rebecca gazed at us sheepishly. "I don't know what that is."

"It's an extremely addictive pain pill," Serena explained. "They had me on it for a while. The worst part of taking it was quitting it."

Calvin furrowed his brow, his lower lip jutting in a troubled pout.

Serena stopped walking, glaring at him, her teeth bared from pain and annoyance. "Get out of my head, freakazoid!" Calvin glanced at me like he wanted to tell me something, but Serena smacked his arm with the back of her hand. "I can do whatever the hell I want!" She recoiled from the movement, her hand clutching her stomach. "Ow."

I pulled from Savanna, hoping nobody noticed our sudden appearance, and grabbed Serena's elbow to keep her from keeling over. Seth grabbed her other arm, her voice full of worry. "Are you going to be able to make it?"

"Yes," Serena said, nodding, at the same time Calvin grunted and said, "No." He crossed his arms, meeting Serena's frustrated gaze. Seth and I guided her to a nearby bench, gently setting her on the cold metal. She gritted her teeth, continuing her staring match with Calvin. "I can make it."

Calvin bent, his hands on his knees. "I knew something was bugging me about your plan." He squinted his eyes. "You had evidence or knew of the evidence to indict Aaron all along, so why add yourself to his collection? At first, I thought it was all a necessary risk when it came to getting close to that prick. After all, real heroes make certain sacrifices for the greater good. But why do anything that would put yourself on the Krauses' radar? How would making yourself a walking target help you gain access to the lab?" He paused, studying her for a second as she grew increasingly more agitated. "I heard it when you were talking to Rebecca." His voice was lower, more concentrated. He hesitated before outing her.

"I don't know about these clowns, but I'm not letting you go anywhere if your intention will get you killed."

I looked at Savanna. Was this so dangerous of a mission that the threat of any of us not making it out alive was so high? Should we have been worrying about more than just ourselves? Had Jay-Jay seen more than one person die—or almost die—in his vision? Were any of us that doomed?

The realization of what Calvin was getting at hit me hard. Serena had originally chosen this as a solo mission. Everything she said or did leading to this moment was intended to make her a martyr. Her inevitable death was intentional. This was more than a solo mission for her. It was a suicide mission. For weeks as she lay in the hospital, she had screamed that she wanted to die. This was her out. Jay-Jay was right to be worried.

"She wants me to save her," he had said. "To prove that I could have changed her future."

I turned to Serena, who was still glaring at Calvin, her eye twitching as her hands gripped the bottom edge of the bench. "We need to get to the lab." She pushed her words through her gritted teeth. "We're running out of time."

I glanced down the street. We were still only halfway to the lab, but we also weren't far from where Calvin had parked his car. Serena stood. Calvin held up his hands to try to keep her from moving.

"Touch me, and I'll scream," Serena threatened.

Calvin froze. She had the upper hand, and he knew it. There were too many witnesses, many with cameras and recording devices at the ready.

Rebecca held a trembling hand to Serena. "I-I can t-take away y-your pain i-if you l-like." I narrowed my eyes at my sister. She always stuttered when she lied, which is why she didn't do it often. What was she planning? Serena didn't seem as suspicious as I felt. The pain must've been affecting her judgment. She grabbed Rebecca's hand. As she had with Aaron, my sister reached with her free hand to lay it on Serena's scalp. At her touch, Serena collapsed onto the bench, unconscious.

"Damn, girl," Olga muttered. "I could use that trick back home."

I rolled my eyes. Yeah, I bet she could.

"You have twenty minutes before she wakes up," Rebecca murmured to Calvin. "Take her somewhere safe."

Calvin glanced at us. "If I go, I won't be able to help you at the lab. Don't you need me?"

"We needed Serena," Seth responded sadly as she studied Serena's peaceful frame.

"You're the only one who can carry her," I explained. He was also the only one who could drive. "We can't leave her here alone."

Calvin wasn't listening to me though. He was zeroed in on Seth. They looked like they were having a private conversation. Seth squirmed a little, shrugging her shoulders. It was a minute before Calvin turned to lift Serena into his arms. "Guess this is kinda familiar to you guys," he said, his lips forming a grim line.

He was right. This was the second time in three months Serena was being carried away from an impending battle. She always did this—got in way over her head, trying to be the hero. Each time, she intended to die, hoped for it actually, and this realization brought a weird sense of sticky guilt in my chest. I should have noticed the growing pattern. Of all of us, I was the closest to her. But I let her continue with her plan. Calvin had made it sound diabolical. If it wasn't for him being nosy…

Olga crossed her arms as Calvin made his way across the street. She cleared her throat. "Anybody else not in the right headspace for this? Leave now or forever hold your peace." She studied me with judging green eyes.

"What?" I shrugged, pushing my thoughts to the side.

She cocked an eyebrow. "Is it me or have you gotten worse since you moved here? The old you would have freaked over the mice thing, sure, but he wouldn't have gone into full-blown panic mode."

Savanna grabbed my hand to squeeze it gently. "That was your second panic attack today, Bradley," she murmured.

I pulled my hand from her grasp. "I'm not going to try to off myself. Geez, how many people do I need to prove that to lately? I'm fine. I fully intend to come out of this thing alive. Panic attacks do not equate to whatever the hell Serena was planning. Frank thinks I have PTSD."

"No shit," Olga nodded and rolled her eyes. She slapped her knee. "So does your little friend Serena. You might even have *Complex* post-traumatic stress disorder, to be specific. I've been dating Chad for two years. I know mental illness when I see it."

"I'm fine," I said again, taking a few steps in the direction of the lab.

Savanna grabbed my arm. "After this is over, promise me you'll get help."

"I don't need it," I argued.

She tightened her grip. "*Promise* me." Her worry clouded over both of us. We were glowing again. In her small inner voice, she thought distinctly, "Your emotions affect me too."

"Fine," I sputtered. "I will. I will, I will, I will," I thought back.

She nodded quickly, turning her head to wipe away a stray tear.

"Can we go now?" Seth asked impatiently.

The lab. Right. Why was it becoming so hard for us to get to this place anyway? I could barely see it ahead— eight more blocks. There were a few flashing lights at their parking lot entrance. Seth picked up her pace, eventually working to a full sprint. We followed her as quickly as we could. She was fast for a gymnast. Rebecca held us back the most.

The building came into full view when we reached South Street. The parking lot began past the light on the opposite corner. Police barricades stood at the entrances to the lot, yellow tape connecting them at the perimeter. A few police officers stood at the barricades, guiding traffic. The building itself appeared to be guarded by heavily armed members of the National Guard.

"It's exactly how your parents described it," Seth whispered in awe as we waited at the crosswalk.

News crews lined the street across from us. I could imagine how sketchy Priori was coming off to the undivine. Their walk had gotten canceled because of an ominous message on a century-old statue—a message intended to place doubt and mistrust in the minds of their supporters. Priori's reaction? Arm the building. Yeah, they weren't guilty at all. They obviously had something to hide.

"A spokesperson from Priori Labs has stated that they're 'simply taking precautions to ensure the safety of their employees,'" a reporter said into their mic as we passed. I rolled my eyes. What a load of bull.

Olga ducked behind a nearby dumpster, beckoning us to follow. The six of us squeezed in between the dark green receptacle and a cement wall. Flies danced around us. Seth wrinkled her nose at the smell, gagging dramatically. After lifting a stray banana peel from underneath my foot, I tossed it.

Olga smiled cunningly, ignoring the rancid smell of week-old food. "Ready to fly?" She cocked an eyebrow, her eyes dancing over us in the crowded space.

Liam grimaced, clutching his shoulder. He tilted his head, the joint at his neck popping. "Oh no. Not again," he whined.

I gulped. I'd never been turned into an animal before and, judging by everybody else's reactions, I knew I'd be in for an unpleasant experience. If the line of militia weren't surrounding the building shoulder-to-shoulder, Savanna and I might have had a chance to slip through them undetected. At that point, though, it didn't seem possible. Even invisible, we weren't Serena. We couldn't walk through walls or people. We knew from our experience in the hotel that invisibility didn't mean we couldn't be heard.

Olga started with Liam, his form shrinking into a gray mourning dove, his head shimmering with a light blue color. He cooed, taking a few awkward steps to test his red-tinged feet. She did the same with Seth and Rebecca.

Savanna squeezed my hand before letting go, the glow disappearing with her touch. She closed her eyes in nervous anticipation as Olga placed her hands on her shoulders. A dove soon replaced Savanna. Olga turned to me, her smile disappearing. "You're okay if I turn you into a bird?"

"No," I answered, cringing at the thought. "But you're gonna do it anyway."

"You're right." She tilted her head, her smile full of insincerity. "Please don't freak." Placing her hands on my shoulders, my vision spun. In a matter of seconds, the world around me grew, my insides transforming at awkward angles, my joints popping with the pressure. It was quick, like ripping off a Band-Aid, but my ears still rung as Olga transformed herself, the shoe in front of my face replaced with another bird.

"Where do all our clothes go?" I tweeted, rubbing my head with a feathered wing. The ringing still hadn't stopped. I could feel a migraine coming on.

"Into the void, I guess. I try not to think about it," Olga answered, but her voice was distant. My other wing tingled as a chill breeze blew through our hiding spot. My vision blurred. I thought birds were supposed to have good vision.

Liam flapped his wings, lifting himself off the ground. Seth soared with him, having too much fun with their temporary ability to fly. Rebecca hobbled to the rest of us, her faraway voice urgent. "We need to get him to the roof so we can turn him back."

"Bradley?" Savanna's voice echoed as black spots appeared in my vision.

Oh. Oh no. "Turn me back," I begged, but Olga was already transforming, shifting into a larger bird. A hawk replaced her dove. Her talons curled around my body, and we flew. I saw the ground below us for a second before my vision went completely black.

22
WHY HADN'T I CONSIDERED THE POSSIBILITY?
BRADLEY

I opened my eyes to darkness. Goosebumps ran along my arms, somebody's hand rubbing against them, trying to warm me. The rough concrete below scraped and burned my skin as I tried to move. "Ow…" I said, attempting to sit so I could examine my arms. The skin felt torn, the muscles in my entire body aching as I moved.

"Stay down," Savanna murmured softly. I could barely make out her upside down face, her long hair tickling my skin. Her cold fingers were in my hair, her blue eyes glistening with tears as they searched mine.

"What's wrong?" I lifted a finger to wipe a stray tear, but someone pulled my hand back.

"Wait—" My sister's voice was laced with urgency as I felt a prick on my index finger—not an unfamiliar sensation, but it shocked me enough to jerk back.

My eyes adjusted to the darkness as I blinked. A golden glow flickered from a light on the wall—unhelpful in its attempts to lighten the room.

"Blood sugar's back to normal," Rebecca murmured, her thin voice barely audible.

"Was it down?" I asked.

Savanna nodded, biting her lip. "You had a seizure."

"That shouldn't have happened," I groaned. My insulin pump was supposed to keep my symptoms from being so dramatic. My blood sugar shouldn't have been that low to begin with. Sometimes it dropped or rose without warning, but that was the quickest escalation of symptoms I'd experienced. I clenched my teeth, my jaw aching at the movement. "Olga." I groaned, this time determined to sit. This was her fault.

Savanna moved out of my way, her arms quickly wrapping around my left arm. I could see the glow from her touch now as well as the scrapes and scratches. My arms must have jerked violently against the coarse material of the floor.

Rebecca zipped my kit closed before handing it to me.

I scanned the room as Savanna helped me to my feet. My legs shook as I stood. Realizing we were in a stairwell, I asked, "Are we in the lab?" I searched for anything labeled with the lab's name, but there was nothing.

Savanna and Rebecca nodded.

Taking a step forward, I tested my weight. It took a few steps before my legs no longer felt like jelly. They were still shaky, but they didn't hinder my ability to walk.

Savanna clung to my arm. "You scared me," she said as she led me down the stairs.

Olga, Liam, and Seth were waiting for us a flight below—Olga pacing in front of a door with her thumbnail between her teeth. Liam and Seth were resting on the steps watching her. Olga stopped pacing when she saw me. "How are you walking right now? You should be in a hospital! Oh my gosh." She resumed pacing again and rambled, "I could have killed you, Brad. I don't care what you think about Chad, but I am not a killer. These two"—she motioned to Savanna and Rebecca—"wouldn't let me fly you to a hospital. They kept saying, 'turn him back, turn him back,' as if that was some magical cure-all. I've been with you when you had a seizure before. I know the protocol, and it is not to wait for your blood sugar to even itself out. That's not how it works." She had her hands in her blonde hair, tangling it with her confusion.

Liam and Seth watched me curiously. Olga was right. That wasn't how it worked.

"Maybe birds require more glucose," Seth pondered. She might've been on to something, but we didn't have time to hash it out. The door behind Olga opened swiftly, most of us freezing in place. Olga skittered before morphing into a bat, squeaking as she flapped her wings. A man's voice mumbled an apology before carefully shutting the door behind himself. He turned to us, taking us in with his round brown eyes. Savanna and I gasped in shocked relief. Rebecca smiled smugly as Liam pointed at the man in the white lab coat. "Hey, don't I know you?" Olga made a clicking sound in the corner as Seth's confused eyes flitted among us all.

"I thought Serena would be with you," Mr. Lindt stated, the absence of his eldest daughter seeming to disappoint him. The lines of his face contorted with heavy concern. His eyes zeroed in on Liam's. They were silent for several seconds of their private conversation. Mr. Lindt's frown deepened. Finally, he nodded solemnly, accepting whatever version of the story Liam's mind had told.

"Remind me to thank him." Mr. Lindt nodded before glancing at the bat. "I didn't mean to scare you. I'm Serena's dad."

Slowly, Olga lowered herself to the ground, readjusting into her true form. She shot me an angry look before setting her jaw. "You didn't scare me." She folded her arms. "I don't scare easily."

Liar. I snorted. *Who is the panicky one now?*

Mr. Lindt raised his eyebrows at her but said nothing.

Seth didn't seem so thrilled by his appearance. Standing from her spot on the steps, she crossed her arms, sliding her tongue between her teeth. "I thought you left her." Her voice was less than kind, her eyes narrowing accusingly.

Mr. Lindt nervously shifted his weight, sizing her up before responding. "I came here to make things right, not to get in the middle of a teenage love chain. We don't have time for drama. Sooner or later, security's going to wonder why I used my key card to access the roof. I've only been working here a few weeks. I'm still on probation. With everything going on, it feels like I've got eyes watching me like a hawk."

"What exactly are you doing here?" Savanna asked, eyeing his lab coat dubiously.

"Statistical analytics. Thought I'd beat Serena to the punch. I heard her thinking of this place, and I wanted to keep her out of trouble." He side-eyed Liam. "Apparently you kids had the same idea." His eyes swiftly shifted to Rebecca's. "You have a plan?" He furrowed his brow in concentration before shaking his head.

My sister's lip twitched as she considered his question. "Some knowledge is a burden—I'd rather not share. There's a time and a place for everything. I can't have telepaths lurking in my thoughts, unlocking secrets. It wouldn't be fair. We don't all get to play God."

Mr. Lindt scrutinized her, seemingly unsure of her motives for blocking his gifts. I forgot she could do that. Mom couldn't always see her future. Rebecca's innate knowledge of the universe made people like them uneasy. Sometimes I forgot she was supposed to be a ten-year-old kid. The extra knowledge aged her.

Rebecca took a step down to answer his question. "Bradley and Savanna need to stay together. As long as they are glowing, they're invisible to the undivine. In the meantime..." She glanced at Olga.

"Are you kidding me?" Liam stood, catching on to Rebecca's plan.

Olga smiled, wriggling her eyebrows. "Lab rats."

I stiffened. Savanna led me down the rest of the steps. "Wait until we're out of the room this time, will you?" she pleaded. For once Olga didn't say anything, watching us maneuver around Mr. Lindt. It didn't take long for us to be out the door and into the warm hallway. We looked both ways, unsure of the direction we should take. Savanna bit her lip. Through her thoughts, she said, "Maybe we should have asked Mr. Lindt where to go." The hallway was devoid of people.

"I can't believe he had a job here this whole time," I responded, randomly pulling her to the left.

An elevator at the end of the hall dinged, and two security guards exited. We held our breaths, pressing against the wall as they rushed past. The door to the roof's staircase swung open, and I heard Mr. Lindt's relieved voice. "Thank God you're here! I've been chasing these lab rats all day." I cringed, squeezing my eyes shut to avoid seeing the four rodents.

Mr. Lindt's voice echoed in our heads. "You may want to head to the fifth floor."

Savanna reached for the elevator call button, dragging me with her.

Mr. Lindt warned the guards. "Don't let those little boogers bite you. They'll leave you feeling damn near lightheaded."

Savanna held back a giggle as the elevator doors clicked open. We rushed inside, her fingers flying to the fifth button. I hoped the guards would be too busy chasing the rats to notice the elevator doors opening and closing all on their own.

When the doors clicked shut, I opened my eyes and watched as the lights moved down the numbers, counting backward from twenty-three.

"What do you think's on the fifth floor?" Savanna asked, clinging to me as if our lives depended on it. Her thoughts raced with the possibilities: Could it be Marcie? The cure? Mila Walker-Krause? Important paperwork and research?

What was our plan, anyway? Like the bunker, we had gone into this building not knowing what to expect. We were lucky Mr. Lindt had thought to run interference. We were lucky he knew to check the roof. But wait—how did he know to check the roof? Serena's plan couldn't have been to enter from there. She had other plans that didn't involve flying, plans that might have involved Aaron, plans that were thrown out the second we appeared on the scene. She had to have known the floor plan, right? She knew where everything was—or where it was supposed to be. Serena was excellent at digging up information. She and Jay-Jay both knew how to hack. But then again, her plan couldn't have been *too* solid if Calvin had heard what he heard. How far had she planned to get before—?

The elevator door opened. My hand couldn't get to Savanna's mouth fast enough to muffle her screams. Not that it would have helped. The soldiers with the large barrels pointed at our bodies had us right where they wanted us. It didn't take long for them to shoot.

★

We weren't dead. I knew that much. Savanna and I had folded into each other, our eyes clenched shut. Our lungs and noses tickled, and we coughed, sputtering for clean air. I thought bullet wounds were supposed to hurt more. My hand blindly flew to my side, touching something soft and powdery clumped in the spot where I'd been hit. I didn't have time to process before I was ripped from Savanna's arms.

My eyes flew open along with my fists as I struggled against the two soldiers. They dragged me through the elevator doors. Savanna's blue eyes were terrified as she stood uncharacteristically still, her skinny arms held by another pair of soldiers. Clumps of powdered sugar dusted her body, some of it lingering in the air like smoke. My stomach sank. They were expecting us. They knew we'd be invisible. They knew we'd be in the elevator. They knew we'd be arriving on the fifth floor. This was a trap.

I honestly hadn't considered the possibility.

I wondered how they could use the powder to see our bodies when it seemed our clothes disappeared with us. Wouldn't the sugar have disappeared too? Or was that the point? Could they somehow see through the cloud enough to figure out where the sugar was disappearing? Or was the powder loose enough of a substance that it didn't stick to our skin well, therefore unable to disappear with us? Whichever way the science worked it was still enough for us to be captured.

The soldiers led us into a large conference room—an elongated table dominated the center. The walls were lined with television screens, blinking as they flickered among various live feeds. I caught sight of replay footage from an hour or so before, Olga's dark dragon form circling above the reformed monument. Spikes arced along her back and her tail. She was so large, her shadow spanned multiple buildings in the square.

After shoving me into a chair at one end of the table, the two soldiers who had brought me in stood at my sides, their hands on my shoulders. No cuffs, no restraints, just... hands. The other two sat Savanna at the opposite end. She didn't fight them as she closed her eyes and breathed, her hands shakily resting on the shiny surface of the table. I tried to focus on her emotions, tried to get a better reading, but it was hard to sense past my own fear. Was she struggling to find her emotions too? Were mine overpowering hers? I couldn't imagine my fear being any different from hers at the moment. The task seemed to be distracting her. Couldn't she fight? Couldn't she use her powers? Why wasn't she?

Heels clicked on the tile floor outside, along with the heavier footsteps of others. The wide glass door swung open, and three figures strode in. An elderly gentleman in a suit led the way, hunching over the table to scrutinize my face as Jeremiah Krause and his wife took seats in the middle. The old man's jowl trembled in anger, and I clenched my fists in response, anticipating a fight.

"What will it take to stop you Chamberses from attempting to ruin my laboratory!" Rage shook the man so violently, I thought he would flip the table.

I considered his question. He had to be the ex–attorney general. He was the one who stole the lab and the research from my grandfather. He was the one who destroyed my grandfather's reputation, stripping him of his medical license. He was the reason thousands had died every year for the past eighteen years. I was face-to-face with one of the most selfish men in the world. I was face-to-face with evil itself. If he wanted to make a deal, it wouldn't be with me. I'd learned not to make them with the devil.

Setting my jaw, I refused to answer his question. In response, he slammed the palm of his meaty hand on the tabletop, the sound causing everybody except the soldiers to flinch. "Tell me what you want, boy!"

I slid my eyes away from his gaze, examining the many flashing screens on the wall behind him. They didn't just show news footage. Security cameras seemed to catch every inch of the building. For a brief second, I caught sight of the stairwell to the roof. It was devoid of people. I hadn't noticed any cameras when we were there, but I also hadn't thought to look. They'd known about us since we arrived. Is that how Mr. Lindt knew where to find us?

I returned my gaze to the old man. "I want this place to disappear." My voice shook with my fists, the white powder falling from my skin, sprinkling the furniture.

"We want Marcie." Savanna finally spoke, her eyes glancing accusingly at Aaron's dad. Jeremiah cleared his throat but otherwise ignored her. What a coward.

The old man squinted in response to my answer. "Let me rephrase my question." He pushed his words through gritted teeth. "What can I do to make *you* disappear?"

Well, for one, you could let Savanna and me near each other again, I thought sarcastically, brushing excess powder from my hands. Even though hearing Savanna's thoughts wasn't all it was cracked up to be, I was hoping the long-distance telepathy would kick in. Maybe we could hatch a plan of escape. I could see how useful Calvin's powers would have been to us, or Mr. Lindt's for that matter.

Glancing at another screen, I froze. The others—all except Rebecca—were in their human forms talking to… no one. There didn't seem to be anyone standing where they were all staring. The picture changed before I could confirm what I had seen. Something strange was going on. Slowly, I looked at the old man, unsure of what to say to him. After a moment of silence, I finally said, "I want the lies to stop." My eyes kept flickering to the screens, hoping I'd catch another glimpse of my friends.

The old man leaned back, nodding. "I'll tell you somethin', Mr. Chambers. I'd like the lies to stop too." I cringed, hating the fact that this guy already knew who I was, despite the lack of introductions. I guess it made sense. My family had assumed Priori was watching us. Especially since they had caught me talking to Marcie. My real question was how they seemed to know about our powers. The news footage was still showing the monument as snow fell lightly from the sky, dusting the cemented words. The snow reminded me of the sugar that still covered Savanna and me. The powdered sugar was a dead giveaway of their knowledge.

Finally, Olga, Liam, and Seth reappeared on the security camera footage, this time in a small room. One of the walls seemed to be made of clear glass. Olga and Seth banged on the walls, begging to be let out as Liam stood in the center, repeatedly snapping his fingers. Something shiny sent a glare that temporarily obstructed the camera's view—a familiar round bracelet on Seth's wrist. It wasn't just on her wrist though. They all each wore one on their wrists. I gasped, the picture changing.

The Krauses observed my horror with the same satisfied smirk on their faces. Savanna looked at me confused, her back to the screen.

Clamping my mouth shut, I became hyperaware of the soldiers' hands on my shoulders. They had the upper hand—literally. I couldn't afford to make a scene—a scene would risk Savanna's life and mine. If one of us died, the other died. Maybe that was why Savanna wasn't bravely fighting like I expected she would. Rebecca had promised to keep her alive, but at the moment, Rebecca was AWOL. I hadn't seen her in the footage once.

"Those bracelets." I swallowed. "Where'd you get them?"

The old man smiled wide, showing his teeth. "Military-grade technology. Priori does more than mass-produce a lifesaving serum for diabetics. We also created a serum that inhibits a gene found in your mother's people's DNA. We thought it might come in handy one day. We didn't want to be defenseless if her people came after us. Especially if her son was in our target demographic."

Damn. He had done his research.

I'd seen those bracelets before. Neo-Nazis had secured one to Rebecca's, Savanna's, and my wrists in the bunker. This must have been where they got them from. I was hoping I knew something Priori didn't though. For unknown reasons, those bracelets didn't work on my sister and me. Why hadn't they clasped them on Savanna's and my wrists yet? I guess they had the soldiers to scare us into compliance. Risky. I mean, I couldn't do much from where I was sitting except make the table disappear, but Savanna, on the other hand…

Her eyes darted across screens on my side of the wall. Her blue eyes widened before she cringed in her seat. An eruption of sound came from somewhere several floors above, the fifth floor shaking slightly. Mrs. Walker-Krause gripped the table to steady herself. The old man wobbled but quickly corrected his stance.

I smiled, the familiarity of the situation brightening our chances. Gazing at the old man, my eyebrow cocked tauntingly, I let him know what I suspected. "Guess that serum doesn't work on my sister. And guess who just royally pissed her off?"

23
I MEET THE SPIRITS OF THE PAST
REBECCA

Bradley was trapped. I could sense it. I could sense something else too. I sensed it in the stairway when my godfather had entered. Häns'che le Yoskasko, telepath, born in Tennessee thirty-four years ago, the first of three children. The information popped into my head the minute he popped into my view. In my godfather's case, his name always came to me in its Romani form instead of as Hudson Lindt.

I have memories with my godfather—new and old, although most of them were from when I was littler. He would sing me an old Sinti lullaby his mother had sung him. I would lounge sleepily in his cushiony arms, feeling the vibrato in his chest. The song was beautiful, flowing in and out of the notes, stitching the melody the way my mom stitched booties for Jesse and later for my godsister Kendra. My eyelids were heavy with sleep, but still I saw my mom smile my way. "Blessed are the children," she had said, squeezing my godmother's arm. Mom had years of knowledge and friendship at her fingertips. She was a source of wisdom. I let my eyes flutter shut at the comfort, my godfather's strange language lulling me to sleep. He was warmth. He was light.

In the stairwell many years later, I was overwhelmed by a sensation of cold darkness. Although my mind was fed his *anav Rromano*, along with a short sentence of information, I knew this wasn't the godfather I had known and loved. This godfather knew more darkness. It was true that my godfather had experienced suffering since that time. To anyone who isn't me, his darkness wouldn't be suspicious. The rumor was, he had left his family—that he and his wife would be divorcing. He believed he was the reason for his eldest daughter's torture. She was not protected. She was *maljardem*, so much so that she wanted to be dead. I could see her nearness to death when I looked in her eyes. I could clear it for a little bit, but it would come back with her pain. Pain was tricky like that. Separating physical pain from emotional pain wasn't something I'd mastered.

There was an importance in the ability to bear children. A phrase existed in the Romani culture—*but ĉhave but baxt*—many children, much luck. Serena would never have that luck. Still, my godfather loved her as he should. This godfather—the one in the stairwell—did not hold guilt. He held dark power.

He switched feet. His eyes—the same as Serena's— were squinting at Seth. "I came here to make things right, not to get in the middle of a teenage love chain. We don't have time for drama."

I winced despite myself. I knew Seth's secret better than she knew it herself. This godfather had sensed it too. Seth's worry for Serena was hiding the fact that she admired her.

Seth didn't know what I knew. Serena didn't want to admit it, but she'd secretly hoped my brother would look at her the way he looked at Savanna. It was sad to me—she would never get that happy ending. It made me never want to love.

"Sooner or later, security's going to wonder why I used my key card to access the roof," Godfather said.

As he continued to explain, a cold rush of wind blew against my back, a word whispering itself into my ear. I smiled at the voice's familiarity. I missed hearing it every day. It had been haunting me for months, feeding me information in dark times.

This must've been a dark time.

"Camera," the voice whispered to me.

I didn't dare look. I knew the voice wouldn't lie to me. It hadn't lied when we were in the bunker. There *had* been a camera watching us. If this godfather had the wrong darkness, I couldn't let on that I knew about the camera.

The muscles in my forehead tightened, my temples throbbing from an invisible pressure.

"You have a plan?" Godfather asked. I knew it was him trying to get inside my brain. Calvin hadn't made it to the lab with us.

When I first got my powers, I didn't know how to block other people's gifts. The more knowledge I gained, the more reason I had to protect it from greed. I had to stay blocked most of the time, especially to telepaths, mind readers, and psychics. This godfather sensed the resistance. His eyebrows furrowed.

In the past, he wouldn't have tried so hard. He respected boundaries. If he asked a question out loud, he expected an answer out loud. This godfather was digging.

I kept smiling, feeling my lips falter slightly. "Some knowledge is a burden—I'd rather not share," I explained. "There's a time and a place for everything. I can't have telepaths lurking in my thoughts, unlocking secrets. It wouldn't be fair. We don't all get to play God." I took a step down, creating a plan I wasn't sure would work in our favor. "Bradley and Savanna need to stay together. As long as they are glowing, they're invisible to the undivine." I hoped that wouldn't be too predictable for the people running the lab. I knew my brother wouldn't like the idea of having to go along with what the rest of us would be doing. Turning to Olga, I said, "In the meantime…" I didn't need to finish my thought. Her green eyes brightened, reflecting my idea back to me.

Liam caught on just as quickly and stood. "Are you kidding me?"

That plan was what led the four of us—Olga, Liam, Seth, and me—into a literal trap. As soon as Bradley and Savanna were out of the room, we were scurrying along the floor as lab rats. When the door to the hallway opened, Godfather pretended to be relieved. "Thank God you're here! I've been chasing these lab rats all day." He bent, grabbing at us for good measure. His large hand cast a shadow over my little rat body, and he scooped me into his unfamiliar hand, coldness chilling my spine.

"That's not him," the voice said. My heart sank. I had suspected that. In one quick motion, I bit the strange look-alike's hand, being sure to bite hard enough to draw blood.

He jumped. "Don't let those little boogers bite you. They'll leave you feeling damn near lightheaded."

I watched the bitten skin, waiting for the blood to appear. It didn't. "Turn us back!" I squealed to Olga before the fake version of my godfather cupped his free hand over me. The sounds were muffled—voices and scuffling. Clinging to the stranger's hand, I worked to keep myself balanced as he moved.

Olga shrieked. "Let me go, you asshat!" She must have heard me. She must have turned back. The others' voices weren't as clear. I couldn't tell if she had returned them to their normal forms.

It was a long moment before I could see again. When I did, nobody I knew was in sight. It smelled like a pet store—all cedar and urine. Soft flecks of paper tickled my feet. Metal creaked and squealed as it whirred in the background at uneven intervals. Something—or multiple somethings—chittered noisily. I blinked, adjusting to my rat eyes, and saw thin white bars—bars intended to keep me trapped. Past them was a face—a man several years older than Calvin. His blond hair was cut into fringe-like spikes, not sharp and sticking up, but calmer somehow, the gel in it keeping it tame. He smiled darkly at me, his name and information popping into my head. *Wystan Reece, illusionist, born in Illinois twenty-three years ago, the first of three children.*

Illusionist? I stepped closer to the bars—to his face—curiosity burning. That wasn't one of the thirteen powers of the diviners. How could he have a power that didn't exist?

"There's something special about you," he said, his hazel eyes studying me.

Funny. I thought there was something special about *him.*

"Tell me, what gave me away? How did you know not to trust me? I honestly thought the telepathy would sell it," Wystan said casually, as if we were long-lost friends catching up. "It was the dialogue, wasn't it? Did I slip? Say something Mr. Stats would never say?"

Interesting. So was he suggesting it was him in the stairway with us? I sniffed the air and shivered. He did emit the same darkness I had sensed before. How powerful were his gifts? In theory, I didn't think illusions could mimic telepathy. If Wystan were that powerful, maybe we had met our match. This wouldn't be a fight we would win. This didn't make any sense, though. How did Bradley end up with the cure in Mom's vision?

At the thought of my brother, something tugged at my little rat gut—an uncertainty I had felt only one other time. When Bradley had been kidnapped in August and held in an airplane hangar, this tug of uncertainty had twisted my insides. In the lab, the sensation had returned. Bradley was trapped too. It was all a trap. We had miscalculated the power our enemies had. It was easy to think we were invincible.

Wystan burst into laughter, his head craning toward a door. "Your friends will trust anything they see, won't they? They're making this too easy."

I forced myself to look past him—to study the room. There were several cages lining tables. Some mice ran on wheels, others slept. Some of the cages held rats, but none of them seemed to be humans in disguise. *Where were the others?*

Wystan was still focusing on the door. "Capture and release, only to capture them again." He shook his head, chuckling to himself. "Works every time."

I stood still, focusing on feeling for Olga, Liam, and Seth. I couldn't. Another cold chill ran along my spine. Something was blocking me. I eyed Wystan, who turned to me in that instant. Was he doing this?

He slammed his hand on the tabletop. The floor of the cage rattled. "My work here is done for now. I'm late for an appointment with a certain scientist." He winked before leaving the room.

I didn't like this. I didn't like this at all.

Gnawing at the bars, I tried to think of how to escape. My tongue brushed against the cold metal. It wasn't exactly bendable. Giving up, I watched the other creatures for a while, letting my mind fill with horrible ideas. If only I could turn myself back without Olga's help. All I had at my disposal were my powers of materialization, which wouldn't help me if I didn't have opposable thumbs. I looked at my feet. Wait a minute. What if I made the cage disappear? I'd seen Bradley dematerialize objects. If he could do it—as well as Ursula and Savanna—then I definitely could.

I dug through the paper bedding until my feet felt the plastic at the bottom. Closing my eyes, I focused on the trick. There was a brief jolt as the floor disappeared, replaced by the tabletop. Yes, freedom!

Scurrying to the edge, I peered over it, woozy from the height. Backing up, I took a minute to focus again. Even if I was able to reach the door, I needed a way to open it. Maybe if I made a run for it. I could be like a competition horse, except in rat form. If I could leap from the table to the doorknob, maybe I'd weigh enough to turn it. Who was I kidding? That was a stupid idea. I needed my human body.

"Shapeshift," the voice said.

I shook my head. I couldn't do that. That wasn't my ability.

The voice chuckled and quoted *The Little Engine That Could*: "I think I can, I think I can."

I laughed a little with the voice. I used to read that book to Jesse. Standing at the edge of the table, I took a few deep breaths. "I think I can, I think I can," I thought before taking that leap of faith.

My hand grasped the door handle—all five opposable fingers curling around it. That would be a handy trick to remember. *Haha, handy.* I smiled to myself, pleased with what I had accomplished.

I stepped into the hallway—it was empty. I knew better than to be too confident about the lack of patrol. The knowledge of Wystan's powerful abilities reminded me not to trust everything I saw—or didn't see, for that matter. A sign above the elevator doors told me I was on level thirteen, ten stories from the top. I wasn't sure where to search.

Sticking to the walls, I inched forward, reading the plaques by the doors. I couldn't help but stop short at one. "Dr. Clayton Sauer," it read, the name churning my stomach. Was this what had originally brought the lab to Serena's attention? Her tormentor and Bradley's old doctor was still alive. Did Dr. Sauer know he was working with an illusionist? The doctor wasn't exactly a friend to people like us. What had been Serena's plan anyway? Was she planning to confront the Krauses, or was she planning to confront the doctor? Something told me she wanted to take as many people down with her as she could. This building was swarming with our enemies.

I wandered the halls of the floor. There had to be a sign that Olga, Liam, and Seth were somewhere. My hand traced the wall before halting at two large double doors. There wasn't a sign next to this one.

"That one," the voice whispered to me.

I pushed, the door swinging easily to let me through.

I stopped cold in my tracks.

A large soundproof box with a single glass wall contained my siblings' friends. When they saw me, they gathered to the front, pounding on the glass. They looked like they were shouting. Sitting in front of the box, coloring in a book, was a four-year-old girl. Olga pointed at the girl and then motioned to slice her throat. I never liked Olga. She wasn't afraid of violence. Seth's eyes pleaded with me to do something. It would be easy to step around the child and dematerialize the wall.

Or so I thought. The second I stepped forward, an invisible force shoved me back. The child giggled, brushing at her paper. She smiled at me, the world stopping the second our eyes met. My friends had frozen in place as information flooded my mind. Daphne Nicholson-Reece, lie detector, *matrona* of the Druids or captivators, born in Kansas four years ago, the first of one child.

The room became crowded and cold. People dressed in various fashions throughout time, their bodies translucent, stood around us. They were all different ages—some old, some young. One brushed against my hand, and I jumped at the cold touch. They had to be spirits, *mule*, there to guide us. Was it smart to be that close to them? Could they bring judgment?

The girl—Daphne—seemed surprised as well. She stood. The crayon she had been holding to the page stayed upright when she let go. Gawking at the figures surrounding us, she pointed at each one, saying their names with a sense of prideful awe. "Jonas!" She shrieked in delight. "Margaret! John! Mary!" She kept going until she had named half the spirits. I looked at the others. Although their names—most of them long—popped into my head, I didn't know them. They were strangers to me. However, the boy standing next to me was familiar.

"There are so many people here," Daphne said excitedly.

Like a reunion, I thought, peering skeptically around the room. Were these ancestors?

The six-year-old boy next to me spoke, his voice the same one I had been hearing. "They are our past." *Our past?* I looked at him questioningly, tilting my head.

He pointed at Daphne. "She is a piece of your present. Together, you form two corners of a triangle."

A ghostly woman behind him spoke in the Romani language I had grown to naturally understand.

"Remember that triangles have lines connecting the points. You are a point. She is a point. One other is a point. Those points can never touch. It would upset the balance."

"You must maintain harmony," the spirit of an older man grunted.

"No, you listen to me." A woman floated through the crowd until she was in front of me. "The Druids are notorious for upsetting the balance." She threw a harsh glare across the room. "They're selfish. They want all the power for themselves. Their greed consumes them."

A teenage boy shouted at her. "We wouldn't be in this mess if you hadn't killed your Druid counterpart! You're the reason we've been cursed!"

"He would have killed us all," the woman said defensively. "Would you rather be dead?"

"I *am* dead!" the boy said, waving his hat.

I stared through them at the four-year-old who was watching my siblings' friends in their box. "Why are they frozen?" she asked, stepping toward them to tap the glass. The spirits started to fade the second she turned her back to me. Ignoring the argument between the two spirits, I made my way to Daphne's side. The voices faded altogether by the time I reached her. Placing my hand on the glass, I willed it to disappear. Olga, Liam, and Seth unfroze, jumping in shock as the panel dissolved.

Daphne shrieked, jerking her hand away as if the disappearing glass had burned her. She turned on me, shoving her hands in my direction, another invisible force pushing me away.

"You are a meanie!" she shouted, storming toward me. The others ran past, stopping at the door.

"Go find Bradley!" I told them. They couldn't help me, not with her. They left, sprinting down the hall. I ran straight at Daphne, extending my arms to push her back. She fell backward off her feet as if I'd used a brand of telekinesis on her. That wasn't an ability of mine. I skidded to a stop on the linoleum as she propped herself on her elbows.

Her face scrunched, her nose wrinkling, she shook, her teeth clenched. "My daddy said not to let them leave!" Daphne leaped to her feet, the floor beneath her cracking as I watched in horror. Her anger was gonna get her killed. I charged at her, my only focus on keeping her from the hole that was sure to form. My hands grabbed at her shoulders—the movement had us flying across the floor.

When we landed, my skin began to burn and flake. I noticed Daphne's shoulders were too as she wailed in pain. I tried to crawl off her, but we seemed to be stuck together. Joining her screams, I writhed as the pain became too much. My ears started to ring. She covered her own. Heat built between us until suddenly I was flown across the room, my back hitting the wall.

Boom! The building shook, the wall behind me slowly crumbled. I couldn't move forward. I could only move back. Army crawling my way to the door, I silently prayed Daphne was okay. I'd have to leave her—the only person I'd ever met like myself—in the crumbling room.

A foot blocked my path. I cringed, angling my body to see who it belonged to.

24
SAVANNA STOPS BEING SELFISH
BRADLEY

The explosion had to be Rebecca's doing. I was sure of it. Some of the security cameras had gone down, static replacing their picture on the screens. I couldn't tell what was happening from where I was, but with Rebecca being the Chosen One, I was sure our side was winning.

Mrs. Walker-Krause raised an eyebrow, straightening paperwork on the table. She didn't look at me as she spoke. "Bold of you to assume we don't also have extraordinary abilities on our end." Her calmness flared a sense of doubt in my core. Maybe I was wrong. Maybe Rebecca hadn't been the one to cause the explosion. After all, this *was* a lab. The wrong chemicals could mix and *boom!* My smile disappeared.

She raised her head, her expression unreadable. "Jumping to conclusions could get you killed." My eyes flickered to Savanna, her hands no longer where I could see them. Her arms were pressed to her sides, her shoulders tensed. She didn't blink as she continued to stare ahead at the screen.

For the first time since he entered the room, Mr. Krause glanced her way. "It looks like you've seen a ghost, Miss Huckleberry. I didn't think you would recognize our friends at all."

Savanna's lips pressed into a thin, hard line. Slowly, her facial features hardened. I could feel her fear expelling from her body, like steam in a sauna. The fire of her fury heating both our insides replaced that fear, our arms tingling from the metaphorical flames. I had a strong urge to flip the table. This is what I had been waiting for. My hands gripped the edge.

"You. Are. Working. With. Monsters." Savanna groaned through her words.

What the hell had she seen? I tried to lean forward over the table, my body trembling from her fury, so I could get a decent angle of the screen she had been staring at. The soldiers held me back, their free hands gripping my upper arms so tightly my fingertips tingled.

Mr. Krause laughed mockingly. He turned to his wife. "I thought we were the monsters."

She snickered with him.

What. Had. She. Seen? I tried to pull myself forward again, my sweaty hands squealing as they slid across the tabletop.

General Krause gripped one of my hands, yanking it forward. Something popped in my shoulder, and I couldn't help but cry out in pain. *Dammit. Dammit. Dammit.* One of the soldiers let go.

"I don't appreciate liars in my presence, boy." The old man spat.

I rolled my head against the table, attempting to hold in my agony as he threw my hand back. Savanna sobbed. Closing my eyes, I tried to tune it out.

General Krause leaned over me, his breath leaving condensation on my cheek. "Your telepath friend neglected to share some relevant information with us regarding you two. Too bad we figured it out on our own." His index finger hit the tabletop in front of me, dipping into a clump of sugar. He played with it between his fingers, sprinkling the powder. "I don't like liars." His voice was farther away, his footsteps loud and thumping as he paced. "Maybe it's time to say goodbye to our new hire."

I closed my eyes, defeated. None of this was making any sense. Hot tears rolled off my face.

"Of course"—the man's hot breath was back on my skin—"you and your friends could give up, forget your siege. Maybe we won't have to kill your friend."

Frick. He wanted me to choose between my godfather's life—potentially *all* our lives—and the millions of others we could save on the off chance we could find a way to take down Priori and distribute the cure? Mom and Dad were right to be afraid of these people. I didn't know why we thought this would be easy. They knew about us. They knew about our powers. They knew Savanna and I could turn invisible when together—

a fact we had only discovered that day. Mr. Lindt wouldn't have known that. He couldn't tell them what he didn't know. He didn't know anything about us being fated.

Slowly, I lifted my body, every movement causing a new flare of pain in my shoulder. My eyes locked with General Krause's. "What monsters know our secrets?"

The man smiled.

"The captivators." Savanna's voice trembled. I angled my head toward her, pain shooting up the right side of my neck. Her left hand was gingerly holding her right shoulder, as if the touch made her pain both better and worse. The soldiers weren't holding her anymore. Instead, they watched her warily from a few inches back. My gut sank. Had she felt him break my shoulder? Anger welled inside me. By hurting me, he had hurt her. My glare followed the old man as he strode toward her, dropping his meaty hand over hers. She yelped at the touch before closing her eyes to breathe deeply.

"The captivators love their secrets. Tell me, Miss Huckleberry, how did you come to know of them?"

She gritted her teeth, opening her eyes. "They're a fairytale," she spat. "Old legends that have lost their meanings over the centuries. After all, how can one be scared of a people who don't exist?"

"Oh, but they do," Mrs. Walker-Krause taunted, stealing a glance at her husband.

He smiled, an evil glint in his eye as he looked across the table at me. "You've known of their existence for a while. I'm surprised you never thought to warn the rest of your tribe."

Tribe? We weren't a tribe. I grit my teeth.

He continued. "You must have had a reason. Something to hide, perhaps?"

I had no idea what he was talking about. I had never heard of the captivators. Savanna knew the legends better than I did. She grew up with some of the stories and the folklore of the diviners. I had only just begun to learn of our history.

"You don't give the captivators enough credit," Savanna accused the Krauses. She mimicked Mrs. Walker-Krause's earlier words. "Bold of you to assume they let Bradley remember the real story." What the heck did she know that I didn't? What could I possibly not be remembering?

Savanna took a deep breath and for a second, I thought she was going to answer my unspoken questions. Instead, she divulged the folklore. "They died to become what they are—haunted by fifth-century spirits. They were originally Druids who practiced dark magic, cursing their family lineage for centuries. They were regarded higher than the Romanichals in England, perhaps for their wisdom or skin color, who knows. Regardless, the captivators were a powerful people both in their gifts and in society. They were primarily manipulators, only interested in exercising and maintaining power. Secrets weren't their forte, but I guess our Chosen One at the time was able to put the fear of God in their descendants. How else could they have survived all these centuries?" Her eyes narrowed.

"Your folklore needs some updating," General Krause said, patting her shoulder. She winced. He leaned so his mouth was level with her ear. "As you could see, they are very much alive and well. They don't seem fearful of you at all, even with the Chosen One lurking about. You know what that tells me?" He paused. "The diviners aren't nearly as powerful as they once were."

His theory floored me, watering the ever-growing seed of doubt in my stomach. I had once said that having powers didn't necessarily make us powerful. I was a fair example of that. Half my powers were locked away, and I didn't have the key to unlock whatever metaphorical door they were hidden behind. The fortune-tellers couldn't seem to predict the more important events of our future—otherwise they would have seen this coming. Few diviner families trained like they once had—Savanna's being the exception. I had thought the entire concept paranoid and ridiculous. I hadn't known how real our enemies were. I hadn't known the danger.

Mrs. Walker-Krause smiled at me, pushing a small stack of papers. A ballpoint pen rested on top, waiting to be used. I stared at her, my doubt and confusion leaving my mind reeling. "Now that you understand how truly unmatched you are, perhaps you will reconsider your motives for being here," she said.

I glanced again at the security footage. A good chunk of the cameras still seemed to be down. I wanted a sign that surrendering was the better option. Had that explosion really not been my sister's doing? Could we really not escape? Was there zero chance of walking out of here with a cure?

The camera showing the front entrance flashed on the screen. Aaron, in all his six-two glory, strode through as if the last several hours hadn't happened. Bile gathered in my throat at the sight. I scowled. Of course, we wouldn't be able to send him to jail. His family held way more power than we knew. We couldn't touch them, and they knew it.

All three of their gloating smiles were angled at me. I looked at Savanna, silently pleading for her to do something, but she was preoccupied with another screen. Her eyes were wide, her mouth gaping. She tore her eyes away to meet mine. "I found Mr. Lindt," she said, her voice trembling, "… and Mrs. Thomas."

"They will be free to leave with you and the rest of your posse as soon as you sign this contract," Jeremiah promised me, tapping his index finger on the stack of papers. "Agree to never come within three hundred feet of this lab, any of its employees, or a member of my family again, and we'll agree to do the same with you."

"Does that mean Aaron will be switching schools?" I asked. Serena and Marcie might as well get something good from the deal.

"Indefinitely," Jeremiah nodded happily.

"What about Marcie?" Savanna asked, her long hair flying over her shoulder with the speed she used to whip her head in his direction.

He scowled. "Don't pretend you don't know your people have her in custody. Feigning ignorance doesn't suit you."

"We don't have her," Savanna retorted.

Jeremiah rolled his eyes. He pressed a finger to his ear, sighing heavily. With a bored voice, he asked, "Can we see replay footage from Sniper Eleven."

A blank screen at Savanna's end of the room flipped on. Camera footage that, I assumed, was shot from the helmet of a sniper looked downward on Monument Circle from several floors above. The tip of a rifle was aimed directly at the Thomases' booth. The circle was active with chaos as people ran from the shapeshifting statue. A shot rang out. A figure came from nowhere, tackling Marcie to the ground. The bullet flew past them, straight into Mrs. Thomas's lower abdomen. We watched as the figure dragged Marcie away with great difficulty. The short clip replayed.

"That doesn't prove anything!" Savanna shouted.

I squinted at the figure who had taken Marcie. The circle had to have been crawling with Priori personnel. It would have made sense for Priori to have nabbed her. Besides, all the diviners who had come with us had been accounted for at the time of the shooting. What did Priori have to gain by lying? It was clear Savanna didn't plan on leaving without her friend, and I wasn't going to sign the papers if she didn't agree it was for the best. But Priori always lied. That's why we were there in the first place. The Krauses were greedy, lying bastards. I joined in on Savanna's piercing glare.

General Krause stepped back. "I can see we're getting nowhere with negotiations. I assume you would prefer to all die." He raised his eyebrows, addressing me. "Are you willing to put your friends' lives at risk all so that you can be cured?" Though the raid wasn't about me being cured, he had a point. I wasn't willing to risk anybody's lives—not after we had lost the upper hand. I didn't know much about the captivators, but I'd heard enough to be afraid.

Sliding my left hand across the table, I dragged the papers in front of me. My right arm stung with every movement, my hand cold from lack of blood flow. I'd have to use my left hand to sign. That wouldn't be pretty. My eyes skimmed through the stipulations of the contract. In signing it, I represented every diviner—whether I knew them or not. If any diviner broke the restraining order— and Priori found out—the responsibility would befall me. I would suffer the consequences.

"This is ridiculous," I muttered, continuing to skim. "I'm fourteen. In no way do I represent every diviner."

General Krause took the seat across from me, interlacing his fingers. "You're a Chambers, a diviner, and type one diabetic. If anyone has a special interest in taking us down, it's you. We have a right to assume from now on that any diviner who tries to do so in the future has a direct connection to you."

"I didn't realize I had become such a threat," I said.

"You're only a threat to my time," he corrected. "You can't defeat me."

My eyes floated to the final line of the contract. "If the signatory of this document violates this contract in any way, the captivators will reserve the right to terminate the life of the signatory in any way they see fit." My entire body ran cold. Stammering, I said, "I-I'm signing my death certificate?"

"Think of it this way. As long as your kind doesn't bother us, you get to live." General Krause said, sounding more like a mob boss than an ex–attorney general.

I looked at Savanna, whose fear had returned, leaking from every pore. Did they know that by signing this contract, I was not only putting a target on my head, but hers as well? If I die, she dies. Ugh. Why did this have to be so complicated?

She surprised me by nodding, tears streaming down her cheeks. "Do it."

I stared at her, incredulous. "Even with the off chance that they're lying about Marcie?"

Savanna glanced at the footage once more. She wiped a stray tear away. "Whoever has Marcie is the same height as her." She turned to me. "It could be one of us."

"You realize we can never cure diabetes," I said, my voice cracking. I knew her intentions with joining our mission had been selfish. If I couldn't be cured, her life expectancy stayed lowered to mine or whatever bull crap she had spun the day before.

She nodded, her lips trembling. "If you're okay with it, I'm okay with it."

I stared at her for a long moment, my heart sinking lower. No. I wasn't okay with it. But what other choice did I have? If we died failing to rid the world of this disease, what was the point? "We'll die before all our friends." I couldn't prove that fact as truth, but it was likely, with or without the contract. I had a knack for attracting danger. Tears were spilling down both our faces.

She nodded. "At least we'll die together."

"Like Romeo and Juliet?" I asked, remembering her saying those exact words the night we discovered we were fated.

"Exactly like Romeo and Juliet."

I so wished I could have kissed her then.

25
THAT DID NOT JUST HAPPEN
BRADLEY

I couldn't believe we gave up. Just like that.

"Talk about people using secrets as weapons," Savanna said as the soldiers walked us past Aaron on our way out the front door. When the cold air hit us, I jerked my head north toward the monument, hoping to catch a glimpse of it, but I couldn't see it past the other buildings.

The National Guard was gone. The helicopters were gone. The news crews were gone.

It was like signing that contract reversed the entire day. The monument may have been our only proof that any of this had happened. That and the five o'clock news that would undoubtedly retell the morning chaos in Monument Circle.

We stood in the parking lot to wait for our friends. Although the Krauses had promised us their safe return, I hoped our friends wouldn't put up too much of a fight.

"I feel kinda bad for suggesting Rebecca had anything to do with that explosion," I confessed, attempting to ignore the pain in and around my shoulder. "What exactly did you see if it wasn't her?" She opened her mouth to answer, but I intercepted with another question. "And why didn't you fight back?"

Savanna shook her head, her chin trembling. "We didn't account for who all is in that building."

I inched closer, wanting to comfort her, but a soldier cleared their throat, their gun aimed at me. I backed away. They didn't want us turning invisible this close to the lab. "The captivators?" I pressed.

"Them." She nodded before pressing her fingers to her lips. "There are children in there too. I saw the signs to the daycare when we were taken off the elevator. Priori takes excellent care of their employees. Providing childcare is one way to harbor loyalty. It's a perk lots of employees don't want to give up. So they stay and they keep silent." Her conclusion sounded familiar. Kase, Serena, and I had learned about this concept in our business class. Savanna shook her head. "I couldn't incite violence when there were children in the building, especially when they were on our floor. I'm shocked we didn't hear them." Her hands wrung through her hair. "I kept thinking about your brother."

My brother.

I closed my eyes. It had been almost seven months since Jesse was shot, but it felt like longer. He was in the wrong place at the wrong time. Kind of like those children. If an innocent child was caught in the crossfire, it would have been our fault.

"Do you think that's why they were pushing so hard for negotiations?" I asked. "They knew if they killed us, there'd be war?"

Savanna's blue eyes gazed at the tall building. "It's hard to see them as monsters when you put it that way."

"But they *are* monsters, Savanna," I said, clarifying.

She looked at me, cocking her head to the side. "Do you think that's why Olga doesn't see all the harm that Chad causes because he also does stuff like this? Do you think he's sweet and apologetic and protective? So much so that it's easier for her to forgive him?"

I stared at her, not wanting to answer.

She continued. "Do you think that's also why all the employees stay? Because even though Priori does questionable things, at least they have a steady income and childcare and all that?"

The front doors opened with Mr. Lindt and Mrs. Thomas hobbling out. Jagged lines of dried blood ran down Mr. Lindt's face, an eye swollen shut. Mrs. Thomas limped, her hand pressed to her side. Savanna ran to her, trying to get a better look at her bullet wound.

"It's okay, darling. They stitched me up." Mrs. Thomas said, pushing Savanna away. "I just want to see my daughter."

Mr. Lindt squinted at me as he held an icepack to his head. "When did you kids get here?"

"Y-you let us in," I reminded him, suddenly unsure. Maybe he sustained too much trauma to the head.

Savanna bit her lip. "I don't think that was him."

I quickly turned to her, the movement feeling like an extra tear in my injured shoulder. My heart thudded in my chest. I didn't like where she was headed with this theory.

She glanced warily at Mrs. Thomas. I knew she was trying to decide whether it was necessary to clue her in on our abilities. "The captivators," she finally explained, "some of them can play mind tricks. They can make you see and hear things that aren't there."

I felt sick. Not knowing what was right in front of me, losing my grip on reality, that was a definite fear of mine. I liked the truth—I liked being able to see the truth, to hear the truth. I wasn't so sure of myself anymore, not so sure of what the truth was. I paced, biting my left thumbnail, before I stopped, struck by a memory.

"The others thought they were with him," I said. "I saw the security feed. They thought they were talking to Mr. Lindt, but there wasn't anybody standing there. The illusions didn't show on camera."

Mr. Lindt sat on a curb stop, heaving a defeated sigh. "The captivators, huh?" He winced, adjusting his ice pack. "That explains a lot. Thought that Wystan kid was a diviner like us. Even his thoughts played out to a tee."

Savanna cringed.

"What?" I asked.

She chewed her lip. "About that explosion—"

Olga's loud empty threats interrupted her. "We are not leaving here without that cure! Come on, Becca, do your thing, show 'em who's boss!" She struggled against the grip of a guy in his early twenties as he shoved her out the door.

A tall woman with blond hair and blue eyes leaned nonchalantly against the entryway. "You're no threat to us, sweetheart," she said cockily.

Appearing as if they'd merely been scolded, the others shuffled out of the building like pouting toddlers. Olga was the only one putting up a fight. "Why aren't you guys fighting?" Olga screeched.

"I told you." Rebecca crossed her arms, furrowing her eyebrows. "Bradley signed a treaty. If we break it, he dies. Savanna dies."

How did she know that? Had the guards explained?

The young man let go of Olga, shoving her forward on the pavement. She propped herself on her elbows, glaring accusingly at my sister. "I can't believe you're gonna take the word of a four-year-old over everything! Bradley would never do that! This was *his* mission! Besides, if there was gonna be a treaty between the lab and the diviners, wouldn't *you* be the one to sign it? Aren't you our fearless leader, oh mighty Chosen One?" She said those last words mockingly.

Rebecca gritted her teeth. "Bradley's signature is as good as mine."

Olga jumped to her feet as Seth and Liam joined us in the parking lot. She wasn't going to let this go easily. Storming toward me, she jabbed an angry finger in my direction, reminding me of my father. "Please tell me you did not sign some stupid contract that made all our hard work and effort futile!"

I stepped back and tried to justify myself. "We weren't going to win this one."

"So… you gave up?" Olga shouted. "Without consulting us?"

I wanted to grab her by the shoulders and shake some sense into her, but it hurt too much to move. "The captivators are here," I said through gritted teeth.

"The capti-who-now?" Olga asked, confused.

Rebecca rolled her eyes. "That four-year-old was a captivator," she explained. I wasn't sure who she was talking about, but Olga seemed to know. She squinted her eyes as Rebecca continued. "She's like their version of me. The captivators are born with their gifts. They don't develop them over time like we do. There is always one who knows more, who possesses the knowledge of their ancestors, who is more powerful than the rest. She may only be four, but Bradley is right. We weren't going to win. She's unstable. Her dad's not much better." She sent a wary glance to the guy who had escorted Olga out of the building.

He smirked. Something about him seemed familiar, but I couldn't—

I froze.

He and the woman disappeared inside, and the soldiers moved to cover the door. It was time for us to leave.

"Is that who I saw on the security footage?" Savanna asked. "That little girl caused all that damage?"

Rebecca moved her gaze to Savanna, nodding slowly.

I couldn't move, couldn't breathe.

Savanna looked at me, her lip once again captured by her teeth. "You recognized him, didn't you? Is he who I think he is? I'd only seen him once in your memories, but when I saw him on the tape, I-I knew it was him."

I moved my mouth, but no words came out. It was like that for several long moments until I finally managed to choke, "He's dead."

She stepped toward me instinctively, her hand flying to mine. The soldiers perked up, drawing their guns and shouting for her to step away. We needed to get out of there.

Mr. Lindt dug his car keys from his pocket and handed them to Mrs. Thomas. "Some of you may have to squeeze into the trunk and pray no one pulls us over." He stood, using a nearby SUV to steady himself. "I'm surprised Serena isn't here with you guys. Is she off on some other errand?"

Liam furrowed his brow. "We had this conversation, Mr. Lindt. My brother took her to the hospital."

"You had that conversation with Wystan Reece," Rebecca said in a small voice, leading the way to the car.

Wystan Reece. Yeah, I knew him. Or I did. Before he died six and a half years ago. He was sixteen. He'd be twenty-three now. His brother was my best friend during the brief time we lived in Niles. The age difference between us had him keeping his distance. He was kind of a jerk sometimes, but that's how big brothers are—or so I've been told. I didn't know him more than that. How could he be alive after all this time? I'd seen his death so clearly. I remembered the car veering off the road. I remembered all five of his family's dead, bleeding bodies. I remembered my broken wrist.

"Ow." I groaned, snapping to the present. All four of us teenagers had squeezed ourselves into the back of Mr. Lindt's sedan. Seth and Rebecca had opted to hide in the trunk. My shoulder was screaming as I tried not to bump it against anyone or anything, but the task proved impossible.

"You were friends with captivators?" Liam asked. I must have been muttering to myself.

I nodded, staring at my numb wrist. It hadn't taken long to heal after the car accident. I was starting to wonder if there had been an accident in the first place. If Wystan could create illusions—and judging by the events involving Mr. Lindt, he could create exceedingly elaborate illusions—then couldn't he have created an artificial car accident? Wystan had the power to fake deaths—fake his death, fake others. Could his brother be alive? His sister? Mr. and Mrs. Reece?

I wasn't sure if I wanted them to be alive—not if the captivators in general were as terrible as Savanna led me to believe. Could my childhood best friend really be a monster? Could he be as terrible as his older brother? Would he make Chad look like an angel in comparison? Had I really been that terrible at picking friends growing up?

26
JAY-JAY KNOWS WHICH WORDS
WILL HURT
BRADLEY

Seth slumped in her chair in the hospital waiting room. Her arms were crossed, her eyes focused on the ceiling. "This all feels very anticlimactic." Minuscule dots had formed on her wrist from where the bracelet had clung to her skin. Rebecca had removed the bracelets in the hospital parking lot.

Mrs. Thomas was arguing with Savanna in the corner, her whispers harsh and not at all subtle. "You know where my daughter is. Why won't you tell me where my daughter is? What more could you kids possibly be hiding?" Savanna tried to shush her, but Mrs. Thomas's words were drawing the attention of too many curious ears. It wasn't exactly a quiet day in the emergency room. Although half the people waiting seemed physically okay, every once in a while, someone would wail about aliens or other government conspiracies. A few couples were checking all the area hospitals for their missing children they had lost in or around the square. At least the events of Mile Square gave us an excuse for our injuries. They had admitted Mr. Lindt right away, but I was still on hold, my injury not urgent enough for immediate assistance. Mom and Frank had arrived before they had admitted half the waiting room.

Frank glared pointedly at Savanna, his disappointed frown deepening as he spoke. "Your parents are going to have my head on a stick by the end of the day."

Savanna shrank, a guilty grimace forming on her lips.

Mom took one look at my right arm, the pallor lighter than usual, and made a beeline to the front desk, demanding to know why they hadn't admitted me yet. She slammed the palm of her hand on the tabletop. "If he loses that arm waiting in *your* waiting room, I will sue the roof off this place!"

Olga whistled. "I forgot how feisty your mom gets in hospitals."

Frank took the empty seat next to me, letting out a breath of air so quickly, his lips flapped obnoxiously. "What were you kids thinking?" At first, his tone came as forced calmness, but he quickly lost his cool, his anger evident by the end of his question. He tried again, his voice low. I wasn't sure all of us could hear him. "I realize that these past few weeks have been chaotic. I know what's been happening between Serena and Aaron is distracting. I know that as her friends you have been punished for trying to protect her—even gotten yourselves suspended." His eyes flickered to me and then back at his hands as he repeatedly cracked his knuckles. "I know some of you have lost loved ones and are still trying to process that grief. I don't know you two"—he pointed his fingers in different directions at Olga and Liam without looking directly at them—"but I'm sure you had your own issues that brought you to this point. I was expecting some rebellion." He lifted his head to glare at Savanna again. "What I was *not* expecting was an unexcused absence from Miss Perfect over here. I spent two hours on the phone with your parents trying to figure out where you were, only to be interrupted by the news of a 'terrorist attack' downtown. 'Course, I knew better." He side-eyed Rebecca. "Question is do you?"

Rebecca opened her mouth to protest, but before any words could come, Mom rushed over to let me know they had a room for me.

"So does Frank know the whole story?" I asked the second I was alone with Mom.

She pursed her lips as a nurse came to examine my shoulder. I winced at their cold touch.

"That thing's not in place." The nurse *tsk*ed. After a few seconds, they patted my uninjured shoulder. "I'm going to set you up with an x-ray so we can get a better look at what we're dealing with." They disappeared.

Mom looked like she'd been holding her breath through the whole ordeal. She sighed, shaking her head. "I don't understand how you kids didn't succeed. I saw you holding the cure in your hands. If I hadn't, I wouldn't have let you go. What happened?"

I closed my eyes, breathing in through my mouth, then out through my nose. It was hard to breathe without jarring my shoulder. "We started the day without a decent plan and pretty much everything that could go wrong went wrong." I opened my eyes, staring at my lap. "I guess that's the danger of relying on a vision… or two." I crinkled my eyebrows, remembering Jay-Jay's vision of Savanna's near-death experience. "Savanna didn't even need to use her powers."

Mom mirrored my confusion.

"I think we need to know exactly what Jay-Jay saw," I said after a long silence.

It was dark outside by the time Mom pulled the van into the Joneses' driveway. Savanna and I were the only ones with her. Liam had gone home, but we sent everybody else to our house. Mom wasn't so sure keeping Savanna with us was going to earn us any brownie points with the Huckleberrys, but she figured it might be safer that way. At least until we found out what Jay-Jay had seen. If their visions were bound to happen—and they always were— we needed to decipher why they hadn't happened yet.

"Your shoulder hurt?" I asked Savanna, my right arm in a sling.

She snorted. "You missed the dramatics in the waiting room. I felt them pop that sucker back in."

Mom rang the doorbell.

Ms. Jones jabbered inside, her voice growing louder as she reached the door. Her voice stopped suddenly, and there was a pause before the door handle slowly turned. She opened it a crack, peering warily at my mom. "Can I help you?" I looked at my left hand entwined in Savanna's. The glow lit the darkness, bathing us in light. Ironic that the undivine couldn't see something so bright. I let go, the glow immediately disappearing. Ms. Jones started, her hand jumping to her chest as she backed away. "Oh, kids, you scared me!"

Mom smiled sweetly, her voice calm and content. "I'm Clarinda Chambers, Bradley's mom. We were hoping to speak to Jay-Jay."

She extended her hand, and Ms. Jones took it tentatively in hers, barely shaking it. Jay-Jay's mom let go, seeming to snap out of her daze. "They're in the living room."

They?

She opened the door all the way to allow us to enter. "Poor Marcie's shaken."

At the sound of her friend's name, Savanna bolted inside, shouting for Marcie. Mom and I quickly followed, pushing the door closed and locking the bolts. Mom peered through the peephole.

Marcie came into the hall, and Savanna rammed into her, gathering her in a bear hug.

"They have to be watching this house," Mom murmured.

I considered the possibility but then told Mom what Mr. Krause had told us in the lab. "They acted like they had no idea where she was."

"Keyword: acted." Mom said before pulling Ms. Jones to the window. "Do any of these cars look unfamiliar to you?" I walked toward the sobbing girls. Jay-Jay appeared behind them.

"Is my mom okay? Did you see her?" Marcie cried. Savanna was crying so much, she couldn't answer.

I answered for her. "She's okay. She's at my house."

Marcie would have fallen over with relief if it wasn't for Savanna's tight grip keeping her upright.

"Have you really been here all day?" Savanna asked, barely coherent, her voice pitchy.

"Do you really have special powers?" Marcie asked, half-laughing through her tears. Savanna pulled away, nodding as she tried to wipe away her tears. Marcie giggled. "Jay-Jay said you're kind of like that cartoon." She snapped her fingers, trying to remember the name. "Kim Possible?"

Savanna couldn't help but burst into laughter at the comparison. Her hand landed on Jay-Jay's shoulder as she used him to support her weight, bending at her waist from uncontrollable fits.

Jay-Jay managed a weak smile, the healing bruises on his face not distracting enough to hide the deep blue crevices underneath his eyes. He looked like he hadn't slept in days.

"It was you on the tape?" I asked him before realizing that was a dumb question. Of course it was him. "It was you who saved Marcie?"

He nodded, his head bobbing in a slow, subtle movement. His tiredness made him unusually quiet.

I felt bad for keeping him awake. "You should get some sleep."

His eyes dropped to the carpet as he slid from Savanna's grip. I followed him as he shuffled to the kitchen. "Can't sleep," he mumbled, grabbing a bag of coffee grounds. As he poured them into the coffee machine, he explained, "The visions come when I close my eyes. I can't stop them."

Well, that didn't sound normal. Let me rephrase that. That didn't sound like a common problem for precogs.

"What do you see?"

He punched a few buttons on the machine. "Nothing I haven't already seen a million times—things that have already happened and things that haven't happened yet." He folded his arms tightly against his chest. "The universe won't leave me alone."

"Are you allowed to tell us about your vision of Savanna?" I asked tentatively.

He glared at me. I guess not. There was a moment of silence between us before he said, "Let me ask you something, Bradley. Do you care about me at all as a human being?"

I was taken aback by his frustrated words. Of course I cared about him. I wasn't a complete garbage person.

"'Cause I don't think you do," he said. "If you did, you wouldn't be asking me the same question that landed me in the hospital over a week ago."

I stared at him as he shook, his trembling hand reaching for a ceramic mug. He was right. Maybe I *was* a trash human being. In fact, I knew I was. I'd stupidly thought being friends with Jay-Jay and dating Savanna automatically proved I was better. I thought maybe that somehow meant I was good.

"Look, man." Jay-Jay shoved the mug underneath the spout to catch a fresh stream of coffee. The aroma filled the air. "All I know is that I didn't have to see horrible things before *you* came around."

I backed against the wall, the air rushing out of me. Jay-Jay didn't have to physically throw a punch. This was exactly what I had been afraid of, and he knew it. I'd come into all their lives like a wrecking ball.

Jay-Jay didn't look at me. His eyes focused on the stream of brown liquid filling his mug. He knew how much those words—that truth—would hurt me, but I needed to hear it. I didn't recognize him anymore. Ever since the bunker, he'd transformed into this bitter person. He never laughed. He stopped trying to pitch random story ideas and titles. He'd transformed from this happy, carefree guy to a bitter creature of despair. That was my fault. That was on me. I'd ruined his perfect outlook on life. Now, he was so… broken. So was Serena, who could have angered the Nazis in the four years before I had arrived in Indianapolis but had decided to wait until I came on the scene—a force of great destruction, harbinger of death and pain and darkness. I'd thought about leaving so many times in those four months, cutting all ties with anyone and everyone who I ever cared for or who cared for me. It was worth it, maybe, just so they could experience some semblance of peace.

That was the moment I decided. It was so quick I didn't have time to think through all the repercussions of it. In my mind, there were no adverse consequences if I left. Their lives could only get better from there.

27
THE SECOND LAW OF
THERMODYNAMICS
SAVANNA

Stepping away from Marcie, I gasped in a lungful of air, trying to breathe against dense fog. I'd felt this before, the memory of it stinging my eyes with fresh tears. My heart sank, darkness clouding the bright relief I had been feeling moments before. My vision blurred, Marcie's red hair the only color I could see before I bent over, sobs erupting from my lungs. I blindly felt in the dark for a solid object to keep me upright, but Marcie's hands gripped my arms instead. I could hear her voice, but I couldn't make out the words. My legs shook from my weight. I wanted to fall, to hit the ground with so much force I would crash through the floor and sink into the dark abyss of the underground. Something tugged at my gut, like an invisible string was attached to it, and someone was pulling, the material expanding, stretching like a rubber band. *Snap!* I felt the pull of the rubber suddenly bounce back, slamming into me with full force.

Something was wrong. Something was very wrong.

Jay-Jay had once tried to explain to me the second law of thermodynamics. It's easy to destroy something— not so easy to put it back together. It's exactly how rubber bands work. The molecules that make up rubber are chaotic, entropic. We could try to stretch them, to align them, to try to straighten the molecules, but if we let go, if we give up on holding them in place, the rubber returns to its entropic state. That's exactly how I felt in that moment—entropic. Complete and total entropy. With that realization, I knew where it was coming from.

The muscles around my heart constricted, aching of my own volition. I squeezed my closed eyelids, willing myself to focus on my heartbeat. It ached at the idea of blocking Bradley, but his emotions were so overpowering, I could hardly think.

Footsteps approached, more worried, frantic voices accompanying them. Someone asked where Bradley was, his name once again tugging at my gut, but lightly this time, and I realized the person who had been holding the other end was my boyfriend. He had let the rubber go. It was easy for him to destroy something. Not so easy for him to put it back together. How effortlessly the second law of thermodynamics could be applied to our relationship. We were elastic. I heaved another sob, my breath continuing to catch and release in quick spurts. Bradley was gone.

Slowly opening my eyes, I didn't bother focusing on any one person or thing. The tears still blurred my vision, but I didn't care to see. Hands were on my back, on my shoulders, on my arms, but none of them belonged to the boy who had captured my heart, the boy whose fate was entwined in mine. How could he leave me? He'd promised.

Red flooded my vision. Not the same red as Marcie's hair, but red-red, bright scarlet or candy apple. Flinging my tears in a hurried flurry of frustration, I stepped out of everyone's reach, my eyes refocusing on the last person I knew to have spoken with my boyfriend.

Jay-Jay blanched, his eyes widening. I'm sure my face must have looked extra terrifying to him. I tried to keep it that way, the roughness in my voice menacing. "What. Did. You. Say to him?" He stepped back, wide awake now, and I quickly followed his movements, my hands flying toward him, getting ready to shove. He didn't answer, his eyes pleading with the people behind me for help. He wasn't getting any. Not if I could help it.

I shoved him, right into the wall. I don't think I've ever been this angry with Jay-Jay in our ten years of friendship, let alone done anything to harm him, but these were extenuating circumstances.

"What did you say to him?!" I screamed again. Various hands failed to grab my arms, to pull me away. He twisted, his hands held defensively, one leg lifted in a half crouch. Finally, Mrs. Chambers bent to wrap her arms around my waist, dragging me backward. If she wasn't Bradley's mom, I would have resisted more, but I let her remove me from the source of my rage.

"Are you okay, baby?" Ms. Jones stroked Jay-Jay's hair, shooting me a short-lived glare.

Jay-Jay elbowed her away, grimacing, his dark eyes finding mine. "You think the world revolves around you and him! You can't see the bigger picture because all you're worried about is how Bradley feels! I've been your friend for ten years. Marcie's been your friend for three. You've known Bradley for three and a half months, and he's all you ever talk about now. At first, I was fine with that, but you've become infatuated with each other. It's unhealthy, and it needs to stop!"

I went still in Mrs. Chambers's embrace. Some of his words sounded as if they had come straight from my father's mouth. My dad didn't understand. My mom didn't either, but my dad was more vocal about it. He hated Bradley, ever since the day we marched into the bunker. The neo-Nazis coming after us wasn't his fault, but Dad didn't see it that way. "Ever since you started talking to that boy—" he would complain. I expected it from my father. I didn't expect it from Jay-Jay. After all, he'd been the one to see Bradley coming. He'd been the one to tell us we were destined. How could he be mad when this was all his doing? Why was he trying to rip us apart?

"You still think I'm going to die." The words were gentle, empathic, my heart sinking a little at the realization. We never filled Jay-Jay in on what was going on. He had no idea.

His eyes widened. "I know you're going to die. I've seen it. Every time I close my eyes, I see you die, over and over again." His breath caught in his throat, capturing his words. "It's inevitable," he choked. "You're in an office shuffling through desk drawers, your cell phone held to your ear. You say you're running an errand for Bradley. Your hand curls around some type of sealed test tube." His chin trembled, his eyes overflowing with saltwater. "The building explodes."

Even though I'd been reassured by the Chosen One herself that I wasn't going to die, my heart still sputtered at the thought. It was so real to him he couldn't convince himself otherwise.

My blood ran cold. "What office?" I asked.

He looked at me like everyone had looked at Serena earlier. "You're gonna go do it anyway, aren't you? Because that's how my visions work. I shouldn't bother trying to stop them or change them. Even after hearing the specifics of your death, you still want to know where? So, what, you can be like Serena and sacrifice yourself to the cause? I don't think so."

"Wait, how do you know about Serena?" I asked. He hadn't been there when Calvin took her.

He jabbed an angry finger at his temple, snarling. "Visions."

I shook my head, squinting my eyes. "Whatever. Did you tell Bradley any of this?"

"No, I…" he stopped, biting his tongue. He looked at his feet, his hands patting his chest as if he had lost track of a pen. "Wait a minute—I didn't seize this time."

"That's 'cause I'm not dying," I replied, unwrapping Mrs. Chambers arms from around me. "Not if Bradley doesn't die." I stepped closer to him to peer out the back window. The darkness shrouded any hope of tracking Bradley's whereabouts. His emotions were faint, burrowing quietly in my chest. Wherever he was, he was still alive—sad, but alive. I sighed, a single tear slipping down my cheek. I wanted to stop his hurt, but I wasn't sure how.

"Are you seriously crying over him right now?" Jay-Jay said, judgment seeping in his tone.

I swiped at the tear. "You can't tear us apart." My lips trembled. "Our hearts are connected—they beat rhythmically with each other. When one of us is hurt, the other feels it. Don't act like our love for each other is imaginary. It's real. Even at fourteen, we know each other's souls."

"That's bullshit," Jay-Jay said.

His mom slapped his shoulder. "What did I tell you about using that kind of language?" He cringed but didn't say anything.

The silence lingered as I stared into the nothingness of the night.

Marcie broke the silence, her tone small, tentative. "If you're talking about the cure, I know where they keep one of the vials."

Jay-Jay closed his mouth, the rows of his teeth snapping against each other. His eyes rolled to the ceiling. I stared at him quizzically, trying to decipher his body language. He addressed Marcie. "I didn't save you so you could spill all your secrets."

She guffawed. "My mom was shot right in front of me today because the Krauses were afraid we told Bradley their secrets. Then you showed up, telling me this crazy story about how you have these visions and how my best friend also has superpowers. If I hadn't seen that statue morph before my eyes, I would have thought you were pulling my leg." Her eyes shifted between Jay-Jay and me. "If you two really have superpowers, if you can take down the Krauses, then I want to help. I don't want to have to keep looking over my shoulder every second of every day for forever."

Jay-Jay rolled his eyes. "You and Bradley need to form the 'let's get Savanna killed' club."

I glowered at him before aiming my full attention at Marcie. "What do you know?"

She leaned against the back of a living room chair. "Jeremiah Krause keeps a vial in his downtown office." She bit her lip, her fingers nervously intertwined. "There's a sensor in the box it's in. If it's opened by anyone but him, supposedly explosives in the walls will go off."

Jay-Jay raised his eyebrows, his arms crossed against his chest. "The explosives in the walls *will* go off."

Marcie's gaze flashed to his and then mine, her eyebrows drawing near to each other. "His visions aren't all or nothing, are they?"

I didn't realize I was biting my nails until I had to take them out of my mouth to answer. I shrugged. "All I know is Bradley's and my lives are connected. If he dies, I die, and vice-versa. Mrs. Chambers also has visions, and she knows Bradley will still be alive in months to come, so I can't die in that explosion. Besides, I can self-materialize now." I nervously scratched at my leg with my foot. "I should be able to disappear for a few seconds in the case of an explosion."

"You can what?" Jay-Jay sputtered. "And since when are Bradley's and your lives connected?"

I ignored him, analyzing the potential plan in my head. According to Jay-Jay's vision, if I leave to fetch the cure and there is an explosion, I should be able to self-dematerialize. The question would be for how long. If it was only for a few seconds, I would be rematerializing in the fire. I couldn't imagine that ending well. Still, I had to try. Rebecca had told me my self-dematerialization would be what saves me.

Mrs. Chambers spoke for the first time since my physical altercation with Jay-Jay. Sighing, she said, "It's not that I don't trust my daughter, but I don't know how I feel about this plan, Savanna. Sending a fourteen-year-old—even one who is not my kid—into a building rigged to explode does not sit well with me."

I crossed my arms, challenging her. "You were fine with it when we all went to the lab without any adult supervision."

She chewed on her lip. "The diviners are stronger in groups, and you had Rebecca on your side. For the record, I was not okay with it. I'm never okay with you kids putting yourselves in danger. But I also know my kids. I know when they get an idea stuck in their heads, there's no stopping them. I see the future, Savanna—I know, okay? I know you'll make it out alive. It's the how that scares me. It's the possibility of you getting hurt in the process that terrifies me. You kids tend to underestimate the consequences of your actions. My best friend's daughter is under observation in a psych ward right now—and while that's preferable to her being dead and I'm glad you kids intervened to get her the help she needs—I wish she didn't have to be. As a parent, I wish that on all of you. I hate how dangerous some of your lives have become. You caught the attention of the captivators today and that's not a good position to be in."

"Who are the captivators?" Jay-Jay asked.

I huffed, rolling my eyes. I would have to remember to explain everything to him later, but at that moment, I needed to focus on getting the cure. I had to make sure I wasn't within three hundred feet of the Krauses while doing it too. The only building they had listed in their contract was the lab. What a fun little loophole. I thought they were professionals—98 percent success rate and all that. It looked like I'd have to be in that two percent. Maybe they didn't want to place suspicion on the downtown office. Did they know Marcie knew about the vial's location?

"How far is his office from the lab?" I asked Marcie.

She shrugged. "Maybe a mile or two? It's north of Mile Square."

"And the lab is south," I recalled. "I'm gonna need a 10-20 on the Krauses locations at all times. I can't risk breaking the contract."

"You watch too many cop shows," Jay-Jay muttered, scratching the back of his head.

"How are we going to pull that off if all diviners are bound by the restraining order?" Mrs. Chambers asked.

Jay-Jay guffawed. "There's a restraining order now? Great. We're gonna have to move." He didn't used to be so sarcastic. He was getting on my last nerve.

I eyed Marcie and Ms. Jones, an idea forming in my head. "The contract specified that *diviners* couldn't come near them."

Marcie flinched a little, knowing immediately what I was getting at. Under normal circumstances, I wouldn't have considered asking her. Marcie and Aaron had known each other for a long time, almost as long as I'd known

Jay-Jay, and their history wasn't a great one. We'd met them in middle school at a time when too many boys fantasized over the girls who'd already developed breasts. Marcie had hit puberty early—a couple years before— and while some of the other girls were jealous, I knew better. Big-chested girls were always bullied, and I saw secondhand how horrible some of the boys were to her.

Aaron was the worst. He hung around her a lot—at first it seemed sweet. I was even jealous for a little bit. An eighth-grade basketball player in love with a normal sixth grader? It seemed like a fairytale. I thought they would be together forever—hoped for it, really. I daydreamed about their wedding, how I would be a bridesmaid or—if I were lucky—maid of honor. Her beautiful red hair would fall in perfect ringlets at her shoulders. Her bouquet would be huge—baby's breath spilling out into the aisle. She didn't seem so fascinated by her relationship as I did, but she nodded along with everyone else's interpretation with a tight smile. It wasn't until the rumors started that I let my fantasy of their future melt away.

It started when someone's older brother overheard some other boys talking about "sharing" Marcie. Supposedly, Aaron disagreed at first, but that doesn't give him a gold star in my book. He did, however, contribute to rumors about her being a slut. She would cry to him, and he would tell her boys are stupid, and she would believe him and continue to go along with whatever he wanted. When Aaron realized he could make money off her, he gave in to the other boys' offers. One day she came crying to him, thinking he would beat up a guy for harassing her, but he turned around to tell her that it was her fault.

"If you weren't so sexy," he'd said, as if that were a compliment. "You can't be upset that other guys want to be with you." Another backhanded compliment. "Stop acting like you don't ask for this stuff to happen."

The final straw was the day they were caught in one of the school bathrooms. I won't go into the details, but I came home crying, telling my mother that Marcie had been suspended and how Aaron hadn't gotten more than a slap on the wrist. I told her all that I knew about their relationship, and my mother took my hands and decided that that would be the day she talked to me about consent and the reality of toxic patriarchy—she didn't think she'd have to give that talk to me for a few more years. She invited Marcie and her mom over for dinner, and we cried and laughed and talked all night.

I glanced at Marcie again, guilt beginning to choke me. Was I really going to ask her to track the whereabouts of her abuser? To distract him if necessary? Maybe Jay-Jay was right. Maybe I *was* letting the whole fated business with Bradley cloud my vision.

She set her jaw, a look of determination lining her face. "I'll do it. Whatever it takes."

I opened my mouth to protest, but Jay-Jay beat me to it. "No." He swiped his arm in a slicing motion through the air. Turning to me, his voice practically flowed with venom. "You did not seriously ask—"

I cut him off, my voice rough. "I didn't. It was a stupid idea." Tears burned at the rims of my eyelids, the lump in my throat refusing to shrink. Marcie and I stared at each other, a silent conversation flowing between us.

When she spoke again, her hand shook at her side. "Will I be in danger?" she asked.

Ms. Jones crossed over to her, taking her hands in hers. "I'll be with you, sweetheart. He can't try anything if I'm there."

28
I ALMOST KILL JAY-JAY... AGAIN
SAVANNA

We were taking too long. That's what Olga said when she rang my cell. She demanded to know where we were. Frank had stopped by Jay-Jay's to find the house empty. He thought maybe we'd been kidnapped by the captivators. The truth? We were back on Meridian Street, Mrs. Chambers's van parked outside the bright beam of light piercing the night from a nearby streetlight. I'd never felt more like a criminal, casing the sidewalk in front of the brick-and-mortar buildings of several lawyers' offices for witnesses. Olga would have loved this, but I didn't dare give her any specifics. Ms. Jones and Marcie had driven around the block, searching for any sign of the Krauses. Maybe they'd get lucky and never find them. Maybe the Krauses weren't anywhere near us.

I was still on the phone with Olga when Mrs. Chambers's phone rang. She checked the caller ID before answering. Mrs. Chambers answered, then nodded to me—Jay-Jay's mom gave the all clear. I glanced at Jay-Jay, whose eyes were frozen in a state of horror, and I hoped with all my might that Rebecca had been right, that this wouldn't be the last time I saw my oldest friend. I took a deep breath before stepping out of the vehicle. Olga was still talking my ear off, listing ideas and plans as I crossed the street. I listened, allowing the normality of her voice to distract me from my racing heartbeat. Placing my hands on the door of Jeremiah's office, I closed my eyes, willing the door to disappear. It took a few seconds before the inside heat touched my palms. Opening my eyes, I peered inside the space belonging to one of the best criminal defense attorneys in the state. Too bad he couldn't represent me if I got caught breaking and entering. *Was it technically breaking if I made things disappear?* I took a deep breath and slowly took a step into the dark office. A waiting room appeared to be inside the entrance, an ominous closed door beyond it. I couldn't help but tiptoe toward it like one of those cartoon thieves, jerking forward with large, overly cautious steps. When I reached the door, I took a moment to breathe. Olga mentioned something about cybersecurity, wanting a confirmation that Jay-Jay knew how to hack.

"Yes," I answered quietly, my voice breathy. Placing a shaky hand on the door, I dematerialized it.

Olga's voice was suspicious, suddenly extra interested in what I was doing. "What are you doing?" she teased. I quickly leaped to the large desk in the center of the room.

"I'm running an errand for Bradley," I answered, then cringed. That's exactly what Jay-Jay told me I would say. I was closer than ever to being blown up. I rattled a few desk drawers.

There was a smile in Olga's voice, her words dragging suggestively. "You two aren't making out or something, are you?"

Heat flooded my body, my face burning from the accusation. We hadn't told the others what we were doing in case anyone tried to stop us. With a shaky hand, I grabbed a letter opener to jimmy a drawer.

She wasn't satisfied with my silence, wanting to embarrass me further. "Make sure he wears a condom."

Oh, please, no. Was she saying this in front of everyone at Bradley's house? I mean, they at least knew we weren't doing *that*—Mrs. Chambers was with us—but still, her lack of a filter was embarrassing.

"Shut up!" I meant to sound menacing—my voice came out high-pitched instead. The drawer slid open, and I placed the letter opener back where I found it. Gritting my teeth, I gently moved a few sticky notes and pens, searching for the vial. "I am not doing what you think I'm doing." My breath caught at the same moment my eyes caught sight of the clear casing in the back of the drawer. "I gotta go," I quickly said, hanging up and pocketing my phone. With my hands, I carefully slid the case closer to the front, holding my breath in anticipation of the impending explosion. Closing my eyes, I focused on making the casing disappear—hoping for the best, preparing for the worst. The second I felt it go, I curled my fingers around the test tube and braced myself.

I felt the heat first, and my eyes squeezed shut, my grip tightening around the tube. The sound of the explosion ripped through my eardrums, but I didn't have time to cry in pain. I knew I had dematerialized myself when the air suddenly felt cleaner, my skin chill from a neutral temperature. My ears rang violently. I wasn't sure where I went when I did this. My eyes were always closed. Trying to open them, I attempted to see where I was—to see limbo—but I couldn't bring myself to. I knew I'd be back in the fire any second.

Holding on to the test tube, I considered the implications of having it in my possession. It was one large vial—not enough to cure the world or even the country of type one diabetes. I knew that was Bradley's real hope. I knew he didn't want to use it solely on himself. He wasn't selfish like that. He truly wanted to help others. That was something I revered about him.

The wind shifted, the ringing in my ears dying, and I tensed further, anticipating smoke and heat, but all I felt was cold. Letting out a breath of air, I refused to open my eyes. I'd once heard that sometimes intense heat could feel cold as it activated cold temperature receptors in our skin. It took me a moment to realize I could breathe clearly. I could smell coffee and exhaust. I thought I smelled flowers, like the perfume my mother sometimes wore on Sundays when she went to Mass with Jay-Jay's mom. Slowly, I opened my eyes.

This wasn't the office.

My feet balanced at the edge of the curb, a few cars passing in the street. A coffee shop was straight ahead, the employees probably getting ready to close for the night. I knew this coffee shop. The mall was just beyond it. Stepping from the curb, I turn to confirm that Union Station was behind me and let out a shriek of surprise. Standing there, less than five feet from me, was Bradley Chambers.

He gawked at me, bewildered by my appearance, unsure of what to make of it. I switched the vial to my left hand before ramming into him. I burrowed my face in his neck and hugged him tightly. A Greyhound bus pulled to the curb, an elderly lady climbing on. Bradley's uninjured arm moved so his hand could grip my waist, pushing me away. I obliged, trying not to be hurt by his reaction. He studied my face for a long moment, the muscles in his expression taught. "I left you," he said.

"You did," I acknowledged, my heart ricocheting between my ribs.

"I'm not sorry." His breath hit my face, a cloud of strange, slightly sweet warmth in the coldness of night.

I squinted, examining his brown eyes, unable to hear his thoughts. I didn't need to, though. Our proximity returned our empathy for each other, his heart swelling in mine. There was a slight pressure around my eyes as the tears returned, glazing my sight.

How could it be possible for one person to feel so much? How could Bradley not feel his heart ache for my presence? How could he be so good at denying—so afraid of admitting—that he could not live without me? How could he stand there and lie to my face?

My voice shook when I argued, trying to smile through the emotions. "You are sorry," I told him. I reached for his hand, pulling it from my waist to hold against my cheek. I felt his heart sputter and smiled a little at the reassurance.

The bus pulled away.

His brown eyes searched mine, his lips upturned in a cringy sort of way, as if he didn't want to feel what he felt. His hand slipped from under mine, allowing it to fall at his sides. His eyes darted to the ground but soon returned to mine as if some magnetic force kept him from looking away too long. "I-I…" he began, but stopped, his mouth staying open as if he had more to say but couldn't quite get the words out.

I placed a hand on his chest, feeling his pulse quicken—both in my own heart and under my hand. "You being here saved my life tonight," I said.

His heart stopped this time, restarting a second later. "What are you talking about?"

I pursed my lips, rescanning our surroundings. We were less than a mile from Mr. Krause's office. I hoped we weren't in range of the captivators' senses. This was South Street after all—the same street that passed north of the lab. "Did you hear the explosion?"

His eyebrows knitted, his hand gripping my wrist. I felt his heart beat erratically beneath my touch and in my chest. Mine quickened as well. "That was you?" Fear crept along the edges of his gut, worry affecting his nerves. I lifted my left hand, trembling from the intensity of his shock. Flipping my hand so the palm was facing up, I released my fingers from their death grip, revealing the large vial in its entirety.

His eyes nearly bugged out of his face. Letting go of my wrist, Bradley lifted the vial from my palm, holding it delicately. "Is this what I think it is?" he half whispered.

My hand drifted from his chest, meeting my other hand. "It wasn't in the lab," I said, pride and joy sparking within me, shooting off like mini fireworks. "It was in Mr. Krause's office near the federal courthouse." My words spilled faster than ever. "There was a loophole in the contract. They said we couldn't come within three hundred feet of the lab or themselves, but no one was at the office. Marcie remembered seeing a vial in his office once. I'm not sure why he kept it there. Maybe it would be less incriminating if anyone ever searched the lab or maybe it was less of a loss for them if someone stole it since they rigged the entire place to blow. They wouldn't want a huge explosion of that entire laboratory building. It would be expensive to rebuild, so they rigged the downtown law office to explode—less casualties and all that if there were ever a robbery. And Bradley"—I gasped in a lungful of air—"you being here saved my life. I think I teleported to you."

His thoughts still hadn't returned to me, but I could see the gravity of my words hit him. He stumbled, his eyes flicking back and forth between me and the vial. He let out a burst of air. It was cold enough to see. "Y-you teleported to me." He didn't say it like a question—more like a confirmation. The cure was still cradled in his hand, begging for attention, but he couldn't tear his eyes from mine. "Is that another fated thing?"

I stared back at him, shrugging. "All I know is that I can't die without you. Fate said it wasn't our time."

Bradley turned his gaze toward the cure, his eyebrows furrowing once again. "Kase said being fated was a curse. He said the closer we get to each other, the closer we get to death."

"Isn't that how all couples work, though?" I asked. I didn't like the way his tone sounded, and I couldn't let him try to leave me again. I was worried another bus would come and Bradley would take it no matter where it led, just for an escape. He was always trying to escape the things that made him feel.

He notched an eyebrow but didn't look at me.

I continued, "Every day we get closer to death, no matter if we're in a relationship or not. That's how life works. Nobody is immortal. So why should that be a deciding factor in whether or not you want to be with me?" I could feel the tears coming back. I tried to hold them at bay but knew he could feel them too.

"I want to be with you," he said quietly, still watching the cure as if it might disappear.

"Bradley," I said, closing my eyes. "I want to be with you too. You know that. You can feel that. I wish you would stop pretending."

"I'm not pretending." He was angry. Good. I knew he'd hate my assumption. His eyes flashed to me. He tucked the cure into his jacket pocket. His left arm pulled at my waist, beckoning me. I obliged, my heart fluttering violently in my chest. I felt his anger subside, his face inches from mine. His brown eyes searched the depths of my soul. "I know you know I love you." He let go of me, reaching to pull a few strands of my hair from my face.

It was hard to breathe and think with him so close. "You said… haven't said… me… to me."

He chuckled. "I love you." Plain and simple. His head bowed, his lips pressed to mine. I closed my eyes, letting myself savor the moment. I knew he loved me. He just never said it before. I thought I didn't need to hear it, especially when I could feel everything he was feeling, but the words sparked a new kind of shock to my system. Although it was necessary, it was tough to be patient with Bradley. I wanted to skip to the good parts, the good parts like that moment, like every other moment like it, that would inevitably occur in our futures. I wanted to marry this boy—even if we were only fourteen. I knew my parents would never go for it. I would have to graduate from high school first, maybe complete a few years of college before my mom would ever give us her blessing. My dad would never in a million years, so convincing him would be hopeless. Still, I could wait.

I didn't realize I was hearing Bradley's thoughts again until they interrupted mine. "Your dad would never go for it," he agreed.

I smiled. That was a case I would willingly fight. It would take a few years, but I'd do it. In the case of our fate, our destinies were already written in the stars.

My cell phone rang. I was going to ignore it, but I thought better of it. Reluctantly, I pulled away, digging my cell phone from my pocket. "What?" I huffed impatiently into the phone.

Jay-Jay let out a strangled sound. "You're not dead," he panted.

My veins ran cold. Oh, shoot. I'd been torturing him all night, for weeks actually, and when his vision suddenly came true before his eyes, I vanished? I'm a jerk. "Jay-Jay, I'm so sorry," I apologized. "I got so distracted. I didn't think to call or—"

He interrupted me. "Call? Savanna, the least you could have done was call! I watched you get blown up! My ears are still ringing from the explosion!"

I cringed. "Sorry," I said again. "I didn't know I would teleport to Bradley."

There was a long silence on the other end before Jay-Jay said, "Wow. Maybe you really are fated."

The line went dead.

EPILOGUE
BRADLEY

"Maybe I can reverse engineer this baby," Grandpa Chambers told me when I showed him the cure during his Thanksgiving visit. We were sitting in the dining room, trying to ignore Mom and Grandma arguing about the proper way to baste a turkey. Mom always liked to spice things up. Grandma was more traditional.

"Honey, we white people cannot handle all that cayenne," Grandma chastised.

Grandpa and I laughed. I knew Grandma didn't mean it like that. What she meant to say was that *she* couldn't handle spice in the nth degree, but sometimes she speaks without thinking. She loves Mom, she really does, but Mom being Romani was always a staple conversation when they were over. Mom's too kind to make a big deal of it, but I know it bothers her. She tries to use it as an opportunity to share her culture.

Grandpa returned his attention to the vial I had handed him. "Boy, I didn't think I'd see another one of these in my lifetime." He looked at me proudly. "You know why I created this cure?"

I shook my head.

He smiled. "I was just like you. Had type one for several decades before I cured myself." Grandpa tapped the tube on his knee. "Are you sure you don't want me to administer this to you?"

I nodded. We'd already had this conversation. I didn't want the cure for myself. "I have other things I need to worry about," I said. "Besides, I'd much rather see hundreds cured before I ever take the cure myself."

"Trust issues, eh?" he asked.

I ignored him. It wasn't that, but it was an interesting way to look at it. I grabbed a pamphlet from the table—the Restoration Story Recovery Center. It was for youth who had suffered trauma. Frank thought it would be good for me. His girlfriend—did *not* know he was dating—worked there. "I have a friend there now," I explained to Grandpa. Serena had been admitted shortly after her overnight hospital stay.

"You thinkin' about joining them?" Grandpa asked.

I shrugged.

He leaned forward, his hand on my knee. His eyes searched mine for a long moment before he said, "I think you have a long road ahead of you, but you're not going to learn how to deal with it if you don't deal with your past first. Go. See what that place is all about. If it isn't for you, it isn't for you, but at least put it to the test. You deserve the potential to be healed."

"I don't think I'm ever going to be healed, Grandpa," I told him.

He furrowed his bushy gray eyebrows. "I tend to look at life as if everybody can be healed. I was a doctor for a few decades. I've seen my share of miracles. Heck, I created my share of miracles. If you don't look at life like there's potential for positive change, then what's the point? I'm telling you, sometimes healing is inevitable. Especially in your case. Don't forget that."

The doorbell rang. Paige screamed that Marcie and her mom were here. Mom must have invited them.

Marcie popped her head in, excited to see me. I tucked the pamphlet underneath my leg so she wouldn't see it. I knew it was stupid, but I didn't want anyone to know. Not yet. She leaned to hug me. "Savanna's family doesn't celebrate Thanksgiving," she mentioned, pulling away. "We thought celebrations at your house would be more fun anyway."

I'm not sure when Marcie and I became friends. Maybe it was when I decided to try to save her life, though that did more harm than good. Savanna said she'd made a real sacrifice for me. Or rather, a real sacrifice for the cure. She had to come face-to-face with Aaron one last time. Marcie hadn't given me the details, but I'm not sure I wanted to know this time. I just hoped that the Krauses were out of her life for good.

She plopped into a nearby chair. "Did you ever learn why Jay-Jay's visions were causing him so much trouble?

Everyone seemed to act like that wasn't normal." Marcie sure was taking the diviner thing well.

I sighed. "No. My mom has a couple of theories, one of them having to do with Savanna and me, and another having to do with my sister. You know—pick out the weirdos among us."

"You're all weird to me." Marcie blinked, smiling crookedly.

"I guess you would see it that way."

She nodded. "Well, at least he's finally sleeping now."

I nodded in agreement.

The phone rang. Mom answered it. She appeared in the entryway between the kitchen and dining room, her caramel eyes wide with worry. Her hand clung to the frame. "W-wait, slow down. It's not our fault that—" With every word from the caller, her face fell further away from her holiday cheer. "I would hate to lose you all because of a misunderstanding." She frowned, listening. "I know how scary it is, believe me, but we need diviners like you in the area—" Another interruption. Her voice was calmer, softer. "I guess I can understand that. I hope one day we can be friends." She put the phone back in its cradle.

"Who was that?" I asked.

She stared at the phone for a while, troubled. "That was Juliet Schwartz. They're unhappy with the attention we've brought to the area. They're packing their belongings as we speak."

"Kase is moving?" Marcie asked.

Mom frowned. "I believe so."

"The world is a ladder, in which some go up and others go down."

— Romani proverb

ALPHABETICAL INDEX OF DIVINERS

Brown, Calvin *[Telepathy]*
Brown, Jaime *[Precognition]*
Brown, Liam *[Pyrokinesis]*
Burnett, Karston *[Teleportation]*
Burnett, Sage *[Telekinesis]*
Burnett, Seth *[Telekinesis]*
Chambers, Bradley *[Materialization]*
Chambers, Clarinda *[Precognition]*
Chambers, Paige *[Telekinesis]*
Chambers, Rebecca *[Materialization]*
Cornell, Olga *[Shapeshifting]*
Huckleberry, Macie *[Power Mimicry]*
Huckleberry, Milo *[Quantity Manipulation]*
Huckleberry, Savanna *[Materialization]*
Huckleberry, Ursula *[Materialization]*
Jones, Jay-Jay *[Precognition]*
Lantern, Frank *[Telekinesis]*
Lindt, Hudson *[Telepathy]*
Lindt, Nancy *[Precognition]*
Lindt, Serena *[Mass Manipulation]*
Schwartz, Kase *[Mass Manipulation]*

ABOUT THE STORY
DISCLAIMERS

It is unlikely that a cure for diabetes would exist in a single vial. The disease is much more complex. Due to the nature of their differences, it's also a common assumption that type two would have to be cured before a cure for type one could be created. However, medical researchers around the world have been tirelessly working toward a cure, along with various treatment options for managing the different forms of this disease. As it is pointed out throughout this book, diabetes is a manageable illness, despite its chronic nature. Years ago, a diagnosis for type one was considered a death sentence. There weren't ways to manage it—no insulin vials, no glucose tablets… nothing. In another time, Bradley would have died of his illness as a child. He wouldn't have been able to narrate this story. That's what I like so much about writing from Bradley's perspective. There is a certain type of magic in this fact. He is a survivor, a warrior, a person who perseveres. He has overcome so many obstacles and will overcome many more as the series progresses.

I didn't cure Bradley in this book. Part of me is a little sad for that. It would certainly be easier on me as the author not to have to worry how Bradley's disease may impact the rest of his story. However, I feel I would be doing my readers a disservice if I were to rid the rest of this series of this representation. At the same time, I still will never be able to give that part of Bradley's life the level of accuracy it deserves. Like Savanna, I see type one diabetes from the outside. At one point in the story, Bradley rambles a bit about her seemingly displaced concern. "She is not the one who," he begins, and in allowing him to rant about her, I allowed him to rant about me too. I am not the one who has to experience all the effects of this disease. I only know the science and the statistics. There is no personal experience I draw from. There is only what I have observed from others. I don't want to mislead readers in believing otherwise. For readers searching for Own Voices books depicting type one diabetes, I have created a growing list on my website.

I also want to make it aware that Priori Labs is a figment of my imagination and does not represent a real place or business entity. It has zero affiliation with insulin distributors like Eli Lilly, whose real-life headquarters are located in Indianapolis. This was merely a coincidence.

On an unrelated note, I would also like to address the topic of child marriage. Child marriage is not a practice specific to any one culture, but often accompanies cultures where women are treated as inferior to men. While child marriage does continue to be a practice in some Romani families and vitsas, it does not exist in many others. It is the same way for other cultures. There have been reports of young women being forced or talked into a marriage in their teens even among primarily white evangelical cultures, despite many in those same cultures believing that this problem is nonexistent in their countries, let alone their communities. While some of these marriages work through laws and loopholes in their country's legal system, many are not legal in the eyes of the law, but still hold value in the eyes of their families and communities.

In this book, the topic of child marriage is introduced through Chastain, as he shares the story of his consensual, unarranged marriage to his wife, who was previously arranged to be married to a Romani man in her vitsa. Clarinda comes from a conservative Romani family in the southern United States, but her story is not meant to demonize the Romani race nor some of the cultural practices within their ethnic vitsas, especially when this particular practice is neither representative of all Romani vitsas nor exclusive to Romani culture.

The same goes for any other aspect of Romani culture that is represented in this series. Every vitsa, community, and family has a set of values and customs that may differ from the representations in this series.

GLOSSARY

Most of the Romani words used in this book are from the Vlax or Romanichal dialect. Please note that the Romani language is sacred to many of its speakers. This glossary is only intended to help with words used in this book and is not here to help teach the language to non-native speakers. Please be respectful in your use of this glossary.

ROMANI WORD	ENGLISH WORD
ANAV RROMANO	ROMANI NAME
BAXT	LUCK
BENG	DEVIL
BUT	MANY/MUCH
ĈHAJ	UNMARRIED FEMALE
ĈHAVE	CHILDREN
DEL/DEVEL	GOD
GADJE/GADŽE	NON-ROMANI PEOPLE
GADJO/GADŽO	NON-ROMANI PERSON
KINTALA	SPIRITUAL BALANCE
MALJARDEM	MADE DIRTY
MARIME	UNCLEAN/IMPURE
MULE	SPIRITS OF THE DEAD
PORAJMOS	DEVOURING/HOLOCAUST
PRIKAZA	RETRIBUTION *(AS A RESULT OF UPSETTING THE SPIRITUAL BALANCE)*
RROMANIJA	THE ROMANI WAY OF LIFE

OWN VOICES
RECOMMENDATIONS

Two of the major themes in this series—racism related to the Romani people and type one diabetes—were not written from the author's personal perspective. However, they were depicted with a great amount of research. As the author, I would like to urge my readers to actively add Own Voices books to their reading lists and bookshelves as authors like me can only provide limited views on certain subjects.

For a growing list of Own Voices books depicting type I diabetes and the Romani people, please visit
www.ekbarnesauthor.com/ownvoices

US National Suicide Prevention Lifeline
800-273-8255

ABOUT THE AUTHOR

For nearly a year-and-a-half, E.K. Barnes owned and operated *Scribe Stash*, a personalized subscription box service for readers and writers, where she also participated in writing and editing book, movie, and product review articles. She has been interviewed by Outlet Publishing Group and Double the Books Magazine regarding her writing endeavors and her work with *Scribe Stash*, respectively. Prior to and alongside this short endeavor, E.K. has written and performed several speeches and presentations across different topics—specifically regarding people, events, and mental health.

E.K. is a member of the Independent Author Network. She is a 2014 graduate of Olathe Northwest High School in Kansas and has been a student at Johnson County Community College, MidAmerica Nazarene University, and Southern New Hampshire University.

E.K. comes from a family of creatives—her brother is a musician with dreams of becoming a film composer, her sister has a degree in graphic design, and her parents both hold degrees in music.

She currently resides in Kansas with her dog, Nikki.

www.ekbarnesauthor.com

Instagram & Tik Tok: @ekbarnes_author